I0588675

So Perilous, my Love

Clarissa Ross

CRIMSON
ROMANCE

F+W Media, Inc.

This edition published by
Crimson Romance
an imprint of F+W Media, Inc.
10151 Carver Road, Suite 200
Blue Ash, Ohio 45242
www.crimsonromance.com

Copyright © 1979 by W. E. Dan Ross

ISBN 10: 1-4405-7291-7
ISBN 13: 978-1-4405-7291-3
eISBN 10: 1-4405-7292-5
eISBN 13: 978-1-4405-7292-0

This is a work of fiction. Names, characters, corporations, institutions, organizations, events, or locales in this novel are either the product of the author's imagination or, if real, used fictitiously. The resemblance of any character to actual persons (living or dead) is entirely coincidental.

Cover art © 123RF.

CHAPTER 1

It was a gray, late afternoon in the melancholy autumn of 1861. Thick fog had seeped up from the docks to spread all over the great city of London. In the mean, twisted streets close by the docks where the families of seamen and shipbuilders lived, the yellowish cloud was at its thickest. Already both pedestrians and vehicles were having difficulty getting about the area, and most of the public houses had lit up their windows. Gas lamps on street corners glowed bleakly in the fog and could be seen only a short distance.

In a ramshackle, two-story wooden house in one of the streets near the Gregg and Kerr Shipyard a young woman was busy at the kitchen stove. Becky Lee, an attractive, golden-haired girl with large, wistful blue eyes and an oval face. She wore a pert cap and apron over a dark dress as she opened the door of the oven to check on the progress of a kidney pie which she had prepared.

The aromatic odor of it satisfied her that all was well. The kidney pie would be ready when her father arrived home shortly from his work as a laborer in the nearby shipyard. Since the death of her mother a year earlier, the nineteen-year-old Becky had taken charge of cooking the meals and looking after the meagre flat in which they lived. Her sister, Peg, only a year younger, was a lively, rather vacant-minded redhead with a pretty face of a milk complexion dotted with a charming array of freckles. Peg had never been as interested in studies or housework as her older sister. Instead, she spent much of the time mooning over herself in the small mirror above the dresser in the bedroom which she shared with Becky.

"I want to marry a rich man and live in a big house," she'd often confided to Becky as she stood by the mirror. And looking into it with a satisfied smile, she'd added, "And my beauty will make it easy!"

"Don't be all that sure!" Becky had warned her. Becky was the realistic and hard-headed one. Her father had much the same easy-going dreamer's personality of his younger daughter. He had once aspired to being a shopkeeper, but he hadn't the talent for it. He had wound up a common laborer in the great Gregg and Kerr shipyard. "You're full of dreams like our Dad, but like him you haven't the ambition and drive to see them through!"

Peg showed indignation at this time. The pretty girl grimaced and flounced her shoulder-length auburn curls. "You're jealous of me, I do believe! You're afraid I might marry better than you!"

She would then laugh. "That's the last thing I worry about." Then she'd go on to tell Peg, "You need guidance. Perhaps a good, steady boy like Bob Reeves!"

This would cause Peg to indignantly inform her that she would not be satisfied with poor Bob, who worked side by side with her father and had a widowed mother and several younger brothers to help support. He lived in the same street of small, ancient houses and twisting cobblestones. Perhaps because he'd shown more interest in Becky than Peg, the younger girl always spurned the idea of his showing interest in her.

On this grim afternoon with the aroma of the kidney pie following her into the sparsley furnished parlor of the flat, Becky came upon Peg seated in the one armchair they owned reading a tattered copy of the *London Illustrated News* which she had spread on her lap.

Becky reminded the younger girl, "Time for you to be getting the plates on the table! Dad will soon be back from the yard!"

Peg glanced up at her indignantly. "Plenty of time for that! I'm reading the story of the Prince Consort's death! Real sad it is! Victoria's taking it badly!"

Becky's pretty face showed impatience. "We've enough misery here on Blade Street without having to get so worked up over the Royal Family!"

Peg stood up and stared at her in a shocked fashion. "Why that's almost unpatriotic of you! And unkind as well!"

"I don't mean to be unkind," she said. "But I do think too much is being made of Prince Albert's death. There were many who didn't show such fondness for him in life. I think we should tend to our own affairs and let them do the same!"

"I had to borrow this magazine from old Mrs. Cardel," Peg said unhappily. "We never have enough to buy more than an occasional paper."

"Go on now and set the table," Becky replied angrily. "Dad doesn't like to have to wait for his food after a hard day at the yard!"

"The yard!" Peg said with disdain. "That's all people living in this street think about!"

"The shipyard provides the food on our table and the clothes on our back," Becky told her younger sister.

Peg looked over her shoulder on her way to the kitchen to set the table, "Scraps on the table and rags on our backs!" she said. Becky was going to follow her to the kitchen and answer her sharply but decided not to. Their father would soon be home, and she didn't want him to find them quarreling. He deserved better than that after toiling long hours in the shipyard. He had seemed to lose much of his interest in life and had gone down hill physically since the death of their mother. She worried much about him and tried hard to make him as comfortable and happy as possible.

Her mother's illness and death had made her postpone her plans for finding a position as sales clerk in some kind of shop. She knew her limited education and coarse manner of speech made her ill-equipped for the more genteel establishments, but she thought she might find a position in a bakery or a fish monger's place. She meant to try as soon as she could, since the extra money she would earn would at least clothe her and pay for her food.

She had no idea what Peg intended to do—beyond her wild dream of marrying someone rich. Becky found this a little sad and wished that it might be possible, but she knew life too well to believe it could happen. She hoped that perhaps Bob Reeves would pop the question to Peg, or failing that, that her younger sister might also find employment somewhere.

These thoughts ran through her mind as she listened to Peg noisily setting the table in the kitchen. She paid no attention to this, though she might have normally reprimanded her sister. Instead, she went to the window of the ground floor flat, in the four-story house and gazed out into the fog-ridden street. The yellow cloud was so heavy that everything was dripping from its dampness. Figures hurried by like shrouded ghosts.

She was about to turn from the window when she heard a voice in the distance. She halted, thinking she recognized it. Then as the voice came closer she realized it was the shrill voice of Jimmy Davis, the dwarf who worked with her father at the shipyard. It was Jimmy's peculiar talent that he could climb into the smallest cranny when it was needed, and do jobs which ordinary men could not manage. He and her father had become good friends, and Jimmy often smoked a pipe or two by their fireside after the evening meal.

Now he was coming running down the street and shouting. And as he reached the house, she knew that he was calling out her name, in a kind of wailing fashion, "Becky! Miss Becky!"

She threw open the door, and he came stumbling down the dark hall to face her in the doorway. Her blood chilled as she stared at the little man and asked, "What is wrong, Jimmy?"

There were tears on the dwarf's weathered cheeks. He was hatless, and he looked up at her sadly, his graying hair in disarray.

He said, "There's been an accident!" He had a fearful expression on his bearded, but not unpleasant face.

"Go on!" she implored him.

"Oh, Miss Becky," he said sobbing. "I ran here all the way, and now I don't want to be the first to tell you!"

"I must know!" she said, feeling sick with apprehension. "An accident? What sort of accident?"

"Your father, poor Barney," the little man said. "He fell from a high scaffolding. All the way to the bottom of the yard. He was dead when we got to him. Died right away."

A pale-faced Peg had emerged from the kitchen and asked in a frightened voice, "Is it father?"

Becky put an arm around her for comfort. "Yes," she said in a taut voice. "Father was killed in a fall! There's just the two of us now!"

"No!" Peg said brokenly and pressed against her sobbing.

Little Jimmy Davis had recovered from his own sorrow a little and stood gazing up at the two girls awkwardly. He said, "I was-confused. I didn't want you to hear it from a stranger."

"You were right, Jimmy," Becky said, trying to suppress the tremor in her own voice, fighting to hold back her own great sorrow for the sobbing Peg's; sake. "Father would have wished it so. He would have wanted us to hear it from a friend."

"Thank you, Miss Becky," the little man said. "Is there anything I can do?"

She soothed the sobbing Peg and then asked quietly, "When will they bring him here?"

"They're on the way now," Jimmy said. "A half-dozen of the best lads bringing him here on a stretcher. You'll be wanting to lay him out in the parlor, I suppose."

"Yes," Becky said, feeling it all had to be a bad dream from which she would awaken in a moment. None of it true, all part of a frightening nightmare. "You'd better go to Gower Street and fetch Mr. Longbeck, the undertaker. We'll be requiring his services."

"I'll go at once," the dwarf said, turning.

"Tell him to bring the same sort of coffin he supplied for my mother," she called after the little man.

Jimmy was already at the front door. "Aye! I'll tell him!" And he vanished in the fog.

Barney Lee lay in his plain coffin in a corner of the tiny parlor looking more at rest than at any time since he'd lost his wife. Mr. Longbeck in his shabby black suit and high hat draped with black crepe had done his usual efficient work on the dead man. The coffin was not lined, but Becky had found a small silk pillow beloved by her late mother, and it seemed suitable that her father's head should rest on it. His worn but almost handsome face showed no sign of pain.

The dwarf, Jimmy Davis, wiped a tear from his eye as he sat on a stool near the coffin and said those very words, "He could well be asleep!"

The soft light of the flickering candles in the room seemed suitable for the occasion. Peg sat very still and silent, obviously still suffering from shock. It fell on Becky to greet those coming to pay their respects and offer them cups of tea. The women of the neighborhood, her mother's friends, came first, a somewhat worn and haggard group familiar with life's sadness. One hesitated to whisper on her way out, "He is at peace! It is you girls who are to be worried about."

Becky listened, and with her pride coming to her rescue, she said, "Don't worry about us. We'll manage. I have plans." Which wasn't precisely true but would suffice for the moment.

Then her father's fellow-workers came shuffling in to pause a moment by the coffin and make some uneasy comment. They tried to show their sympathy, but they were a rough lot who for so long had repressed their emotions that they now had hardly any to call on. Tongue-tied and embarrassed, they came and quickly left.

The funeral was held the next morning with a drizzle of rain and the remnants of the fog. Their father was buried in an old churchyard in the district through an arrangement with Mr. Longbeck, who had found a place for their mother to rest in the same burial ground.

As the small crowd which had assembled melted away and the half-drunk grave-diggers began to fill in the grave, the old Vicar of St. Quentin's shook their hands and wished them well. Then he walked off like one lost in his own thoughts.

Only then did the sallow and gaunt-faced Mr. Longbeck remove his crepe-decorated black top hat and bow courteously. In his nasal voice, he said, "I have not bothered you young ladies with the monetary side of this sad business. Now, I fear, the time has come. Let me tender my accounting of it all." And he rummaged in an inner pocket and produced a folded statement which he passed to Becky.

She opened the statement and studied it. While it seemed fair enough, it was several pounds more than she'd expected. She glanced at the thin man. "It cost more than my mother's funeral," she pointed out.

Mr. Longbeck looked embarrassed. "True, dear girl. But in the matter of a year my expenses have risen most grievously, so I have no choice but to pass the increases on."

Becky folded the bill. "I understand,' she said quietly. "You need not worry; you will be paid."

Mr. Longbeck coughed politely. "When, dear lady?"

She said, "Within the week. My father would wish it done promptly."

Mr. Longbeck's gaunt face at once became brighter. "That will be most satisfactory, my dear. Most satisfactory!" He put on his top hat and glancing back at the grave diggers who'd almost completed their task of filling in the grave, he said, "I think it all went very well, do you not agree?"

"I agree, Mr. Longbeck," she said tautly. "And now, if you don't mind, my sister and I would like to be alone. We need quiet."

"Of course," the thin man said sympathetically. "Within the week then!" And he bowed and marched out the cemetery gate.

Peg, still sick and pale, found her voice and said, "What a horrible man! I expect he charged us double what he should have!"

Becky sighed. "Hardly that, but enough! More than we have, as a matter of fact."

"What shall we do?" Peg stared at her with concern.

"We shall manage," Becky said firmly as they began to leave the cemetery, walking towards the street nearby. "Father would want it so, though we shall likely have to give up the flat and sell our furniture."

"Sell the furniture!" Peg wailed. "Where can we go without furniture?"

"We must find positions where rooms are provided," Becky said. "Perhaps in the household of some rich family. We will have to seek work as maids. This may be your chance. You've always wanted to marry a rich man! Maybe you'll meet one this way."

"Rich men never marry servants!" Peg lamented.

"Wrong," Becky assured her. "They often do. All the romantic novels tell of such matches."

"We are not living in a romantic novel!" Peg said unhappily.

Becky gave her a sharp look as they walked along. She said, "At least you've learned that useful truth!"

When they reached the cheerless ground floor flat which had seemed so happy a home before their parents died, they had another grim surprise awaiting them in the person of Mrs. Medwick, the owner of the building. She had shown the effrontery of letting herself into the flat and waiting for them seated in their best chair.

Mrs. Medwick was large, and had a bloated, red face and wispy gray hair. She reeked of gin no matter the time of day or night. She stared up at the girls sullenly as they entered.

"No need to be surprised," she said roughly. "This is my house!"

"I consider it ours as long as we rent it," Becky said. Peg stood back looking awed.

Mrs. Medwick rose ponderously. "I will not take offence at that. I could, mark you, but I will not. I shall simply tell you that since you already owe for a month's rent I consider the flat no longer yours."

"I'll see you are paid, Mrs. Medwick," Becky said.

The big woman mocked her manner, saying, "Will you, now? And what with? After the funeral expenses are looked after. And I know Longbeck doesn't offer his services free! He always gets his!"

Becky said, "We will pay you. But we shall be leaving here the first of the week. So you may plan on letting the place to someone else."

Mrs. Medwick's bloated face showed a nasty smile. "I've already done that! Party is coming to occupy on Monday. So you be out of here by then. And don't expect to take this furniture with you unless my rent is paid in full! In full, mind you!" And with this threat she ambled out.

When the door closed behind the big woman Peg turned to Becky and said, "What will we do? If we can't sell the furniture, we can't raise the money to pay her."

"It will work out," Becky said with a confidence she did not feel. "We have not heard from the shipyard yet. Father's employers, Gregg and Kerr, may be planning to offer us some money because of father's being killed at work. In any event, we have coming to us whatever wages he had earned to the time of his death."

For the first time, Peg showed a more hopeful look on her pretty young face. She said, "When will we know about that?"

"By tonight," Becky said, removing her straw bonnet. "Jimmy Davis is going to speak to the partners, and he is coming by here on his way home."

"Ugly little dwarf!" Peg said with a grimace.

"Don't say that!" Becky rebuked her. "He was our father's best friend, and he is ours as well. You may be sure he will do all he can for us."

They spent the afternoon making a list of all which was saleable and trying to guess what price each item might bring. The total was not large, even when they were careful to try and set a proper price. They would not make much from the sale. But even a little would help.

A little after five the dwarf arrived. The girls let him in and pulled up the stool on which he always sat. Then they sat facing him, Becky hoping for the best and Peg even showing some signs of interest.

Becky asked the little man, "How did you make out, Jimmy?"

The dwarf looked miserable and tugged at his graying beard with a small hand. He said, "They gave me the wages he'd earned right enough."

"I should hope so!" Becky exclaimed.

The dwarf showed embarrassment as he reached in his pocket and then handed some coins over to her. "Fifteen bob! Not much, I'd say!"

Peg sounded indignant. "Fifteen bob! That's all?"

"That's all," the little man said sadly. "I'm sorry."

Becky looked at the coins in her palm and said, "I can't believe that they wouldn't have at least sent his full week's wages."

Jimmy Davis said, "They're hard men, Miss Becky. It's a cruel company. We all know that."

Becky said, "Did you speak with both partners?"

"Only with Mark Gregg," the dwarf said. "Mr. Kerr's health has been poor lately, and he seldom comes to the shipyard."

"And what did Mark Gregg say?"

Jimmy sighed. "He gave me the fifteen bob and said to tell you he sent you his sympathy."

"I wonder that he could afford it!" Becky said with scathing sarcasm.

Peg complained, "How can anyone be so heartless?"

The little man's large face showed frustration. "They are cruel people, Miss Peggy. This is a cruel business, filled with competition in these days of the new iron ships. Gregg and Kerr are still building wooden ships and the call for them is going down."

"Why don't they build iron ships?" Becky wanted to know.

"I've heard old man Kerr is against it," the dwarf said. "But Mark Gregg has been unhappy with the present policy ever since the *Great Eastern* was launched in 1858. Biggest iron ship afloat! They say she'll make history! Some think there's a curse on her because two workers were lost in the construction, and many claim they were caught between the false bottom and the hull and not noticed until all the section was closed in. They say their ghosts haunt the ship and will eventually doom it!"

Becky said, "So this means Gregg and Kerr are not doing as well as they might?"

"Correct!" Jimmy said. "But they're doing fairly well. They could well pay you some good sum for your father losing his life on the job. Especially considering the facts."

"Facts?" Becky asked crisply. "What are the facts?"

He looked uneasy. And then in a low voice, he said, "Well, I was told the scaffolding on which your father was working when he fell hadn't been properly set up. That it swayed so as to make you ill."

Becky said, "You're saying my father was sent up there to work on a scaffolding which wasn't safe?"

The little man nodded. "That's about the size of it!"

Peg exclaimed, "They are murderers! It's almost the same as if they deliberately killed my father!"

"Mr. Mark Gregg doesn't see it so," the dwarf told her. "But I must admit I agree with you. If that scaffolding had been set up the way it should, I haven't a doubt your father would be alive this very moment."

Becky sat back in her chair with a shocked look on her lovely face. "I shall have to see this Mark Gregg," she said.

Peg gave her a disgusted look. "He'll never agree to see you. Don't you know that!"

"What do you think?" Becky asked their father's best friend. "Do you think he'll see me?"

"I think it's worth a try." Becky said, her young face offering a grim look.

"You could try and talk with him," the little man said with despair. "I did not manage well with him as I've testified. But perhaps the sight of a pretty face might help. They say he is more fond of liquor and women! He'd never done a lick of work until he was left his share of the yard by his father. Now he is the meanest of the lot of them!"

Becky said warmly, "Thank you for all you've done, Jimmy. And for telling me the truth about dear father's accident."

"I thought you should know," the little man said. "And I have some money of my own if you'd let me help you. I've saved it against sickness, but you're welcome to every penny of it!"

"Do you mean that, Jimmy?" Peg asked with delight.

Becky turned on her younger sister swiftly and informed her, "Whether he means it or not, we are not going to take his money!"

"Why not?" Peg asked in astonishment.

"Because he needs it for himself and his own family," she exclaimed. "You are forgetting he has a widowed mother and two spinster sisters to look after."

"They do not grudge you the money," the dwarf promised her.

"Say no more," Becky told him. "We will manage well enough with our own resources, though we do appreciate your offer. And I intend to talk to Mr. Mark Gregg and speak to him of my father's death. It is not to pass without some mention being made of it."

"I agree, Miss Becky," Jimmy Davis said, getting down from the stool. "I wish I had done better."

"You musn't worry yourself," Becky said, escorting the little man out. "We have plans and we'll make out. And I'll let Mark Gregg know he had better not take his workers' lives so cheaply in the future."

"You do that, Miss," Jimmy agreed. "He needs to be told how hard he is!"

After Becky had seen the dwarf out, she found Peg looking angry. The redhead cried, "How could you refuse his money, with us in this terrible plight? You must be mad!"

"I will not rob those as poor as ourselves," Becky told her sister with determination.

Peg sank down into a nearby chair and cried, "We shall find ourselves in debtors' prison!"

"Allow me to worry about that," Becky said, placing a comforting hand on her sister's shoulder. "I'm doing as I think our parents would have wished."

She knew this was small comfort, even though it was the truth. And she was far from being the cool, collected person she allowed Peg to see. Actually she was quaking inwardly and full of fears for what would happen to them. But she knew Peg was of weaker clay than herself, and she did not want her to collapse. So she maintained this facade of knowing exactly what would happen next.

The next morning she dressed carefully in her best and made her way through the winding streets of the dockside area on the route to Gregg and Kerr's shipyard. She had left Peg with a neighbor woman of a jolly nature and hoped all would be well.

Now she was forcing herself to have a confrontation with the legendary Mark Gregg.

It was a fine, sunny day and the gold lettering of the shipbuilding firm's name stood out in gold against a black background. The sign was mounted on a modest brick building at the harborfront within sight of the shipyard. She could glance in the distance and see the yard with the bare hull of some ship in the making, and men swarming about it like ants. The vast size of the project almost took her breath away.

She forced herself to turn from this interesting view of where her father had met his death and enter the offices of the shipbuilding company. She was first to find herself in a bare reception office where a wizened, bald man sat behind a high counter.

The old man paid no attention to her for a moment as he pored over a long, slim book of accounts. Suddenly he sneezed, and after wiping his thin nose, he turned to stare at her accusingly, as if she had rudely interrupted him.

He said sternly. "We do not employ young women, Miss!"

"I'm not looking for employment," Becky said, her cheeks going crimson.

The old man stared at her. "What do you want?"

"To see Mr. Mark Gregg," she said with as much authority as she could produce under the circumstances.

The thin face showed a nasty smile. "All the world wishes to see Mr. Gregg," he said. "That is why I'm here. Let me warn you that few get by me here."

"I cannot help that," she said. "I wish to see him!"

"What is your business?"

"Personal!"

"No doubt," the old man said, off his stool now and facing her like an ancient jackal on his skinny shanks. "May I ask the reason for your visit and your name?"

"My name she said firmly is Becky Lee and I have come to speak with Mr. Gregg concerning the recent death of my father in an accident in the shipyards."

This brought a decided change in the old man's manner. He said, "You are poor Barney's daughter?"

"One of them."

"He was a fine, hardworking man," the old fellow said. "I'll see if Mr. Gregg will see you. He's busy!" And he shuffled off and out a door in the rear of the bleak office.

She trembled as she waited. She tried to picture what the formidable Gregg might be like. From all she'd heard, Mark Gregg must be in his mid-forties, a bachelor, grimly dedicated to business after a youth spent in debauchery. It was whispered that he still absented himself form the business every once in a while to go on a drinking binge. But she did not know how much of this was true, and how much was hearsay!

The door at the back opened, and the old clerk came shuffling back. He lifted a hinged section of the counter for her to join him as he confided, "You are fortunate! He has agreed to give you a few minutes. Follow me!"

She did so, trying to maintain the same facade of cool determination she used to fool Peg. But she was not deceiving herself of her quaking heart, and she doubted that she would deceive this hard man of business, either.

They mounted a dark stairway which gave access to a long hall, off which there were the doors of many offices. She heard the sounds of voices from the various doorways as they went on down to the very end of the hall. There a large door bore a brass plate with the name, Mark Gregg, in Old English script. The clerk rapped nervously on the heavy oaken door, and a brisk voice inside bade them to enter.

The clerk gave her a warning glance and then opened the door to let her in, remaining outside to close the door after her. She found herself in the most elegant quarters she had ever seen. It was a symphony in fine brown woodwork, with all in the best of taste. Seated at a desk with his back to windows overlooking the shipyard was a good looking man in his forties, with strong features and tightly curled brown hair which was graying. He had heavy sideburns, but no mustache or beard. He was dressed well in a dark suit and all in all, he was much more attractive than she had expected. But his eyes warned her this was no ordinary man. The perceptive, steel-gray eyes which burned through her as she stood there intimidated her.

He slowly rose, his eyes not leaving her. He spoke in a cultured voice, saying, "So you are Lee's daughter?"

"Yes, sir. I am," she said.

"Pray be seated," he said brusquely, still studying her in that intent way. "I'm having a difficult morning, but I can give you a few minutes."

"Thank you, Mr. Gregg," she said, ignoring her pounding heart to speak with some sharpness. "I think it no more than right when I recall that my father gave his life in your service."

He stood there staring at her oddly. Then he fumbled with some papers on his desk. "It was a most unfortunate affair. I'm sorry for his death, and I asked that my sympathy be conveyed to you."

"Along with fifteen bob!" She could not hide the disgust in her tone.

The distinguished Mark Gregg raised an eyebrow. Quietly he said, "I believe this was the amount due him."

"Down to the last quarter hour," she said stiffly.

Mark Gregg looked thoughtful. "Perhaps I should have handled it in a more considerate manner. I have lately been experiencing serious business difficulties. I have been much occupied with these problems."

She said evenly, "My father served your firm from your father's day. He was a faithful employee here long before you took over."

"Indeed," the handsome man said coolly.

"And I have been told that his death might have been avoided if the scaffolding on which he was put to work had been more securely built. Clearly, it was built hastily by your foremen; they put my father up there before it was safe. I say they murdered him!"

His steel-gray eyes were focused sharply on her now as he quietly asked, "You believe that? That our negligence brought about your father's death?"

CHAPTER 2

Becky defiantly faced the grim shipyard owner, knowing him to be a proud, unbending man. But she had her own pride and her own desperate feelings of grief in the loss of her beloved father. So after the briefest of pauses, she told him, "Yes. I do think your company is to blame for my father's death!"

Mark Gregg stared at her. Then he pointed to the framed engraving of a magnificent sailing ship with side-wheels amidships and said, "Gregg and Kerr have a fine position in the shipbuilding world. There you see the Royal York, which broke the records for an Atlantic Crossing in 1839 in a voyage which took thirteen days and seven hours! Our firm built that ship!"

"I cannot see that has any bearing on my father's death," she protested.

"Just listen to me, young lady," the older man said coldly. "The point I'm trying to make is that this is a responsible firm. We do not take risks with our vessels or our men!"

"My father is dead," she said. "The staging did collapse."

The square-jawed man rubbed his chin, as if he were in a moment of decision. Then those strange eyes fixed on her again and he said, "So you continue to maintain that neglect on the company's part brought about the death of your parent?"

"I do," she said stoutly.

"Very well," Mark Gregg said. And he unlocked a drawer of his desk and reached into it to bring out a half-dozen golden sovereigns. He tossed them on the desk between them and with a biting sarcasm told her, "You may have these as a recompense, since that is what you're obviously seeking."

The temptation to take the gleaming gold pieces was great. Her need of them was great enough. But her eyes blurred with tears as she gazed at them and saw them as the worth Mark Gregg was placing on her father's life! How easy for him! And how cruel he had behaved in making his offer.

In a choked voice, she said, "I came here hoping you might better understand the loss my sister and I have suffered, the grief our father's death has caused us."

Mark Gregg showed no emotion. In the same cool way, he said, "I did not know your father. But I grant that the company has lost a good worker. That is why I have offered you this compensation." He modified his original gesture by picking up the gold coins and offering them to her directly.

She took the sovereigns and with a curl of her lip said, "I cannot allow you to put a price on my father's life in this way. I came here hoping there might be some repentance on your part and perhaps an assurance from you that you would be careful to try and avoid such accidents in the future. But I see you have nothing but contempt for the likes of my father and myself! Thank you, Mark Gregg, but I can manage without your charity!" And she threw the gold pieces at him.

She did not wait to learn his reaction. Her eyes brimming with tears, she hurried out of the elegant office to the dark stairway. She managed to get downstairs safely, and she almost ran past the old clerk in the reception room in her haste to get outside and away from the place.

It took her a little while to regain her composure. When she did, she began to carefully go over her resources and make some decisions about the future. She wandered along rather aimlessly through the back streets near the docks. Then all at once she found herself staring into the window of a shabby tavern with the ironic name of Seafarer's Rest, and saw a hand written sign in the window announcing that young barmaids were wanted.

She stood staring at the sign for a moment or two and decided that this was in some odd way an answer to her prayers. She had never been in this kind of tavern before, but now she braced herself and went inside, trying to give the impression she was fully at ease.

Inside, the tavern was dark and dank. Standing behind the bar was a weird looking man with a patch over one eye, he had a long, hooked nose and a shifty look. A tousle of dark hair fell about his forehead. He was clearly looking for someone.

She walked slowly to the shining counter, happy that the bar was empty for the moment. She said, "I have read your notice in the window."

The thin man with the black eye-patch eyed her with no interest. "Not for the likes of you! I need barmaids who can sing for the customers when things get dull."

She had a clear singing voice and so had Peg. Her hopes rose a little. She refused to give up so easily. A smile which she hoped might seem enticing crossed her pretty face. She asked, "Do you have any favorite songs?"

The thin tavern owner scowled. "I hate music of every sort, myself," he said. "But the blokes what come in here like a saucy tune. 'The Liverpool Maid' for example."

Now her heart began to pound. There had to be a fate in this! The song he'd mentioned had been a favorite of her late father's, and both she and Peg had sung it for him many times. She said with delight, "I know it!"

"So?" the man with the eye-patch said sourly.

She did what she felt she should. Standing very erect, she began singing, 'Liverpool Maid' in her best voice. She included all the saucy verses which her father and Jimmy Davis had taught her. The bartender was impressed.

Ending the song, she said, "There!"

As she did so a loud clapping came from directly behind her, and she turned to discover a handsome young black-haired man in the rough clothes of a seaman standing there. There was a smile on his handsome, young face and a twinkle of approval in his black eyes. She had assumed the bar was empty, and the remembrance of the verses she'd just sang made her cheeks crimson!

The young man laughed and, removing his peaked, sailor's cap, said, "Davy Brown, at your service, Miss. That's a good song, and you did it well. Can I coddle your sweet voice with a drink?"

"Thank you, no," she said, embarrassed and moving away from him.

"Don't be ashamed," the smiling Davy Brown told her. "You were first rate. Wasn't she, Luther?"

The one-eyed man shrugged. "Not bad!"

"Twice as talented as the last wench you had working here," Davy said. "And twice as good looking! Why not admit it?"

Luther glanced at the young man with his single eye and then leaned over the bar to talk with her. "It's not a fancy place," he warned her. "We get toughs and tarts as part of our regular night trade. You'd have to hold your own with them!"

"I could," she said. "Just so long as I'm not expected to be a tart also!"

The thin man frowned. "I don't ask that! Luther Crown is no pimp! I run a straight place, even if I do get a mixed trade!"

"You do get that!" Davy Brown said jovially.

The thin man ignored him. He asked Becky, "Is your sister as attractive as you?"

"She's more attractive!" Becky insisted.

"Can she sing?" he asked.

"Yes. She knows more songs than I do," Becky said. "And we often blend our voices in a duet which people seem to enjoy."

"I own the place next door," the owner of the tavern said. "Rooms go with the job and whatever you can manage in tips. The salary is ten bob each, take it or leave it!"

"We'll take it!" she said delighted. "Come to work tonight at six, and you stay until the place closes," Luther Crown told her.

"Mrs. Crown will be here to show you how to serve the beer, and I'll tell you when we want a song!"

"Thank you," she said. Turning to the young sailor who had been watching it all with a smile on his handsome face, she added, "And thank you, too, for your encouragement!"

"We'll be meeting again," the young man said warmly. "My name is Davy Brown, remember? What is yours?"

"Becky Lee," she said shyly, noting his bronzed skin and sturdy build. He was a fine figure of a man, and by his speech he seemed educated beyond his station in life. She added, "And my sister's name is Peg."

Davy laughed again. "And according to you, she's prettier than you and a better singer. I don't believe it!"

She laughed with him. "Truly it is so! And she is also a full year younger than I am."

"I'll be here to see you both tonight," Davy said. "And that won't mean changing any of my plans, for I spend most of my nights here in this sinful place!"

"Watch your words, sailor!" the man behind the bar warned him.

"I meant nothing by it," Davy Brown said. "Give me a whiskey to drink this young lady's health. I must do it alone, since she has refused to join me."

"I drink very rarely," she said.

He nooded approval. "That'll make you more valuable to Luther. The last two slatterns he had were lushes who drank on the sly twice what they earned for him!"

Becky saw three other older men in sailor's clothing come through the doorway and quickly said, "I must be getting back home. My sister will be worried about me." And to the glum Luther she added, "And we'll be here for work at six! I promise!"

"I'll take the sign from the window," the one-eyed man said grudgingly.

Utterly delighted with her good luck, she hurried out into the narrow street. In one daring move she had found jobs for herself and Peg, along with free rooms for them both. They could manage with food and be free to leave their present flat and sell the furniture. By being careful, she could just about pay the landlady and the undertaker by the time she'd sold the few things and added her slight savings and the total of their first week's wages at the tavern. Then they would be free of the shadow of debt!

Once again she had a momentary vision of the gleaming, golden sovereigns on the desk of Mark Gregg. But she knew she had done right. Had she accepted them, she would have shown contempt for her father and for herself. A bitterness against Mark Gregg and his kind welled up in her, a bitterness which would always be with her. With it there came a grim determination on her part to succeed, despite the cruelty of the world around her.

She was in so good a mood she bought two oranges and some roasted chestnuts from an old woman street peddler. Hurrying home with these treats, she set them out before an amazed Peg and told her of the events of the morning.

Peg listened, and when Becky had finished she said, "The tavern sounds like an awful place!"

Becky sighed. "It is not Buckingham Palace but it is a place where we can earn our living until we can find something better."

"I thought Mark Gregg might offer to adopt us and take us into his fine house," Peg said with disappointment on her pretty face.

"More of your romantic notions," Becky said with a hint of anger. "You must get over them and adjust to real life."

"I will," Peg promised. And then more brightly, she said "Your Davy Brown sounds nice."

"He could be," Becky said with carefully assumed disdain. Not wanting Peg to get more romantic fancies. "I'll decide that after I know him better. And you'd better remember that! Don't judge anyone until you know them well! And don't trust anyone who is a stranger!"

Peg pouted prettily. "You sound like my parent, not my sister only twelve months older."

"Someone has to put sense into you and try to protect you," Becky told her. "We have a busy day ahead, what with packing and moving. And we must go over all the songs we know. Singing is to be an important part of our work!"

They arrived at the house next to the tavern before six with their scanty belongings wrapped in packages which they carried. They were greeted at Number Eight by a buxom woman in dustcap and work dress. The woman's red face was adorned by warts on the end of her nose and on the sides, as well as in the middle of her cheeks. She was not a beauty.

"You're the girls?" she asked in a whiskey voice. "I'm Mrs. Crown! I'll show you to your rooms and then you can come over to the tavern when you're ready and I'll teach you how to draw the beer properly from the kegs!" She went down a long, murky corridor with them, following as she complained about having to continually instruct new girls.

At the very end of the corridor she halted and opened a door on a tiny cubicle with a narrow, iron-frame bed, dresser, and no window. "That's one of the rooms," she said. "The other is just beyond. They're both the same."

Peg stood in the doorway and studied the first room with despair. "There's no window. It'll be dark all the time!"

"No," the woman said, pointing upward, "There's a glass over the door to open for air and to let in the light." She seemed to disregard the fact that the hallway itself was airless and almost dark.

Becky put her things down on the bed in the second room. She told the ugly woman, "They will do nicely."

"I like agreeable girls," Mrs. Crown said with a frown in Peg's direction. And turning to Becky again, she added, "You have the privileges of my kitchen providing you clean up afterwards. The first mess that's left behind, and that's the end of using my kitchen."

"We will be careful, I promise," Becky said.

The big woman nodded. "We'll see! The last ones was drunkards. You can be no worse! When you're ready to begin in the tavern, come over. I'll be waiting for you!" And she waddled back along the murky corridor.

Peg ran to Becky in her room and said, "These rooms are dreadful!"

"We can manage with them for a little," Becky told her. "We must! And when we've fixed them up a little, they'll seem much better!"

"I don't believe it!" Peg said despondently as she left to return to her own little room.

The tavern was much more brightly lit at night than during the daylight hours. Large lamps were set out in brackets along the back of the bar and also at intervals along the walls. At this time in the early evening it was also filled with many customers, most of them male, and was a much more lively place than Becky had imagined.

Mrs. Crown provided them with pink caps and big pink aprons. She herself wore the same uniform. As her husband kept busy serving their thirsty customers she went about the business of teaching the girls the various types of beer and ale and how to handle the spigots of each great barrel. Peg picked up the knack of serving a beer with a foaming head before Becky. But they both soon felt confident enough to begin taking orders.

Becky looked around to see if Davy Brown was there, but she saw no sign of the young sailor in the crowded tavern. The numbers of customers increased as the evening went on. Peg seemed to take to the work, and her good looks and pleasant smiles won her plenty of tips. Becky was also doing better than she'd hoped. The tips were often small, but they would total up at the end of the night.

Luther plucked her arm and whispered, "Let's have that "Liverpool Girl" now. With all those extra verses, mind you!"

Blushing, she said, "Yes, sir." And taking a stand at the end of the bar, she waited for him to call for order and announce her song. There was some good-natured applause, and then she began to sing.

It seemed to her that every eye was on her and all other activity in the tavern had come to a halt. Of course this was not true—Luther continued to quietly serve drinks, and even Mrs. Crown and Peg kept on passing out great steins of beer. But many of the patrons were giving Becky their polite attention. When she finished the song, there was a loud burst of applause and requests for an encore.

Luther held up his hand, "Later, gentlemen! After you have further refreshed yourselves!" It was his way of getting extra drinks from them.

As Becky went on serving the various tables she became especially aware of a table where a dandified young man with a grey top hat and coat sat. He was not only dressed more elegantly than any of the others in the tavern, but he carred himself with an arrogant air. He had a weak but rather good-looking face adorned by a carefully groomed, drooping mustache.

Whenever Becky brought a round to his table, the man made some suggestive comment about her body, making it seem a cheap compliment but insinuating more in his tone. Four painted young women sat at the table with him and tittered at his supposedly humorous sallies. These young women were coarsely lovely and also dressed much more extrayagantly then the other women of the area.

When she returned from serving the table for a third time, Mrs. Crown gave her a strange look. The big woman asked her, "Did that Alfie say anything evil to you?"

She blushed. "He said several things I didn't understand. And he reached out for me in a nasty fashion."

"Watch him!" Mrs. Crown warned her. "Alfie Bard is the prize pimp of the area! Those painted creatures at his table are the girls who support him!"

She gasped. "Prostitutes!"

"What else?" the big woman said grimly. "Poor creatures! He uses them and then rids himself of them if they get diseased or drink too much. He's a real threat, our Alfie is, always on the look for new talent. So beware, my girl."

"I shall," she said. "I'm glad you warned me." She was most worried about Peg, whom she had seen at the table at least once. She could barely wait to pass the warning on to her sister.

"You and Peg are straight," Mrs. Crown said. "Anyone can tell that! And you'll be no use to the tavern if you decide to change! I'd bar Alfie from using this place as a headquarters, but there are those among our customers who want a bit of what his girls have to offer. Luther thinks we should tolerate him because of that. But he makes my flesh creep!"

Both Becky and Mrs. Crown went back to work again, and she waited until she and Peg sang a duet together to a warm ovation before she took the time to warn her younger sister against Alfie.

Peg looked dubious. She said, "I can't think he's all that bad. It's likely those awful girls who insist on crowding around him!"

"They work for him! Give him their money!" Becky said.

"I still think he's funny and rather nice," Peg said. "You can tell he's a real gentleman by his clothes."

Becky had neither the patience nor the time available to try and argue with her younger sister. She could only put this off until later and hope that Mrs. Crown would make Peg see sense.

She kept working and the night went by quickly. It was fairly late when Davy Brown at last took his place at the bar, a smile on his bronzed face.

The sailor said, "I was delayed. Found a card game and couldn't leave when I was winning and wasn't allowed to leave when I began to lose! I'll never learn!"

She smiled, "You missed my songs. Do you want a beer?"

He nodded. "A beer will do fine. I've already had too many whiskies." He glanced around. "Where is that pretty sister?"

Becky said, "She's coming back to the bar now."

Davy looked and saw Peg returning with a tray filled with empty glasses. He watched her carefully and, when Becky returned with his beer, he told her, "I have news for you. She isn't half as pretty as you are!"

"I'd be worried about it." She smiled. "You'll probably be telling her the same thing about me!"

"No," he said. "I mean it. She's attractive. But she hasn't your looks or manner."

"Thank you," she said. And she noticed that Alfie Bard was waving to her to come over to his table again. She hesitated, feeling resentment.

Davy noticed this. He gave the dandy a bored glance and then told her, "If that fellow ever bothers you, let me know. I'd like to give him a going over."

"He's a customer," she said with a sigh. "I can manage him."

"Just remember," Davy Brown said with a wink to bolster her courage.

She went to the table and noted that two of the young women had vanished, no doubt off to transact some business for the elegant Alfie. He smiled up at her in his knowing fashion.

He said, "You're too pretty to be working as a barmaid."

"What is your order, sir?" she asked quietly.

"Another round," he said with a careless gesture. "My name is Alf Bard, and I can put you in the way of having a real life."

"Thank you, sir," she said. "I'm not interested!" And she hurried away the laughter of Alfie and the two remaining girls mocking her.

When she returned with the drinks he'd ordered, he tried to catch her wrist, but she eluded him. He gave her a wise smile and said, "We're going to be friends, I promise. Even though you won't believe it!"

She said nothing but once again hurried back to the bar where she served Davy Brown another drink. She hoped she would not have to return to the table of the pimp and his girls again.

Davy Brown broke into her thoughts by telling her, "I'd like to know you better. Maybe we could meet tomorrow. I've nothing to do but walk about the waterfront. I'm waiting for a new ship."

She said, "I'm busy. My father died recently. We've only moved here today to begin this job. I've a lot of things to do."

"I'll be glad to help you," the young seaman said.

She hesitated, "I really don't know you well."

He laughed. "Theres little to know. I'm the son of a schoolmaster in Kent, would you believe that?"

"Yes," she said. "You talk like an educated man."

"Thanks to my father," he said smiling. "I've got me a fair education, but I've done nothing with it. I felt the call of the sea and ran off before he'd found me a post suited to my schooling. Can you see me apprenticed to a bank or law firm? I like the open sea and adventure. And that's what I've found."

"You may regret what you've done when you're older," she said. "The sea is a grim master."

"Aye," the young man said. "I know that, too. But I still can't live without it. Maybe the day will come when I'll be content with land and a quiet life. But not yet."

She used the cloth Mrs. Crown had given her to wash up the counter in her area of the bar. She said, "I wish you well—whatever you do. You helped us get work here."

"Then show your gratitude by letting me meet you tomorrow," he pleaded.

She smiled. "Very well. Tomorrow at one. You can help me take some things I have to sell to the second hand dealer close by."

"I'm your man!" Davy Brown said jauntily. "No one is more familiar with pawn shops than yours truly."

Becky laughed and went on to serve another customer. By the time she was free again she was disappointed to find Davy Brown had left.

The customers were beginning to thin now, with only a few left. Alfie Bard and his quartet of tarts had long gone to attend to the business of the evening. Becky felt some relief at this, worried about Peg's approval of the clearly despicable character.

When it came time to close and shutter the tavern, Luther Crown told the girls, "You did well! Continue as you have tonight, and you can work here as long as you like!"

"Amen to that," his buxom, ugly wife said. "And now I'll see you two safely to the house."

She did, and later Peg and Becky sat on the bed in Becky's room and counted up their tips. The total was just a little more than three shillings. The girls looked at each other in rapture.

Becky said, "If we do as well every night we'll soon have enough money to make a proper start somewhere else."

Peg surprised her by saying, "I don't think the tavern is all that bad! I found the work fun!"

"You were the one who complained at first," she reminded her.

Peg tossed her head. "I didn't know what it would be like then. Did your sailor show up?"

"Davy Brown. Yes."

"What's he like?"

"Pleasant and has a good manner," Becky said. "You'll have a chance to meet him tomorrow. He's going to help me gather up the furniture and sell it."

"I'll be resting most of the day," Peg said. "I'm tired and I'll be sure to have one of my headaches tomorrow night if I don't get plenty of rest."

She knew Peg had a lazy streak and avoided work whenever she could. That was why she was quite content to have her and the young sailor do all the hard work of packing the furniture and taking it to the second hand dealer. But she decided it might be best to pamper her younger sister and keep her contented.

Kissing her goodnight, she said, "Very well. I won't expect you to help tomorrow afternoon. But you'll miss meeting Davy."

Peg smiled. "I can do that another time. Or see him in the tavern." And she went to her own room.

At one-thirty the following afternoon Becky and Davy were busy in the flat taking down the beds and getting them ready to transport to the second hand store around the corner.

Becky hesitated over the half-dismantled iron bed and asked the young man, "Do you think we can manage all this by ourselves?"

"I'm sure of it," he said. "We'll take the ends first. Then the spring, with the mattress coming last. We'll make a regular procession through the street!"

"Peg and I would never have managed alone," she said, resuming taking the bed frame apart.

"She's not much like you," Davy told her.

"It's probably good that we're different in disposition."

"I suppose so," he said. "But as the older sister you have more responsibility."

"I know," she said with a sigh. "And Peg can be difficult. She has a lot of romantic notions of meeting some rich young man and marrying him. She sees herself ultimately as the great lady in some fine mansion."

"I hope her dreams come true," Davy Brown said. "Though I'm afraid few dreams do."

She stared at him. "You sound so sad?"

He smiled again. "Maybe I'm beginning to see that I made a mistake in running off to be a sailor. Meeting someone like you makes me always want to stay nearby. To live on land like most people."

"You said that day might come. But you didn't sound as if you expected it to come so soon."

"I didn't," he told her. "But the longer I know you, the more rapid the change in my thinking. I shall hate to lose you, Becky."

She stared at him in wonder. "But we've only just met. We have known each other only a few days!"

His eyes met hers. "I knew when I first saw you that you were the one. I didn't want to admit it. That is why I was late coming to the tavern last night. I thought I could stay away and forget you. I wasn't able to!"

"I don't know what to say! I like you! But nothing like this has ever happened to me before."

"Nor to me," he said with wonder in his voice. "I believe I've fallen in love with you, dear Becky!"

And he rose and took her in his arms. She did not resist him. The feeling of peace and security she knew in his arms was overwhelming. Was she also in love?

After a long moment he let her go rather guiltily and said, "Better get back to business! You're not one of Alfie's girls!"

She stared at him. "You know about Alfie's girls?"

"Who doesn't?"

"I'm worried," she said.

"Why?"

"Peg thinks he's handsome and funny," she said. "When I tried to tell her what he was, she wouldn't listen."

Davy Brown showed concern. "She'd be well advised to listen. If that fellow ever gets her in his hands she's as good as dead."

"I know, that's why I'm so worried," she agreed.

The young sailor was reassuring. "She'll hear more about him and learn the truth soon enough. I can't see a sister of yours getting herself mixed up with that sort. You'll see! It'll be all right!"

"I hope so," she said. "And now we have to start carrying things to the second hand shop."

It was a tiring task which consumed the entire afternoon. The ancient owner of the second hand shop insisted on bargaining over every item, and Becky had to stand up stoutly for her rights or lose the honest value of the furniture. She felt exhausted when it was all over. She paused at the flat long enough to pay the sour landlady her money. The woman took it from her without thanks. But Becky did not mind, since it was a debt settled. There was only Mr. Longbeck, the undertaker, to look after now.

Davy walked her back to Number Eight and promised to see her that night. She went inside happier than she'd been since her father's death. She had found something in her new friendship with the young seaman she had never known before. She secretly believed she had fallen in love, just as he claimed to have done. But she did not dare tell Peg, for it would only make her jealous and perhaps send her to the arms of the dreadful Alfie Bard.

That night was a repeat of the first evening. She and Peg were kept busy from six o'clock on. The place was filled, and Alfie Bard had his usual table, his four girls seated with him. In spite of his rude comments, Becky made it a point to look after his table so that she could keep Peg away from him.

Davy Brown arrived fairly early and took his usual place at the bar. He smiled at her and said, "I'm not late tonight."

"I noticed that," she said as she slid his beer stein to him.

Mrs. Crown came to her and gave her a key. "Go upstairs and bring me down at least a dozen more beer glasses," the woman said. "Some have been broken and we're running short. Mind the steps and take a candle in a holder with you."

She did as she was told, unlocking the door at the end of the tavern and mounting a narrow stairway to the second floor. She put the candle on a table there and began searching for the glasses. They were on a sideboard, and she began placing them on her tray. She was busying herself with this when suddenly she experienced a strange feeling of fear! She was no longer alone in the upper room!

CHAPTER 3

She turned slowly. Standing there in the flickering glow of the candle stood a smiling Alfie Bard! He made a move towards her, and she stumbled back, upsetting the tray of glasses.

"Go away!" she cried.

"You don't mean that," he said. And he made a swift move which made her a captive in his arms. She struggled to free herself and cried out loudly at the same time.

"Shut up!" the usually suave Alfie said angrily. He tore open her dress and bared her breasts. Then he began fumbling with her skirts, leaving no doubt that he intended to rape her.

"No!" she sobbed and fought back as fiercely as she could, but she was no match for the muscular young man.

She was on the floor with Alfie on top of her, a leering smile on his face. Suddenly a figure burst into the room from the stairway! It was Davy Brown!

Davy saw the situation, and with a howl of rage hurled himself at Alfie. The surprised dandy tried to get up to defend himself, but Davy was too quick for him. He seized the startled Alfie by his vest front and dragged him away from her. Then as she crawled over against the wall he began to hit Alfie with a series of punishing blows!

Alfie's face was smeared with blood now, and he crouched in a position of attack as Davy prepared to deliver a second set of punches to his slender body. It was then that Becky saw the gleam of a knife blade in Alfie's right hand and called out a warning to Davy.

In the same instant Alfie plunged forward to bury the knife in Davy's chest. But having been warned by her, Davy was ready for him. He managed to get hold of the dandy's wrist and twist it until he dropped the knife with a moan! Then Davy proceeded to deliver another series of battering punches to his face and body. Alfie fell to his knees in a pleading position, his face a gory pulp!

"Please!" he begged. No more!"

Davy stood over him grimly. "Get out of my sight, you scum!" he ordered him. And Alfie needed no second command. He struggled to his feet and made a weaving exit to the stairway and vanished in its dark depths.

Becky had rearranged her dress to cover her for the moment. With the aid of some pins she would be able to manage until she had time to repair it. She was on her feet now, still trembling from the shock of it all.

She said, "He followed me up here! I couldn't believe it!"

Davy nodded. "I didn't notice until Mrs. Crown told me. Then I came up on the double!"

"Not a moment too soon!"

"Are you all right?"

She said, "Yes. My dress is torn, but I can get pins from Mrs. Crown and fix it."

Davy shook his head. "I didn't think he'd have the nerve."

"He probably thought he could so as he liked with me, and I'd be afraid to tell on him!"

"Well he knows better now," the young seaman said.

"I'm sorry it happened," she said unhappily. "I'm afraid you've made a bad enemy."

"I can protect myself from the likes of that!"

"I hope so," she said. "You proved tonight you can—in a fair fight. But a villain like that is apt to use all sorts of mean tricks to settle a score."

Davy said, "Let him try! Are you ready to go back downstairs?"

"In a minute, she said. "I'll have to put some more glasses on the tray. Most of the others were broken when he came at me."

They went downstairs with Davy leading the way and carrying the candle while she came after him with the tray of glasses. There was an air of excitement in the tavern, which told them that Alfie Bard had created a sensation when he'd come downstairs in his bloodied and dishevelled state. There was no sign of him and his girls now. The familiar table was empty!

Mrs. Crown was waiting for them, and when Becky delivered the trays, the older woman said angrily, "That's the end of Alfie Bard as far as this place is concerned! I've told Luther neither Alfie nor his girls are to be allowed back in here. Not after what he tried tonight. Did he hurt you?"

"No," she said, "just my dress. Davy rescued me."

Mrs. Crown looked at the rips in her dress front and let out a cry of exasperation. Then she fetched some pins and carefully fixed the dress temporarily. Becky at once went back to work again, leaving Davy at the bar talking to Mrs. Crown.

Becky met Peg on the floor of the tavern coming back from delivering an order. Peg looked pale. "What happened up there?" she wanted to know.

She felt she had best put it bluntly, "Alfie tried to rape me."

Peg gasped. "And Davy Brown beat him up for it?"

"Yes."

"Everyone is talking about it," Peg said nervously. "I think you must have imagined it. Alfie was probably just teasing you!"

"Look at my dress!" she said grimly, showing here where she'd had to pin it. "What kind of fun would you call that?"

The frightened looking Peg said nothing but went back to the bar to get another order. Soon the place returned to normal. By closing time everyone but the principals in the melee had forgotten it happened. Davy saw the girls next door safely, and Becky warned him to be careful as he walked the dark streets to his own lodging place.

"I can look after myself," the young seaman assured her.

Still she worried. And she would continue to worry for many more nights. Peg's behaviour also caused her concern. The redhead suddenly had little to say to her and avoided her as much as she could. Becky didn't like this in her younger sister and tried to break down her reserve without any success.

A few nights later Davy came to the tavern with news for Becky. He said, "I've done a lot of thinking. And I've decided I don't want to go to sea. I'm taking a job here in London."

"Where?" she asked, delighted at the news.

"Gregg and Kerr's Shipyards," Davy said. "They're finishing a fine new ship, the *Orient Queen,* and they're taking on extra help. I'm hired as a ship's carpenter."

Some of her joy vanished. She reminded him. "That is where my father lost his life. Be careful!"

"I'm used to dangerous work," the handsome Davy told her. "You needn't be concerned about me."

"You're almost my old friend, my only friend, I can't afford to lose you," Becky said facing him at the bar.

He smiled. "It's to be near you I'm taking the job."

"I hope it works out well for you."

"It will do for now," Davy said. "And while I was at the yards today I met a little man who claims to know you and your sister."

"Jimmy Davis the dwarf?"

"That's the one! Jolly little man and much liked, I'd say."

"Jimmy is a fine person," Becky said. "Did you tell him where Peg and I were working?"

"Yes," Davy said. "He was a mite startled, but I told him you were managing well enough. There was no danger."

"Not since Alfie Bard has been banished from the tavern," she said. "Have you seen or heard of him?"

Davy smiled grimly. "I met one of his girls on the corner. From what she told me he won't be around for a week or so. I broke his nose and made a few other dents in that pretty face of his. She says he is furious!"

"I'm worried about what he may try to do!"

"He's a coward," Davy said with derision. "He can bully those poor girls he's seduced. But he can't fight a man. He'll keep away from us. You'll see!"

"I hope so," she said.

Davy went to work at the shipyards, and she and Peg continued on at the tavern. There were no more unpleasant happenings with Alfie out of the way. But Peg continued to be sullen and resentful of almost everything she said or did. It was an unhappy situation between the two sisters and Becky tried hard to placate the younger girl without much success.

Mrs. Crown noticed Peg's odd behaviour and told Becky, "I can't for the life of me think what is wrong with her. You've been more like a mother to her than a sister and she shows no thanks."

Becky sighed, "I think she's very mixed up and unhappy. I think I should try to find other employment for her. Perhaps a domestic in some fine mansion."

"She won't make the money she is making here."

"But she would be in a more protected position," Becky said. "She's so immature to be exposed to the wild clientele of a place like this."

"We've had no tarts or pimps since I made Luther rid the place of Alfie Bard and his girls," the big woman with the warty face said with annoyance.

"That's one of the reasons I've stayed on," Becky said. "And we have been able to save a little money." This was true. Each week she had put away a good share of their earnings in a tin box with a lock which she kept hidden in the closet of her room. She had paid the undertaker, and already they'd been able to save several pounds. She felt this would give them some security when they went looking for better positions.

A fortnight went by and Becky was singing, "London Lass" by the bar when she saw the door open and the familiar figure of Jimmy Davis enter in the company of Davy. They stayed back until she completed the song and received a generous applause. Then they came forward to congratulate her.

The dwarf said, "I always felt your sweet voice should be heard beyond your own hearth and tonight you proved it! You're a born entertainer."

She smiled wanly. "You're far too generous, Jimmy. And this is not a discerning audience."

The dwarf shook his big head. "I can't agree. The rough lot of men you get here are not easy to hold with any sort of entertainment. You keep them quiet and interested!"

Davy smiled. "True. And I suggest we wash down that truth with a couple of whiskies." He and the little man made a quaint couple as they stood together at the bar, Davy looming up over the dwarf.

Becky paused to tell Peg, "Jimmy Davis is here? Go say hello to him."

Peg looked impatient. "I'm busy! I have three orders to fill!"

"Then speak to him later before he goes."

"All right," Peg said curtly and headed for the other end of the bar.

Becky watched after her with a feeling of dismay. She had lost control of Peg. The younger girl no longer showed any sort of respect for her. And now she was turning her back on someone who had been a close friend of the family. Someone who would be hurt by her not greeting him. She again decided that they must soon make a move. This could not go on.

The dwarf left the tavern before Davy and Becky made a point of having a minute with him to bid him goodnight. The bearded little man asked solemnly, "Is anything wrong with Peg? She's not ill, is she?"

"No," she said. "She's in some kind of a temper against me. I'm sure she will be sorry later that she didn't speak to you."

"I don't understand," the little man worried. "I tried to speak to her once and she hurried right by me."

"She's been doing things like that," Becky said. "I can't reach her at all."

"It doesn't matter," Jimmy Davis said. "I'll be back another night. Only I was worried about her."

Becky managed a forlorn smile. "Don't worry yourself. She'll be all right."

That night Peg went home early. Davy and Becky were alone. Becky confided in him, "Tomorrow I'm going to have a straight talk with Peg and ask her what is bothering her. We can't go on this way. Whatever it is, I must know."

Davy was frowning. "I agree," he said. "And I think she's angry because you were responsible for sending Alfie Bard and his girls away from the tavern. Alfie used to make a lot of her. She liked his exaggerated nonsense."

Her eyes met his. "You could be right. I hadn't linked the two things."

"I'd be worried about it."

"Then I'll certainly talk to her in the morning," Becky said. "I can't let it wait if she's really upset over that awful Alfie!"

But by the morning Peg had gone! Becky discovered this when she went to find her. She hurried to the kitchen to ask Mrs. Crown about her, but Mrs. Crown had not seen Peg since the previous evening. She went back to her own room in tears, and it was then that she remembered the tin box with their savings. She rushed to the closet and found it was no longer there!

It did not take too much longer to arrive at the conclusion as to what had happened. She was almost certain that Alfie had been seeing Peg somehow on the sly and persuaded her to go off with him and bring the money with her! It would be typical of the pimp to want the money as well as poor Peg!

In tears she sought out Luther Crown at the bar of the tavern and told him her story. She ended with, "If I don't get her away from that man somehow, he'll destroy her!"

"No doubt of that," the owner of the tavern agreed bleakly. "I'll see what I can do about locating him. You mind the bar while I'm gone."

So she tended to the late morning and early afternoon patrons of the tavern, anxiously waiting for the old tavern keeper to return. He came back just after two o'clock, and she could tell he did not have good news for her. As soon as they were both free she asked him, "What did you learn?"

"I found one of Alfie's whores drunk in a doorway," Luther told her. "Soaked with gin and full of tears! Her fancy man had run off with a younger girl. She claims Alfie and Peg have taken off for France!"

"Oh, no!" she said in panic.

Luther nodded. "I'm afraid so. According to the girl, they left on an early morning boat for Calais. They're probably there now. From Calais they'll journey to Paris!"

"I'll go after them and find them!" she insisted.

The tavern owner shook his head. "You'd be wasting your time," he said. "The Paris underworld is darker than the one here in London. Once those two disappear into it, you'd have had an easier time finding a needle in a haystack. And you can be sure Alfie knows where to market Peg's body to the best advantage!"

Tears brimmed over in her eyes. "Please don't talk about it that way!"

"You must face the truth," Luther said sternly. "Peg has always been the weak one. Girls like her are hypnotized easily by men like Alfie Bard. He's an old hand at it. You would be better to think of her as dead, for she is now dead to the world."

"How can I save her?"

"Pray," the tavern owner said. "Perhaps she'll come to her senses and escape from him. She'll have to help herself now. You've tried to guide her and failed. Now she is on her own; perhaps she will develop enough character to see Alfie what he really is!"

"I knew he'd have revenge on me," she said tearfully. "And this is how he managed it."

"He was probably planning something like this anyway."

"I worry for Davy," she said. "He'll not rest until he harms him in some way also."

The elderly tavern owner gave her a troubled glance with his one eye and asked, "Are you planning to leave me, now that your sister's gone?"

"I don't know what I'll do," she said. "I must think. And talk to Davy."

"Peg wasn't earning her way," the tavern keeper said. "I kept her on because of you. You're the one the customers like. And Mrs. Crown and I care for you as well. As much as if you were our own."

She was touched by his sudden revelation of his kindly feelings. Normally he was gruff and reticient. It must have taken some effort on his part to speak as he had. She gave him a grateful glance, "I'll not leave you without some serious thought. But I can't bear to think of Peg off there in trouble."

"You'd never be able to find her," the elderly man said. "And if by accident you did, she'd likely refuse to listen to you!"

It was the bleak truth and she knew it. Peg's loyalty was not to her—it was to the pimp who had taken her off to Paris. Somehow she got through the day and, when Davy arrived at the bar that night, she took a moment to briefly tell him what had taken place.

Davy was not startled. He said, "I warned you she was thinking of that villain. Now you know I was right."

"I should have realized it myself."

"Why?" Davy said with disgust. "You wouldn't expect her to turn from you to the likes of him!"

"That is true," she said tautly. "I didn't expect that."

She went about her duties that night in a kind of fogged state. Luther showed his consideration by not asking her to sing. She could not have done so even if he'd insisted, but he didn't. A few people noticed that Peg was absent and mentioned it. Becky said her sister had a minor illness and would return later. This seemed to satisfy them.

Davy had a surprise for her when the tavern closed. He said, "I've made an arrangement with Luther to take Peg's room. I want to be as close to you as possible, in case Alfie tries to strike at you some other way."

Becky couldn't help but he relieved to hear the news. It would mean there was someone close by to defend her if trouble should come. And she'd been worried about his walking the long distance to his lodging place every night.

She said, "I'm glad you'll be close by. Do you think there is anything we can do to locate Peg and that man?"

"Luther is going to try and get some more information," Davy told her. "If he is successful, we may get Alfie's Paris address. Then we could at least try to get Peg out of his clutches."

She cried herself to sleep that night and tried to stifle her sobs in order that Davy in the room next door shouldn't hear her. When she got up the next morning, he had already left for work at the docks. The wet, miserable day matched Becky's own frame of mind.

That night Davy brought his belongings to the room and then came to the bar as usual. At the first opportunity she told him, "There's been no news to help. Luther couldn't find out anything new."

Davy sighed. "We'll have to wait and hope."

"I'm sick with it all," she said, near tears. "I don't know if I can carry on."

"Giving up won't help Peg," the young seaman said. "You must keep yourself in good health to help her. She'll surely turn to you when she needs you."

Becky made no reply but went back to work. Davy was in a quiet, troubled mood as he kissed her goodnight at her door. No sooner had her head touched her pillow than she began to cry in the darkness again. She tried to stop and could not help herself.

Then the door slowly opened and Davy, bare to the waist, in his dark trousers, came silently into the room and closed the door after him. He came and sat on her bed and touched his finger to her tear-streaked cheek.

"This cannot go on," he said gently.

"I'm sorry."

"You must think of yourself," he said. "And of us. I've stayed on land, Becky, because I want to marry you."

"Oh, Davy!" she said, caught between joy and sorrow, tears still filling her eyes.

He stroked her hair lovingly. "We will make a world of our own. A world strong enough to hold up against all the other ugliness and cruelties."

"Davy!" she whispered.

"I need you so!" He said huskily.

And then he was in the bed beside her, holding her in his arms. She vaguely realized he was naked as he pressed his lips fiercely to hers and at the same time carressed her body. He helped her slip off her nightgown so that finally their nude bodies were in full contact.

Her breathing became more rapid, and she knew that the longings she had so often repressed could not be held back now. It was like a floodburst of emotions! He murmured her name in her ear, and then she felt him penetrating her. She gave a small anguished moan which was soon to turn to strong breathing as they frantically moved through the act of love! All other thoughts were vanished from her mind.

It ended in a great feeling of satisfaction and content. She and Davy lay close together long after the actual loving had ended. They fell asleep in each other's arms. And he woke her to tell her of his love and to kiss her gently again before he left for work at the docks.

She afterwards felt that this initiation to love saved her sanity. It made things clear; she felt she could cope with them. And she knew that soon she and Davy would be married and build that haven of a life together far from the troubles of the everyday world. She did not know whether Mrs. Crown or Luther guessed that Davy had come to comfort her in a physical way. If they did, they gave no hint of it.

For her own part, she did not feel in any way betrayed by his making love to her. They were soon to marry.

She even managed a warm smile for him when he appeared at the bar that night. She whispered, "I've thought of you all day."

He nodded. "And I of you."

"Forgive me for being such a child," she said. "But Peg is so dear to me. I think I can face it now and continue until I'm able to help her in some way."

"That's more like my Becky," the seaman said approvingly.

The evening was a busy one, and among the many customers was little Jimmy Davis. The dwarf had learned of Peg's running away and was in a melancholy frame of mind.

"She should not have done this to, you," the bearded little man said sadly.

Becky told him, "I'm determined to find her."

"I pray that you do," Jimmy said and ordered another whiskey.

In fact he ordered too many whiskies, so he was finally in a sadly drunken state. Davy went over to Becky as she waited for the barman to fill her tray with drinks and told her, "He's in desperate shape. There's nothing for it but to help him home. I'll see to it at once and be back by closing time."

"I'll be waiting for you," she promised. "Take care!" She said the last urgently, as she still had fears of Alfie's revenge.

Closing time came and Davy had not returned. Luther stood by the entrance door of the tavern ready to lock it. He eyed Becky who was waiting there and said, "I have to lock up. It's time!"

"I know," she said. "But Davy isn't back."

"Maybe he found a card game," the bar owner suggested. "You know he can't resist a gamble."

"I don't think so," she said hesitantly. "Jimmy got drunk, and he took him home. He intended to come straight back. That was hours ago."

Mrs. Crown came up to them with a wise look on her warty face. She said in a kindly tone, "You go to your bed, my dear. It's not unusual for young men to take a night out on the town now and then. You'll find he's all right tomorrow."

"That's the truth!" her husband agreed.

"Very well," she said, not wanting to keep them any longer. But when she reached her room, she did not undress but lay down on the top of the bed to wait. Eventually she dropped asleep and came to only at the sound of a loud knocking on the street door.

By the time she wakened and was on her feet and out to the hallway, a nightgown clad Luther was already on his way to the door with a candle in his hand. Seeing her, he gave her a warning glance.

"Keep back," he said. "It could be thieves!"

"It may be Davy drunk," she worried.

"He'd not rouse us this way," the old man with the candle protested. And nearing the door, he called out, "What do you want? Who is it?"

A faint voice on the other side, said, "Jimmy! It's me, Jimmy Davis!"

"Jimmy Davis?" Luther turned to give her a questioning look.

"The dwarf," she said, going to the old man. "The one who drank too much and Davy had to see home!"

With some reluctance Luther Crown drew back the door bolt and threw the door open to the foggy night. A pitiful sight presented itself to them in the figure of a battered Jimmy Davis. The little man's face was cut in many places, and his clothes looked as if he'd been rolling about in some filthy gutter.

He said, "I'm near dead!" And he stumbled forward almost collapsing.

"I'll get some brandy," old Luther said and told her, "You help him into the kitchen." And with that he hurried ahead, the candle still in his hand.

She gave the dwarf some support and led him down the dark hall. "Davy! Where is Davy?" she asked.

"I don't know," he moaned.

"What do you mean?" she asked frantically.

"My head! I can't think!" the little man said as he seemed ready to collapse.

"Don't give way," she told him. "Luther will have some brandy for you in a moment." And she helped him into the kitchen. He sat on the stone shelf before the fireplace.

Luther brought him the brandy and put it in his little hand. "Drink it down, it will help you!" he instructed the dwarf.

Little Jimmy gobbled the drink down and then coughed loudly for a second or two. Then he moaned and held his big head in his tiny hands. "They came at us in the darkness," he moaned.

"Who?" Becky demanded.

He looked up at her with his woeful, bruised face and said, "I don't know! I was the worse for drink!"

"Where were you attacked?" the bar owner asked.

"Just a block form the tavern," the dwarf said. "They came out of an alley. There must have been four of them!"

Becky gave Luther Crown an anguished look. "I knew Alfie Bard would get even somehow!"

Luther gave her a motion to be silent and asked the dwarf, "What happened?"

"Davy put up a good fight and I did what I could," the little man said unhappily. "One of them picked me up and threw me in the alley like an old sack!"

"What about Davy?" she asked.

"He was still fighting them and doing a good job when I passed out," Jimmy Davis said.

"And when you came to?" Luther questioned.

"Just a while ago. The street was silent. No sign of them or Davy or anyone! I was afraid to go any further, so I came back here."

She told Luther, "Davy wouldn't have deserted him if he were all right!"

"Don't think the worst," Luther implored her. And he asked the dwarf, "Do you remember anything else about them? Did they say anthing you overheard?"

"I'm not sure," the dwarf worried. "I was awful drunk. But I thought one of them said to me, 'He won't do for for Australia!' And then he laughed and picked me up and threw me in the alley!"

"Do you think any bones were broken?" Luther asked.

"No. But my head is in pain, and I need to rest," the dwarf said. "And my mother and sisters are bound to be worried about me!"

"They'll have to wait until morning. You can go back to them after daylight," Luther said.

"I'll have to go to work then," the little man worried. "I'll send them a message from work."

"You won't be fit to work," she chided him.

The little man gazed up at her gloomily. "When you're employed by Gregg & Kerr, you report for work, or you don't have a job!"

Luther said, "You'd better rest in the room that Davy has rented. I'll wake you early in the morning."

So it was arranged. She spent a sleepless night worrying that Davy might be dead, murdered by the thugs at the order of Alfie Bard. Perhaps his body was dropped in the river or was hidden in some alley. She prayed it might be only that he was too injured to get word to her, that someone might have found him and taken him home or to one of the hospitals.

In the morning Luther Crown went out early to try and get word of the missing Davy. Little Jimmy, still in a sad state, limped off to work at the shipyard. At Luther's request she remained waiting in the house with Mrs. Crown.

It was a long, worrisome two hours before a gaunt-faced Luther Crown returned. He confronted her in the kitchen, saying, "I've found out what happened to poor Davy."

"Tell me!" she said, scarcely daring to breathe.

He said soberly, "You must be brave. There was a group of shanghaiing seamen last night—led by one of the known thugs along the warterfront, a crony of Alfie Bard's."

"I knew he was mixed up in it!" she gasped.

"They set upon Davy almost as soon as he and the dwarf left the tavern," Luther said. "They knocked Davy unconscious and took him away. At this very moment he's on a ship bound for Australia. That is, if he's still alive."

"You think he may be dead?" Becky asked brokenly.

"I'm afraid you'd better accept it," Luther said sadly. "The man who told me about it swore me to not betray him before he'd talk. But he claimed Davy put up such a fight they were rougher with him than they should have been. They collected their fee for turning him over to the captain of the ship, but they all agreed it was a dead seamen they'd sold him, not a live one!"

Becky listened in a state of shock, unable to summon tears. She went to her room and sat there, she couldn't organize her thoughts. Later Mrs. Crown came and told her she might have the night off. She made no reply, still staring blankly ahead of her. Only when the shadows of night came did she begin to cry.

CHAPTER 4

Almost twelve months had gone by since the night of Davy's murder. She had come to think of it as that, and mourned his death as any true wife might mourn her man. They had not been before the preacher, but they would have been had he lived. So she felt right in her mourning for him. The Crowns were sympathetic, as were the regular customers of the tavern.

In all this time there had been no word of Peg or the wicked Alfie Bard. But Becky had not given up hope of finding her sister and saving her. She let this be the motivation for her continuing to live and work. Every penny of her tips was placed in a new tin box, and she felt it might not be too long before she could make a trip to Paris and try and locate the missing Peg.

Jimmy Davis came regularly to the tavern and he was much against her going to seek out Peg. He advised her, "She went of her own accord. So let it be."

"I can't," she said. "However foolishly she has acted, she is still my sister."

"You'll get no thanks," the dwarf warned her. "And you might even place yourself in danger. If Davy were alive, he would not approve of it."

Her smile was bitter. "But Davy is not alive, so that changes everything doesn't it?"

The little man stared up at her shrewdly, his beer glass in hand, as he said, "It's Alfie you're after, isn't it? You want to settle your score with him for what he had done to poor Davy!"

"That may be part of it," she admitted. "But I do want to help Peg if I can."

It was the summer of 1862 and while the winter had been unusually cold, this summer which followed it was sweltering.

The crowded tavern was hot and filled with fetid air each night. There were times when she felt she couldn't stand the heat and noise. But she had come to be fond of Luther and his wife, and did not want to leave them to break in new help in this difficult time. She decided to continue on.

To try and cool off, she took long walks in the daytime, her parasol carried prettily over her straw bonnet while she wore a new blue linen suit which was her best. Often she went in the direction of the docks to watch the great ships tied up there and those at anchor out in the river. Most of the sailing ships now had some sort of steam auxiliary engine. Some of the great vessels had paddle wheels amid-ships, and many ships of iron were showing themselves. The talk was that the day of the wooden ship was limited.

She had heard from many of the men who worked for Gregg & Kerr, that the shipyard was on the point of bankruptcy because the partners could not agree about building the new iron ships. Old man Kerr was determined to continue with wooden vessels since they had made the firm's name. But the younger, Mark Gregg, was just as certain that iron ships were the thing of the future. They were faster and safer.

It was seventeen years since the *Great Britain* had been launched, and now the superiority if iron ships was no longer in question. Further, paddle wheels were being supplanted by screw propellers, a means of propulsion thought to be better than paddle wheels and much more speedy.

But shipping people and seamen were still divided in their views. The superiority of the iron ships with screw propellers was questioned when the 1600 ton *City of Glasgow* sank in 1854 after sailing from Liverpool. There were 480 on board and it was never heard of again. But ships continued to be built of iron and used the new method of propulsion.

In 1858 Brunei built the *Great Eastern* at Midwall—it slid into the Thames to be the largest ship afloat, a record it held for thirty years! It was built of iron, had paddle wheels and a screw propeller as well. It was 700 feet long and had a tonnage of 19,000. Some claimed she was ahead of her time, but all began to agree that ships of iron were the vessels of the future.

Becky had seen the *Great Eastern*. Her father had taken Peg and her to the docks to see it floating down the Thames in stately splendor. She could still recall five tall smokestacks and its five graceful masts; it had been partly under sail at the time. Her father had pointed out the paddle wheel and the propeller. The great size of the ship in contrast to those around her made them gasp! Becky tried to count the many portholes along its side and couldn't begin to! And then they marvelled at the patriotic design on its stern. It had been an afternoon she would always remember.

Now she strolled along the wharves past the red brick offices of Gregg & Kerr to a spot overlooking the giant shipyard. There was only one small ship on the stays under construction. And this underlined the fact that the company was in some trouble.

In the distance the Houses of Parliament, St. Paul's, and other London landmarks stood high in the sky, blue against the fleecy white and blue clouds. In the shipyard the small ship under construction looked lost; the yard was capable of building much larger craft. Men swarmed around the partially finished sailing ship like ants. And she thought with some bitterness that was how they must look to Mark Gregg, who certainly had no more regard for their lives than people generally had for the lives of ants.

She could never forget the day he had tossed six golden sovereigns to her in payment for her father's life. She had thrown them at him and she would do it again if he made the same gesture. She blamed him, to a good extent, for what had happened to Peg. If they had not been driven by poverty to seek work at the tavern, Peg would never have met a man like Alfie Bard.

And she might never have met Davy. She could not deny that she had been lucky in her meeting and romance with Davy Brown. It would always be a sweet memory for her, no matter what fortunes life might deal her. Even if she loved again, Davy would always have a place in her heart. And she would never forgive Mark Gregg for what happened to her father, Peg, and to Davy. In a strange way, all these things were somehow linked with the shipbuilding firm. And for her the firm would always suggest a vision of that grim, square-jawed man behind his mahogany desk, unyielding and uncaring.

It began to shower heavily in the afternoon and Becky, along with all of London, was grateful for the break in the strange hot spell. She hurried back to Number Eight to rest a little before the evening's work began. She had learned to do this in her year alone.

The rain continued through the evening, and the tavern was much more comfortable because of the cooling rain outside. The air had cleared, and a goodly number of the regular patrons were assembled in the big room. At mid-evening Becky changed to the role of entertainer and sang some familiar sea chanties which proved popular. Then she went back to carrying the heavy trays of drinks.

As it neared closing time and the crowd had thinned out, the door opened and a man came in. He paused in the doorway and gazed sternly about the big room. Apparently satisfied that it was safe to enter, he came in. His walk was unsteady, indicating he'd been drinking heavily, and he was well-dressed in a blue jacket and fawn trousers. He wore a blue top hat; he was clearly not of the usual tavern class.

All eyes were fixed on the well-dressed man as he went to take his place at the bar and order a whiskey. Luther poured him out a drink and said respectfully, "The best whiskey in the house for you, Mr. Gregg!"

Mark Gregg's stern face showed a thin smile, "You know me, then?"

"Yes, sir," Luther said in the same polite fashion. "I once worked in the yards."

"Everyone has!" Mark Gregg said and downed the drink. "Another, please!" He rapped on the bar for service.

Luther set the drink before the shipyard owner almost immediately. "We are honored by your patronage, Mr. Gregg," he said humbly.

Mark Gregg offered him an icy smile. "I expect you are," he observed complacently. Then he started on this new drink.

His entrance in the saloon had created a lot of attention. Becky made a point of avoiding the well dressed man slouching against the bar mid way along it. A number of the other patrons were whispering about Gregg and pointing him out. She noticed that a tough-looking group of four near the door seemed to be extremely interested in the wealthy man.

Gregg had one more drink, then almost contemptuously threw payment for the liquor on the bar. "That should do," he said, his words slurred as he turned and made his way unsteadily out of the place.

Luther picked up the money and gave Becky a knowing glance since she had just returned to the bar for some drink orders. He told her, "I've never seen him in here before, nor have I seen him in such a drunken state."

She said, "I have heard from those who know him that he sometimes goes off on drunken binges."

"He surely has tonight," the bartender said with awe. "He drank enough at this bar to make him pass out, and he was drunk when he arrived."

Becky glanced to the door area and saw that the four thugs who'd been sitting there were also gone now. She turned to the bartender and said, "The four who were sitting by the door have left. Do you think they may have followed him?"

The bartender shrugged. "No business of ours!"

"They might try to rob him."

"I doubt it," he said. "And in any case I say let him take care of himself. That's his attitude towards other people. He's not a kind or friendly man, I vow!"

She knew this was true but the pattern of events continued to worry her. However villainous Mark Gregg might me, he had not been in any state to defend himself when he left the tavern. The four thugs could attack and rob him with ease. They might even kill him. It wasn't a pleasant thought.

The tavern closed and Luther Crown and his wife left after asking her and the boy who did errands to close the place. She supervised the locking up, since the boy was young and she felt the responsibility was hers. When all was secure she started home. It was only a short few steps to the door of the adjoining Number Eight.

She and the youth were chatting in a friendly fashion as they strolled along the dark street when suddenly she heard a low moan.

She halted, a worried expression on her attractive face. "Where did that come from?"

The youth asked, "What?"

"Nothing," she said, about to resume walking, and deciding she'd imagined it. Then the voice came once more, the moan of distress louder this time.

She told the lad, "That was clearly a moan, and it came from the alley over there."

The lad looked back at her nervously, and she hastened to tell him, "There's no need to be afraid! No one is going to hurt you!"

"You don't know," the lad ventured. "There's a rough lot here in the streets of late!" He kept close to her and his voice low.

"We can't go on without finding out what's wrong!"

"What about calling Mr. Crown?" the lad hung back.

"He and his missus will be in bed by now," she said. "We must do this on our own!"

"All right," the lad said dismally. It was quite apparent he was terrified.

She led the way across the narrow cobblestoned street and another groan sounded loudly and more clearly. She almost flinched and halted, but she knew if she showed a single sign of fear the lad at her side would turn and take to his heels. So she pressed on until she came upon the stretched-out figure of a man just inside the alley.

"Gor!" The lad said with awe as he knelt by the moaning figure. "It's that Mr. Gregg! The rich toff!"

"Mark Gregg!" she exclaimed and knelt beside him. "At least he's alive! They must have tackled him as soon as he left the tavern! I was afraid they might!"

"What's to be done?" the lad asked.

"He's bad off," she said. "If you help me I can take him to the house. There's an empty room and bed next to mine. We'll see whether a doctor should be called or not."

The lad glanced about him nervously and reminded her, "The ones who did this may still be about!"

"No," Becky said. "They've done their work and taken his money! They'll be as far from here as they can manage! Help me with him! You take him under the arms, and I'll take his feet!"

"It's going to be a dead weight and no easy load," the boy grumbled but he did as she ordered.

Mark Gregg groaned several times as they moved him, which proved he was still alive. They dragged him across the street and into Number Eight. The final step was to get him in the empty room and onto the bed. Almost immediately, the battered man was sick to his stomach!

Becky held up his head so he wouldn't choke on his own vomit. When the session ended, she had the lad bring a pitcher of water and basin from her room. Using this and some old cloths, she cleaned up the mess, did the best she could with his clothing, and washed his bloodstained face. There was cut above his left eye which had caused most of the bleeding, but otherwise he seemed all right.

The lad stood by sleepily and yawning said, "I want to go home!"

"You can," she said. "I'll need no more help."

"Are you going to call the boss and his missus?"

"No," she said. "I'll speak to them in the morning. There's nothing they can do now. I'll stay with him and see he doesn't come to any harm. You go along!"

"Not much of a fine gent now, is he?" the lad said with a glance of disgust at the snoring Gregg. Then he left.

She went to her room and got a blanket. Then she made herself as comfortable as possible in a plain chair in the room with the sleeping man. She wrapped the blanket around her and sat watching him by the single candle's light. After a few minutes, her chin dropped and she slept awhile. She woke up several times and found him still asleep.

"Damnation!" The word came clearly and loudly to wake her from a cat nap, and she saw that Mark Gregg was standing in the tiny bedroom looking around him with blank amazement. His stern face turned her way; he seemed unable to believe what he saw.

She threw off the blanket and fully-dressed from the night before, stood up to confront him, saying, "You're feeling some better?"

"How did I get here?" he snapped at her.

"You were robbed last night and left in the alley across the street," she said nervously. She was beginning to realize he might think her in on the robbery, or accuse her of bringing him to this sad state. "I'm the barmaid from next door. The lad who helps there gave me a hand in bringing you here."

He continued to stare at her, as if he doubted her. "You found me in an alley?"

"Just across from here. You must have been set upon as soon as you left the tavern."

The cut above his eye looked swollen. His face bore bruises and he looked very sallow. He touched a hand to his temple. "I remember," he said in a low voice. "Yes!"

"I could not leave you there," she apologized.

He paid no attention to what she said. He had both hands at his temple now, and he was seemingly making an effort to remember. He said, "I was drinking last night. Went to a tavern. Very drunk. When I came out into the street, four men set upon me. They dragged me into the alley and attacked me and stole my purse!"

"We heard your moans," Becky said.

Now he turned to stare at her again. He said, "You say you are the barmaid at the tavern?"

"Yes."

"And you made this effort to save me?"

"I would have done as much for anyone in your plight," she said. She did not think he recognized her as the girl whose father had been killed in his shipyard, as the one who had thrown his golden sovereigns back in his face.

"Would you, indeed?" he said, rather quietly.

"Any Christian would."

"I wonder," he said. "I believe myself to be a Christian, but I pay scant attention to the problems of those unknown to me."

"I knew you were Mark Gregg," she said. "Mr. Crown, the owner of the place told me so."

Mark Gregg frowned. "I was most unwise last night. I seldom venture into the streets in that manner." He glanced towards the window. "It will soon be dawn."

"Yes, sir," she said.

He surveyed himself with distaste. "I was drunken and ill! My clothes are filthy from the dirty alley. I still have a most monstrous head! It would seem I might have lost my life had it not been for you. I owe you a most handsome ransom."

"I want nothing," she said firmly. "I will accept nothing. I did what I did because I felt it was right. I warned Mr. Crown as you left that you might come to evil, but he did not seem to care."

"Willing to sell me his liquor but not to worry about what happened to me after I left his place," Mark Gregg said with some bitterness. "Well, that is the way of the world, my girl. Only a few take notice of the problems of others, it seems. Fortunately for me, you are among the few!"

"Would you like some hot tea before you leave?" she asked. "I have a small stove in my room."

"That might help," he agreed. "And if you could bring me soap and another basin of water, I might make something more presentable of myself."

"I'll fetch the soap and water for you," she told him.

And she did. When she returned with a tea tray bearing a small pot of tea, two cups and saucers and some plain cookies, she found that he washed both himself and the worst spots from his clothing and did look and smell less repellent than before.

"This is most kind of you," he said. "I will leave as soon as I have the tea. I would not wish to be seen in this condition."

She poured out tea for him and herself, saying, "A gentleman such as you should not wander alone in these mean streets after the midnight hour."

He sipped the tea with relish. "You are right," he said. "I usually travel about in my carriage after dark. Last night I was not myself."

"I understand, sir," she said.

"Do not call me, sir, in that fashion," he rebuked her. "I would hope we are friends. My name is Mark Gregg. You may call me Mark. What is your name?"

"Rebecca Lee," she said. "Everyone calls me Becky."

"I prefer Rebecca," he said, in a return to his rather brusque manner. "I suppose you are used to seeing drunken men, since you are a barmaid."

"There are many who drink unwisely," she said. "Though most of our patrons come for conversation and a bit of beer. To them it is a place for comradeship."

He eyed her sharply. "I suppose the pub is a working man's club. I have no one to blame but myself for abusing the drink. I rarely do so."

"I'm sure of that," she said, not daring to call him Mark nor wishing to annoy him by referring to him as sir.

"Have I ever met you before? You have a remarkably pretty face."

"I'm sure you would remember me if we had met," she said, carefully. "I doubt that our paths ever crossed."

"Why do you work as a barmaid?"

"I have no family," she said. "I'm alone. Work is not easy for a lone female to find."

He finished his tea and held out his cup for her to refill. And he said, "Of course it isn't. There is no dishonor in what you're doing. You are to be congratulated for working hard to make a respectable living."

"Thank you," she said somewhat shyly.

"You have a working class way of speaking," he said.

"I come from a working class background," she told him.

"But your beauty could grace any mansion," Mark Gregg said. "And the equal of your goodness would not be found in many society belles."

She made no reply to this and found herself uncomfortable with his compliments. He seemed more in character when he was sharp and inconsiderate. His face was not all that stern when he relaxed, as he was at this moment. And in truth, the strong, square-jawed face was rather handsome in its own way. It was strange that he had not married before this. He must be in his mid-forties.

He finished his, tea and put the empty cup down. Rising, he said, "I will go now." He moved to the door and said, "I will not soon forget your kindness."

On her feet, she said, "It was nothing."

"It was a compassionate act," he said. "Which I hardly deserved. Like yourself, I live alone. I have no family. There are times when I'm overcome with the futility of existence. A black despair strikes me, and I go out blindly on a drunken binge. That is what brought me low last night."

"You must take more caution in the future," she counselled him.

"I shall try," he said quietly. And with a nod he left.

She followed him out to the street door. She saw him halt and study the tavern, then cross the street to the alley where she had found him. There he retrieved his somewhat soiled top hat. She watched from behind the door as he placed it on his head and then returned to the sidewalk and made his way along the street in what she presumed must be the direction of his home. There were several streets of rich shipyard owners' houses not all that far away.

She did not expect to ever see him again. And for the next ten days it seemed that she was right in this belief. Then, one early evening he entered the tavern and caused the usual stir. He was well dressed as he had been the last time, but on this occasion he was strictly sober!

Becky was carrying a tray of drinks as they met. He removed his hat, bowed, and smiled. "I see you are still hard at work!"

"Yes," she said. "It is a busy night, though some have been busier."

"I wish to speak with Crown for a moment," he said in his lofty way. And with a nod for her he moved on to the bar.

She went on to place the drinks on the table before the group who had ordered them. It seemed that Mark Gregg had recovered from his unhappy adventure and was not inclined to pay any further attention to her. She was relieved at this. She wanted neither his gratitude nor any reward for what she'd done. If she turned back money offered her again, he might remember her—and she did not want that.

By the time she returned to the bar Mark Gregg vanished. Mrs. Crown, busy filling some mugs with ale, turned to tell her, "Luther wants to speak to you! Right off!"

"Very well," she said, puzzled. And she went over to where the bartender stood at the other end of the bar, wondering if she were to be reprimanded.

Luther gave her an odd look when she reached him. He said, "You're off for the night."

Her eyebrows raised. "Off for the night? What are you talking about?"

He leaned close and eyed her earnestly with his one eye. "To be truthful, I don't know. But Mr. Gregg pressed a pound note in my hand to give you the night off. And at this very minute he's waiting outside in his carriage for you to join him."

"I can't!" she protested.

"You'd better," Luther told her. "I promised you would. In my opinion, he wants to give you some gift for your helping him that night he was robbed!"

"I don't want anything!"

"Don't be a fool!" Luther Crown told her. "He has plenty. But do what you like, as long as you go out to him. The missus and me can manage alone. It's not a busy night."

She sighed. "I'll go tell him he's gone to a lot of trouble for nothing!"

Removing her cap and apron, she quietly made her way outside to the summer night. And exactly as Crown had said, Mark Gregg was seated in his carriage with the driver standing on the street. Seeing her, the driver opened the carriage door and Mark Gregg stepped down to the sidewalk.

Unsmiling, he said, "I propose to take you to a fine restaurant for dinner."

Her eyes widened. "I can't go! I'm not properly dressed!"

"You live only next door as I recall," he said in his business like fashion. "I'll give you a quarter hour to dress."

Becky protested, "There's no need!"

"Please don't disappoint me," Mark Gregg said. "I have the private dining room engaged and the menu selected. Let me make at least one charitable gesture in my life."

She said nothing but turned and hurried to Number Eight. She was in a turmoil of emotions and thoughts as she quickly found her best linen suit and donned it. She freshened herself up as best she could in the short time at her disposal, spending long minutes with her hair. At last, she surveyed herself in the mirror and felt she might pass!

Mark Gregg was on the sidewalk talking to the driver of his carriage when she returned. He glanced at her and said, "A most remarkable transformation!"

She sat beside him dumb with embarrassment during the ride from the run-down dock section to the busy center of the great city. Soon they had reached the theatre district, with its crowds in the streets and its blazing gaslights.

"We are going to the Holborn Restaurant in High Holborn Street at Queen," he said.

When they reached the eating place, she was impressed at the magnificence of its entrance. He ordered the coach back in two hours, and a doorman opened the huge door to let them inside.

A white-haired, amiable headwaiter emerged from the great main dining room where concert music was being played in the background and came to greet them.

"Good evening, Mr. Gregg," he said with a bow. "Your private room is ready, and I shall send a waiter up as soon as you are seated."

He led them up a red-carpeted stairway and down a hall to an open door. The private dining room was on a balcony which looked over the main room and through the open window of which music from downstairs could be heard faintly. The table was set with gleaming white linen, silver, and a vase of flowers. Mark Gregg tipped the headwaiter generously. And before he left the waiter took the champagne bottle from its ice bucket and poured them drinks.

Mark passed her a glass and took one for himself. As the old man vanished, he smiled at her and said, "To our second meeting!"

"I'm overwhelmed," she told him.

"I hoped you would be," he said frankly. "Do drink your champagne. Enjoy it while its bubbly!"

The waiter came and Mark ordered turtle soup, boiled salmon with lobster sauce, pigeon and peas, and dessert and coffee to follow. As the waiter left he told her, "You must try the trifle here! It is excellent!"

She had several glasses of champagne before the first course. And more wine with the meal. She felt a little like Cinderella transported from the dingy bar to this feasting and elegance. She noted that Mark Gregg was dressed formally.

Mark Gregg did not have too much to say during the meal. And she spoke little, nor was she able to properly think her situation out. The wine made her feel relaxed and happy, the rich food filled her with content, and the relaxed atmosphere gave her a kind of happiness she had not known in a long while.

Over the dessert, he asked, "Do you approve of the trifle?"

"It is as good as you promised," she said.

"I'm pleased," he told her. And his slight smile made her think again that he wasn't altogether grim. He was truly rather good-looking, if somewhat worn.

She said, "It was a wonderful thought to repay me. And I shall always treasure the memory of this evening."

"That is kind of you," he said. "But surely there will be other evenings?"

Becky stared at him. "I don't understand."

He studied her seriously. "I have a confession to make. I've tried to forget you, but I've not been able to. Your lovely face has haunted me ever since the other night. I can't shut out the vision of it. I'm obsessed by you!"

His urgent tone left her no doubt that he meant what he was saying—it frightened her. She protested, "You think kindly of me because you are grateful to me!"

"There is more to it than that," he said, his eyes not leaving her. "I may as well say it out. I'm in love with you!"

"That's not possible!" she told him. "I'm not a lady! I'm not for the likes of you!"

"You can be the equal of any lady in the land," he said. "All you require is some coaching in speech and manners."

"Coaching in speech and manners?" she echoed him.

"You'll need them," he said quietly, "if you're to take your place in society as my wife!"

CHAPTER 5

"Your wife!" she gasped.

"I have thought it over all this time. I have waited too long to marry. I need companionship, and I need someone I can trust. You have proven your trust and wisdom, and I know full well I can never find anyone more lovely than you."

"Please!" she said, her head reeling with the wine and this unexpected development.

"I'm completely serious," he said. "I shall arrange with Crown to find a replacement for you. And I shall engage a coach to work with you on matters of etiquette and speech. Within a few months we can be married. As proof of my good intent I shall bring you an engagement ring to Number Eight tomorrow. I pray that you will not refuse it!"

"You have taken me completely by surprise," Becky said.

He smiled one of his rare smiles. "Part of my strategy. I have spent hours deciding how to go about this. Winning you is more important to me than any business project."

"You know so little about me!"

"I know the kind of girl you are. I need not know anything else," he said.

"I cannot promise to accept your ring, not without some thought."

Mark Gregg said, "I'm a reasonable man but an impatient one. I shall be at your room tomorrow at two with the ring. You have until then."

He did not attempt to kiss her until he said goodnight at the door of Number Eight. Then he took her in his arms and held her in a taut embrace. His kiss was much warmer than she had expected, and she felt that his behaviour was that of a man deeply in love.

When he released her he smiled and said, "Until tomorrow, Dear Becky!"

"Goodnight," she said in a small voice. And then added a shy, "Mark!"

She went inside in a state of ecstacy and excitement, and to her surprise she was met in the hallway by the warty-faced Mrs. Crown in her nightgown and robe. The old woman had her nightcap on and her hair in curlers. She held a candle in her hand.

"Well, my girl?" she said.

Becky smiled. "We had a wonderful evening. He took me to the Holborn for dinner!"

"The Holborn!" the older woman said, impressed.

"Yes," she said. "And he's asked me to marry him!"

"Glory be!" Mrs. Crown exclaimed. "Do you think he meant it?"

She shrugged. "He's coming with a ring tomorrow."

Mrs. Crown threw her arms around her and sobbed happily. "I couldn't be more happy if you were my own daughter!"

"I don't know," she said. "I may not marry him."

"What?" the older woman released her and stared at her in surprise.

"I have held a hatred for him so long I don't know if I can erase it. But I have truly come to care for him! I'm not sure at all!"

"What sort of talk is that? He is in love with you and wants to care for you for the rest of your life! Oughtn't that to settle any old scores you may have?"

"I'm not sure," she confessed.

"You'd better be," the woman advised seriously. "Miss a chance like this to rise in the world, and it may never come again."

Becky knew this was true and perhaps it alone was the deciding factor in her decision to accept Mark's offer of marriage. She lay awake long into the night thinking about it all. She was the survivor. Her father, Davy Brown, and even Peg were all lost to her. She was truly alone, and this man seemed to love her. It would be madness to refuse him, expecially since she was beginning to see another side of Mark.

So when he brought her a large diamond the next afternoon she prettily accepted it and agreed to become his wife. He at once arranged to pay all her expenses and have a coach come to her at Number Eight.

The coach was Mrs. Lucinda Bell, a woman of some social position, who had made the error of falling in love and marrying an actor. He had died early, leaving her a widow with several children. She now made a modest living teaching elocution and deportment. To her was assigned the task of making Becky a lady.

Mrs. Bell was a fragile woman who had probably been a beauty in her youth, but who was now much faded. Her manner was doleful but firm. On first meeting Becky she made an astute appraisal of her.

"Your face is pretty, and so is your figure," she said. "We must build on them. Your speech is poor and your posture is sloppy. But we can correct all that!"

And correct them she did! After a month Mark Gregg congratulated both the former actress and her pupil. "You've made the most remarkable change in Rebecca," he told the frail woman.

"She is a ready learner. She could go on the stage if she so wished. But I would not want her to do so. I would never marry an actor again not, even if the new stage idol of the day, William Kendall, should ask me!"

Mark Gregg had smiled at her and Becky as he'd said, "You need not be concerned, dear lady. The only stage she will grace will be the living room of my home."

• • •

By the time September arrived she was finished with her lessons and living in a new flat which Mark had found her in Grott Street.

In this more discreet section of the city she posed as a newcomer from Birmingham, and it was as such that she had agreed to be introduced to Mark's relatives and friends. It had turned out that Mark was not as entirely alone as he'd said. He did have an older sister, Elizabeth, a spinster, who lived with him and devoted her activity to working for the London poor.

The wedding was planned for late in September, but first she had to be presented to his sister and the family of Matthew Kerr, his elderly business partner. Mark arranged with his sister to introduce her to these people at an afternoon tea to be held on a Sunday early in the month at his house in Elgar Road, which directly adjoined the Kerr home.

Mark came early to pick her up and take her to Elgar Road in his carriage. He was kind, but he had assumed a proprietary air about her, as if she were his creation. This worried her a little, but she tried to ignore it.

On this Sunday afternoon she wore a pale blue dress and bonnet and looked up into his stern, square-jawed face nervously. "I'm so uneasy, Mark. I'm sure they will see through my sham and know me for the barmaid I am!"

He took her by the arms. "Nonsense!" And in any case, you have become a fine lady under Mrs. Bell's guidance. Just be vague about your background in Birmingham. I've told them you were brought up by an elderly uncle who recently died of a heart seizure. That is all they need know."

"I hate these lies," she protested.

"They will make our life easier and harm no one," he said. "You may find my sister stiff at the start, but if you take no notice she is bound to warm to you."

Elizabeth Gregg, tall, gaunt and as hard-eyed as Mark, was cool in her greeting. Becky pretended not to notice but congratulated the spinster on the nice flair she'd shown in decorating and furnishing Mark's home.

Elizabeth Gregg had responded sourly to this, saying, "But then it will all soon be yours."

Becky had blushed and said, "We shall share it and the running of the household as well. I insist upon it."

"No," her future sister-in-law had said coolly. "That will be your duty. I shall henceforth devote my time to my charities."

Becky realized that her prospective sister-in-law was not enthusiastic about the coming marriage, and that she would probably give her an uncomfortable time. This was borne out a half-hour later when the guests from next door arrived and Mark introduced Becky to all of them.

"Delighted!" Old Matthew Kerr said, a stout, florid-faced man, who had breathing difficulties and who leaned heavily on a cane for support. His wife, Alice, was another prim woman like Elizabeth Gregg, though she was older and had white hair.

"You are one of the Birmingham Lees," she said, staring at Becky. "I was sure I knew every branch of the Lee family there. My mother came from Birmingham, you know."

Becky said hastily, "I fear my family were not old residents. I only lived there with my uncle for three or four years; before that we were in Liverpool."

"Really?" The wife of Martin's partner said, as if she didn't believe it.

Vera Kerr came next, a young version of her mother with pale straw hair, a weak ching, and a generally frigid manner. She managed a smile for Becky and said, "You will be a most envied woman as Mark's wife."

Her brother, James, a young dandy in a purple jacket and bright yellow vest and pants came next. He gave Becky a knowing wink and said, "If you're interested in marrying into the firm, I'm the youngest of the family partners."

She returned his smile, feeling that he and his father would not be as difficult as his mother and sister. She said, "I fear I have made my final choice."

"Great pity," James said. "Since I'm about ready to settle down!"

"Settle down, is it?" his elderly father said from the chair into which he'd sat heavily. "Does that mean you'll only be out gambling two nights a week instead of five?"

Mark smiled tolerantly. "We mustn't be too hard on James. He is still suffering from growing pains."

James, who had moved on to gaze out the window at the street, turned to the others in the living room once again and said, "It doesn't matter; whatever I do, I'll be criticized."

His mother, primly seated on a divan with Vera at her side said, "That is not at all true!"

As if to end the argument, Elizabeth announced, "I shall now pour the tea. Will you all tell me your preference as to milk and sugar?"

Vera spoke up, "I like my tea with plenty of milk and lots of sugar."

"Sure sign of a weak female," her brother James teased her. "I've never seen it fail."

"James!" Vera rebuked him.

Old Matthew Kerr told the spinster Elizabeth, "I like mine straight. Plain black! Though sometimes a bit of whiskey can improve it."

"Hear! Hear!" Mark said with false jolliness in his tone as Elizabeth started to pour and serve the tea. Becky continued to feel miserable, as if she were on some sort of display and not being judged favorably.

With the serving of the afternoon tea and cakes, the party became a trifle more animated. Old Matthew Kerr said to her, "I think you are having a good influence on Mark, Miss Lee. He has been a trifle easier to deal with at the office since his engagement."

She smiled at the old man and then at Mark, saying, "I trust the improvement in his disposition will continue."

Mark looked none too happy at the comments and told them, "I'm sure all will agree I can do nothing but improve."

Young James Kerr came over to Becky and said, "There's one good service you can do the company."

"Really?" she waited politely to hear what it might be.

"Tell him to build iron ships rather than wooden ones," the young man said. "Iron ships are the future."

"I agree," Becky said. "But I understood it was your father who objected to the firm shifting from building wooden ships to iron."

"Not at all," the elderly Kerr said napping his cane on the floor to underline this. "I believe iron ships are with us to stay. It is Mark who doubts it."

Mark showed annoyance. "We had a slack time but now we have orders it will take us a year or two to fill. Why should we change our policy when things are going well?"

The young dandy, James Kerr, ambled up to him and touched a forefinger to his coat lapel as he said, "So that we can get the jump on our rivals. Be first in the iron ship business, just as we once were first in the construction of wooden vessels."

Mark eyed him insolently. "I find it difficult to believe you can remember so far back."

The thin, rather feminine face of James Kerr flushed. He said, "I do not know it at first hand. I heard it from my father." And he turned away.

Old Matthew Kerr glared at his son. "Most of all, you know about the shipbuilding business you have learned at second hand."

Mark nodded. "You'd do better to pay more attention to the yard and less to the gambling tables."

Alice Kerr spoke up in defence of her dandy son. "I think most men have their time of playing at the tables. I know Matthew did before our marriage, and I have heard you are no stranger to gambling, Mark."

Mark's smile was cold. "I bet only on the horses, ma'am."

"Surely that is also gambling," the washed-out Vera said.

"Different thing altogether," old Matthew Kerr said. "But I do agree with what James said, Mark. If we don't soon make a beginning with iron ships, we may well be too late for it."

Mark showed derision. "You're suggesting the firm might go under?"

"Larger companies than ours have been destroyed by a lack of change of policy or for catering to old customers," the old man said. "We do not dare to be smug."

James said emphatically, "That is the straight truth. You should face it, Mark!"

Mark drew himself up very straight and said, "While I'm the managing-director of Gregg & Kerr, the shipyard will build what I see fit. And I see a long future in wooden ships."

Mark's sister, Elizabeth, gave him a scathing glance, "Sunday afternoon tea to meet your bride-to-be is not the proper occasion for business arguments!"

Mark turned pale with rage. "My apologies to all of you, except to James, who began the discussion."

James bowed mockingly, "My strong back is sturdy enough to withstand all blame!"

Alice Kerr glanced over at her stout husband's chair to see that the stout man's eyes were closed and he was snoring faintly. With exasperation she turned to the thin hostess, Elizabeth and asked her, "Dear Elizabeth, may I enquire about the state of your various charities?"

This launched the prim Elizabeth into a long, boring account of her efforts to assist the children of the poor. Behind her James Kerr stood smiling and winking for Becky's benefit. She pretended not to see him, but it was most difficult.

Then old Matthew Kerr awoke with a start and looked about him in surprise. He reached in his vest pocket and brought out his solid gold watch, and studied its face. "Close to five," he said. "Time we were on our way home."

The ladies rose to leave, and there was a general saying of goodbyes and polite good wishes for her. She stayed at the door with Mark, and they exchanged polite words with the Kerr Family as they made their way out. The last to leave were Vera and young James Kerr.

Vera held Mark's hand a trifle too long and said in a sad voice, "You know I wish you happiness."

"To be sure I do," Mark said to Becky with what seemed like feigned admiration.

James Kerr concentrated on her. With his sly smile, he said, "Mark is far too old for you. Think about my offer."

She laughed. "I'm much flattered by it, but since I'm already engaged, I cannot believe you are serious."

"He's never serious," Mark said harshly and gave James a curt nod as he left. When the Kerr family had all been herded out, he closed the door. With an annoyed look on his stern face, he told Becky, "Well, now you have met them all. Husband and wife and son and daughter. You had best accept them, since Kerr is my partner and there's no escaping that!"

"I should hope not," Elizabeth said as she rose from her tea set. "The Kerrs are fine people! Moreover, Matthew Kerr controls sixty per cent of the firm's stock, which gives him controlling interest; he could well override your desire to stay with wooden ships if he wished. And he must feel hurt that you have spurned his daughter, who counted on becoming your wife, for another young woman!" The spinster marched off down the hall, and there was the sound of a door slammed closed as she entered her own room.

Mark was white with anger. "I fear Elizabeth has gone a bit too far this time!"

Becky said, "Were you ever engaged to Vera Kerr?"

"There was a time when we went out together, but there was no agreement between us."

"Still, she must have expected there to be one, since you were taking her time."

"If the girl was stupid enough to read anything into my actions, I cannot be held accountable for it," Mark said in his stern way.

"No. I suppose not."

"Any more than I can be held accountable for Matthew's senile notion that iron ships will sweep sailing vessels from the ocean. It's an old man's idle desire to appear young-minded."

Becky was embarrassed. She said, "In truth, I thought the argument was the other way around, that you were the one who wished to build ships of iron, and he was the partner who insisted you stay with wood."

"You were wrong."

"I do not know anything about it," she said. "But from the many conversations I heard in the tavern, the majority of seamen appear to favor iron ships and think they will one day compose the majority of commercial craft."

Mark eyed her coldly. "You are supposed to have forgotten you ever served in a tavern. Will you please remember that? I thought you had learned your lessons well from Mrs. Bell!"

"I'm sorry," she said, her face turning crimson. Not only did the reprimand hurt her but she felt ashamed that she had so agreed to hide her past. Mark had not been fair in asking her to assume a false identity, and she had not done right by herself in agreeing to his demands.

This afternoon had worried her and filled her with fear that she would be accepted neither by his sister nor by the Kerr family.

In a lowered, taut voice, she said, "Perhaps the barmaid in me can never be erased. It is still not too late for you to take back the ring and end the whole affair."

"Rebecca!" he said sternly and seized her arm so tightly that it hurt. "Never let me hear you say such a thing again."

She winced with pain but still said resolutely, "You may have your freedom! I do not hold you to anything!"

"I want you !" he said hoarsely. Then he let her arm go and said, "I will take you back to Grott Street now."

As they rode back in his carriage he discussed the plans he had made for the wedding. It was to be a quiet affair in a nearby chapel. He did not feel they should have many guests—just his sister and the Kerr family. She listened, bleakly thinking of little Jimmy Davis and the Crowns, knowing that they would not be invited even though she might wish it, and that they could not fit in with her fake Birmingham past, even if they wanted to attend.

He brought her into the pleasant little flat which he'd provided. He seemed in a strange, restless mood. Normally he left almost at once, but now he lingered and showed no hint of going.

She removed her bonnet and offered to get him a drink. He quickly accepted and asked for a whiskey. She brought it to him and he downed it.

Then, his eyes burning in a strange way, he said, "I heard what James Kerr said today. That I was too old for you. Do you feel that way?"

She shook her head. "I would not marry you if I did."

"Perhaps you might," he said in the same taut fashion. "It could be you agreed to marry me merely to improve your lot in life!"

"You cannot believe that!" she protested, though in her own heart she knew there was some truth in it. She had fought the idea and told herself the hatred she'd once felt for him had turned to love and respect. But had it? She worried about this as she face the angry older man.

"I'm a man of strength," Mark went on angrily. "Not a foolish fop like young James! I will show you whether I'm too old to wed or not!"

And before she could say or do anything he lifted her up in his arms and carried her struggling into her bedroom. He threw her on the bed. Tears filled her eyes as she stared up at him and saw him grimly removing his jacket and then his other clothing. In a moment he was tearing at her clothes without consideration. He was deaf to her protests as he prepared to rape her!

He penetrated her with the same air of cruel dominance. His lovemaking was fierce; it frightened her, for there was no hint of gentleness in it. He was perspiring and breathing heavily as he finally finished with her and abruptly left her!

Shamed and hurt, she covered her tear-filled eyes with the back of her hand, thinking that she was no better than his paid harlot. All the fine manners and kindness to her had ended in this ugliness. She had not been wrong about him! Under the veneer was a streak of cruelty which could ruin anyone.

After what seemed like a long while, so long she hoped that he had silently left the room, he spoke to her in his stern voice, "Rebecca!" And when she made no reply. "Rebecca, please look at me!"

She raised her hand and looked up to see he was fully dressed again, though she lay there partially nude, her clothing torn and dishevelled.

He eyed her grimly. "I'm sorry. That was not the way I wished to take you. But I had to show you I am a man! A man of strength who takes what he wishes."

"You have shown me that and much more," she said in a broken whisper.

He looked down at his shoes. "I will not remain here begging your forgiveness. I only ask you to try and understand. This afternoon was not easy for me. This is what came of it." And with this rather lame apology he turned and left the flat.

Becky lay there as he'd left her for a long while. She was too stunned and hurt to make even the slightest physical move. She could only wonder if the unhappy life she had known this far might be going to lead to a still more unhappy future. Had she allowed herself to be lured into an impossible position with a selfish and cruel man?

Only once in her short life had she been truly happy. That was when Davy had appeared. But Davy was dead and she was alone.

The next morning a lad arrived at the apartment with a huge bouquet of roses for her and a note which said, "My dearest Rebecca, forgive the madness which my love for you made me exhibit last night. If you will forgive me, I promise nothing of the sort will ever happen again, your loving Mark."

She read it sadly and gazed at the lovely flowers. There was no doubt that be believed he meant what he'd written, but she could not. She wished now she'd told him when they met that she was the one who had tossed back his golden coins offered coldly for her father's needless death. But she hadn't told him then, and now it was too late.

For more than a week she refused to see him. Then she had a surprise call from his sister, Elizabeth. The gaunt woman entered uneasily and sat with awkwardness in the chair she offered her.

After a long pause, the spinster said, "I am here on behalf of my brother, Mark."

She stood rather coolly, listening. "Oh?"

"Yes, Miss Lee," the thin-faced woman said bitterly. "Is it your wish to destroy him?"

"What do you mean?"

"He is shattered by your turning your back on him. Mark is a proud man!"

"We all have some pride, Miss Gregg."

"You do not understand!" Elizabeth said in a near-hysterical manner. "It is a near madness with Mark. Since you've refused to see him, he has been drinking to such excess that I fear something dreadful will happen to him."

Becky said, "That would seem to me to be weakness in him rather than strength. He claims to be strong!"

"He isn't!" Elizabeth said. "Inside, he is not strong. I know! It was the same when he was a boy! Do not let him destroy himself, I beg you. Save him!"

Becky went to the sobbing woman and attempted to comfort her. "I'm sorry we had this misunderstanding. I will talk to Mark. Tell him I will see him whenever he wishes."

Elizabeth dabbed at her eyes and nose with a hankie. "I thank you, Miss Lee!" And she got to her feet. "I must seem a silly woman to you but Mark is important to me."

"It is all right," she said wearily. "Have you a carriage waiting?"

"Yes," Elizabeth said. "I will tell Mark what you said as soon as he is in a state to listen."

"Please do," she said, seeing the woman out.

After Elizabeth left, there was a terrible let down. Becky went to the window and watched the carriage with its two gray horses drive away, and it seemed that all her hope was fading with it. She had agreed to see Mark and try to reason with him. But she knew that nothing would satisfy him but her submission. That he must conquer or be enraged. It wasn't a pleasant prospect.

So she did see Mark as she'd promised. He looked so bad from his drinking binge that she was shocked. He was humble and pleading, and in the end she forgave him and agreed to go ahead with the marriage. She would later think of this as one of her major mistakes.

They had the quiet ceremony he'd suggested and afterwards a reception at the Kerrs, with old Matthew Kerr making a speech of congratulations while his wife and Mark's sister Elizabeth, stood grimly by. To cap the occasion, Vera Kerr sniffed all through the ceremony and reception as if it were Mark's funeral, and not his wedding. Young James Kerr seemed heartily amused and entertained by it all. And the only emotion felt by Becky was that of taking part in a strange charade.

Their wedding night was spent at the Strand Hotel. It was not surprising that the groom fumbled in the consummation of the event and that she was not at all aroused. This was an unhappy beginning of a pattern that made any joyous loving between them an exception rather than the rule.

But for many weeks he was on his best behaviour in every other way. She took over the running of the house, and Elizabeth discreetly spent most of her time working at the East End Mission which she had established for the poor. For a while Becky thought there was a possibility of a modest amount of happiness in her marriage.

She was tortured by one thing, though—the memory of what had happened to her sister, Peg, and an urgent desire to find her and try and save her. One evening when she felt Mark was in a good mood, she told him about Peg. He listened with impatience, and when she finished he delivered his judgement.

"I think you should forget all about her," he said.

"She is my sister!" she pleaded.

"I would say she has forfeited that relationship," her husband said coldly.

"I can't get her out of my mind," she worried.

"That is unfortunate, but you must discipline yourself in this matter," he said. "Now if you will forgive me, I have some business papers to go over."

She made no further protest. But that night she came to a decision. She had an allowance to run the house and for her own dress purchases. She would stint on everything and gradually save enough money to do what she had in mind. She would hire a private detective agency to try and find Peg.

It was about this time that labor trouble broke out in the shipyard. To meet the threat of a strike, Mark enlisted the help of a young man who'd gained a reputation in management circles as a strike breaker. He had his own band of hoodlums who would fight the regular workers and take over until the laborers gave in.

Mark had the young man visit him at the house one evening. He explained to her that he did not want to be known as hiring a strikebreaker, and it was more discreet to have meetings with him at home than at the office.

So she came to meet young, sullen Bart Woods. He was a muscular young man with a handsome face, dark hair, and lively dark eyes. He said little, but when she smiled at her, she could not help but be thrilled at his masculinity. At Mark's bidding she left them together.

When Mark had finished with him and joined her in their bedroom later, he looked weary. He told her, "That young man struck a hard bargain with me."

"Really?"

Mark Gregg nodded grimly as he stood in the glow of a rose shaded lamp. "He will only agree to break the strike if I make him works manager."

"You already have a works manager."

"Aye. And a good one. But there's little I can do. I cannot afford the strike to go on. So I'll have to give this fellow his way."

"He's a strange person. He's very silent, but he exudes power," she said.

Mark gave her a troubled look. "I would rather not hire him. He has a black background. Before he became a strike breaker, he was the leader of a gang of thugs who shanghaied seamen for a fee! But I cannot afford to lose! So it must be!"

Becky was no longer listening. Her thoughts had wandered to other days and the man whom she'd loved, the man who had been shanghaied and delivered dead on a ship bound for Australia for blood money!

CHAPTER 6

A thin coating of snow lay over London on that sunny December afternoon in 1862. From the great dome of St. Paul's to the round pilings of the docks, the snow had lightly touched everything. The trouble at the shipyards was still continuing, and Becky had decided to go down and see for herself what was happening. She summoned the carriage, which was always at her disposal for her shopping or other errands, and had the coachman take her down to the red brick building which housed the firm of Gregg & Kerr.

She left the carriage intending to go inside and see her husband. But almost the moment she stepped onto the sidewalk she observed the impressive, tall figure of Bart Woods walking towards her. He wore no hat and his dark hair rustled in the wind. He walked with his head down slightly, wearing a heavy black coat.

As he came up to her he recognized her and bowed. "Mrs. Gregg!"

"Yes," she said, with a small smile. "I have come down to take a look around."

"Don't venture near the yard," the young man warned her. "We had serious trouble there yesterday, and we've only a small gang working today."

She gave him a worried look. "So the trouble drags on?"

"It does," the handsome young man said in his curt way. He stared at her with those sharp, black eyes, and she found herself wondering if in his career as shanghai artist he might have been the one who murdered Davy Brown.

"Is there no hope of ending it?"

"Soon. If they meet our terms," Bart Woods said. "You will excuse me—I'm on my way to make a report to Mr. Gregg. Were you planning to see him?"

"No," she said. "I won't bother him now. I'll just drive by the shipyard and return home."

"Very well," the dark man said, With a slight nod of his head he went on to the entrance door of the building and then inside.

She stood for a moment speculating what to do next. She had changed her plans at the last moment. She'd meant to see Mark but knew he would think her in the way if she went up there now; so it was better to move on. She instructed the coachman to take her by the roadway which led directly to the yards. She sat back in her seat during the short drive, bothered by the knowledge that the strike was continuing.

The carriage halted and she glanced out. Bart Wood's words were underlined by the fact that although there were two small ships on the stays, the full work force was not present. Just a tiny group were busy at the ship while several others stood guard not far with rifles in their hands.

The yard looked bleak on the windy December afternoon. She was watching the doings at the yard and in the harbor and river beyond when a familiar figure in a heavy gray coat with fur collar and a jaunty gray hat came smiling up to the carriage, It was James Kerr, son of old Matthew Kerr. He looked up at her pleasantly.

She quickly opened the door and said, "I didn't know you ever came down here."

He removed his hat and laughed. "I happen to have a share and interest in the business through my father."

"Of course! It's cold!"

"Yes. May I join you in the carriage?"

"Please do," she invited him in and moved to give him room. He stepped in and took a seat beside her. Then he opened the tiny window behind the driver's seat and gave him the address of a restaurant. He closed the window and settled back as the carriage got underway: "No reason why we shouldn't have a hot drink and something to eat!"

She was a little upset by his taking her for granted. "I hadn't planned to go to a restaurant," she said. "Certainly not with you!"

"Your husband won't hear about it," James said with a smile on his weak but pleasant face. "And what if he does—it is all perfectly innocent."

"Just so long as he understands that," she said.

"I promise to bear all the blame," James Kerr said. "What brought you down to the yard?"

"The same thing that brought you, I suppose. I was interested in the strike."

"Ladies aren't supposed to take an interest in business."

"No one has told me it is a crime," she replied. "My husband is deeply involved in the trouble. It is bound to concern me."

"Miss Lee from Birmingham," James said mockingly. "You are truly an original!"

"What do you mean?" she asked. Paying all her attention to him and none to the passage of the carriage through the cobblestone streets.

His top hat was resting in his lap and he said, "You are different! You have beauty and a good mind! You deserve better than Mark! Vera, my sister, would have done for him. I am sure he'd intended to marry her."

"I do not find that a pleasant topic."

"Sorry," he said. "But I expect you've noticed how she moons about whenever Mark is nearby."

"I prefer not to notice such things."

"Very wise," he said. "Father brought this new chap home for dinner the other night. The new manager, Bart Woods, and I must say he is something!"

She glanced at James. "You don't like him?"

He shrugged. "I think he is a powerful, young man with ambition and no scruples. He has a record of being a waterfront thug. Now he's trying to turn respectable as a strike-breaker, and

Mark has made him manager of the yards. It seems Mr. Wood is on his way to becoming respectable."

"He struck a hard bargain to settle the strike—and it isn't over yet."

"It will be," James said. "I was talking to some of the old hands. They can't hold out against Woods and his thugs. So it'll be a new day for the company. And Woods, like my father, sees the future of shipping in iron ships. Maybe they'll join together against your husband."

Becky had to resent the reckless young man's impertinent remarks about her husband. She said, "I do not think any new manager, not even Bart Woods, will break up the allegiance your father has for Mark."

"Maybe not," James said. "More's the pity."

"You don't like my husband," she challenged him.

"Few do."

She stared at him. "How dare you say that? I could easily tell him of your opinion."

"I don't think you will."

"He is my husband, remember."

"But you are clever enough to see through him," James taunted her. "He gives everyone the impression of his strength. But he is not a strong man; he's a cowardly one. That is why he tends to be cruel and corrupt! Worse than that, he corrupts everyone with whom he comes in contact!"

"Please!" she said sternly.

"I beg your forgiveness," James said. "But it is true. To an extent he has corrupted my father, making him engage in labor practices which are unfair to the loyal men who have worked for us over the years. He has drawn this Bart Woods to him because he knows of his corrupt background and hopes he will be of use to him. Even you must have corrupted your moral values to become the wife of a Mark Gregg!"

"If you were not the son of my husband's partner, I would ask you to leave the carriage," she warned him. "I do not like your conversation."

"You are right," he said. "I should not so loudly express what are merely my opinions. I'm probably jealous of Mark for taking the place I might otherwise hold in the firm. If you will overlook all that I've said I will pursue another tack in my conversation."

"You must, or leave my company," she warned him. But while she could not agree with him, she knew much of what he'd said was true. This cut deeply. Especially his comments about her. She had compromised in marrying Mark, and perhaps now she was getting her proper pay for it in an unhappy married life. For she was truly not happy with the stern, middle-aged tyrant.

The carriage halted and James helped her out. The restaurant was a popular one in a fashionable street. But it was small and rather intimate. She was relieved at this and pleased when they were quickly seated at a small table somewhat hidden by a false waterfall in the middle of the dining room. They ordered and then faced each other over drinks.

She said, "No prudent wife would be doing this."

"Your reputation is safe with me."

"Mark is jealous of you, I must tell you that And of me."

"Don't worry," the good-looking James said. "Soon after the New Year I'm leaving England for America."

Becky was surprised. "You've made your mind up?"

"Yes. My father is still well enough to look after his share of the business. And Bart Woods joining the firm means there will be no active place for me. I don't agree with Mark's policy in any case."

"What will you do?" she asked.

"In America?"

"Yes."

"I have a few things in mind," James said airly. "If I wish I can live on the family money."

She said, "You must have more ambition than that."

"There is much shipbuilding going on in America and in Canada," James told her. "I intend to look into the firms and perhaps make some agreement with one of them. Unlike Mark, they are all much interested in iron ships."

"I see," she said.

"Samuel Cunard has established a regular mail service across the Atlantic," James said. "Passenger traffic is increasing every year. Steamships are beginning to come into their own. But they will be ships with hulls of iron!"

"You should try to convince my husband of that."

"He won't listen," James Kerr complained. "But perhaps Bart Woods will be able to make him see sense."

Their food came and they had an enjoyable lunch. Then she and James parted, and she went back home in the carriage. It had been an interesting and not unpleasant afternoon. She found James extremely intelligent and felt it a pity that his lack of ambition made him so indifferent about what he did with his life.

When Mark returned that evening, he brought up the subject of her visit to the yards. He asked her, "Why did you not come up to the office to see me?"

"I met Bart Woods on his way to you. I thought it might be an important discussion and I'd find myself in the way. So I simply continued on." She omitted any mention of meeting James or having lunch with him, trusting that Mark would not hear of her mild adventure.

Her husband's stern face was lined with weariness. "The strike will end tomorrow, but on Bart Woods' terms."

"Isn't that what you wished?" she asked.

He stood before their log fireplace with his back to it and his hands clasped behind him. "Yes and no."

"I don't understand."

Mark frowned. "I'm worried about him. I need his firm hand to keep the laborers in line, but I think he is overly-ambitious. And worst of all, he agrees with Matthew Kerr; he thinks we are wrong in not turning to the construction of iron ships."

"Perhaps you should consider it?" she ventured.

"Never," he snapped. "The company will be operated my way—and that is that!"

She made no further mention of business to him. But she noted from that evening on that he began to drink more. He sometimes came home from the office with whiskey on his breath and in a surly mood. And he would continue his drinking through the evening, being no company for her. Then he would drop sodden into bed to sleep drunkenly through the night before beginning another day in the same way.

The way his drinking was aging him alarmed her. But when she made a small protest to him about it, he accused her of being a meddling wife and not knowing her her place.

• • •

The holiday season was at hand. A time for Christmas festivities and saying an end to 1862. Becky had first read Dickens' *A Christmas Carol* while her father was still alive, and it had changed customs in England a great deal. More than ever, Christmas had become a great family tradition with a tree, a feast of turkey, and many parties. Mark Gregg informed her that he and Elizabeth had always held a dinner party for the Kerrs on Christmas night, and that they, in turn, entertained on Boxing Day, the day following Christmas.

"I want you to see that this is the best year of all," he told her in one of his more sober moments, and he gave her a wad of pound notes to cover the expenses.

She was excited at the prospect. But one thing concerned her more. She was still haunted by the knowledge that Peg had not been found. With the money she had put aside each week and some pound notes from the Christmas money, she made a journey to the business section of the city one afternoon. There, in a small office up three rickety flights of stairs, she met a most peculiar man.

Mr. Phineas Pennifeather was thin with round shoulders, and he had a mass of long, gray hair which was always wildly askew and thick-lensed glasses shielding small blue eyes. He had a pinched face and in his shabby, dark clothes, he could have been anything from fifty to seventy. He was the sort of old man whom no one looked at twice. And that was the secret of his success, for Mr. Pennifeather was a private detective.

He sat at his rolltop desk and listened to her story. Then in a gravelly voice, he said, "It is an old story, Mrs. Gregg, and a sad one. I have often been engaged to find missing girls."

Becky leaned forward, the face under her cranberry shade bonnet pale as she said, "Have you had much success?"

"Sometimes," the old man said, drumming bony fingers on the desktop.

"Sometimes these girls vanish in the underworld without a trace."

"I assume this Alfie Bard and Peg are still in France," she said.

"I doubt that," he told her.

"You do?" She was surprised.

He nodded. "It is a familiar trick to throw the family of the girl off the track. No doubt he has made use of her in Paris to his advantage. And then when he has felt it safe, he has returned to England with her."

She said, "So you think she might actually be in London?"

"More than likely, she is," Phineas Pennifeather said. "But it will take a good deal of seeking out."

"I'm prepared to pay."

"You must not be impatient," the private detective warned her. "This could take weeks, months, or perhaps as long as a year. I could even fail altogether."

"I have confidence in you."

"Thank you, ma'am," the old gentleman said. "I have a good name in the city. I'm known as honest, which is a rarity in my profession. I will undertake the search and will contact you when I have any news. In the meantime you can generally find me here when you wish to talk with me or look after additional fees."

"I shall press this until we find her," she promised. "I will find the money to pay you."

"My fees are modest for a prosperous lady like yourself," the old man said with a sniff. "There is just one thing I must warn you of."

"Yes?"

"This could turn out unpleasantly."

She frowned. "You mean?"

Phineas Pennifeather's ancient face was gloomy. "You could wind up discovering your sister dead."

"I can face that better than not knowing where she is or thinking of her living a life of shame and misery."

"Ah!" he said, tapping the side of his nose. "That is another aspect of it. The sister who left you was in the full bloom of youth and health. The girl we may find will surely not be in that state."

Becky hadn't thought of this. She figured Peg would look exactly as she did when she had run off with Alfie Bard. She said, "You are saying she may have become a different person? It is not all that long a time!"

"Life lived as a drab ages one fast," the private detective said. "Degradation erodes beauty and character. Disease sickens and changes a personality."

"You frighten me!"

"I cannot be less than truthful with you," he said. "You may locate your sister and find her with lost beauty and ravaged with some social disease. She might also be a drunkard or an opium addict. Favorite escapes for prostitutes. And under that man's tutelage she has surely become a prostitute."

Becky said desperately, "I will not accept that she cannot be saved."

Phineas Pennifeather sighed. "Yet she has made no attempt to reach you."

"She might find it difficult. He may be threatening her. Or she may be too ashamed!"

The old man nodded. "I can see that you must find this Peg. You will have no peace until you do."

"Thank you for understanding," she said gratefully.

The old man rose to see her on her way. "I hope it will turn out well. But I have to warn you of the other possibilities. I do not wish to bring sorrow to you without at least a warning."

She stood up. "I want you to begin the search. And I will see you every fortnight to take care of your fee and find out what progress you've made."

"Do not come back until after the holidays," he advised her. "Neither I nor my agents get much accomplished during that period."

"So it is likely I shall have to spend still another Christmas without Peg," she said sadly.

"I would expect so," the private detective said. "But perhaps next year."

Becky gave the thin, stooped man a wan smile. "That thought will sustain me."

And it did. She now went about preparations for Christmas and the New Year blithely. Elizabeth Gregg was away a great deal of the time, as she was planning to hold extra dinners at her mission for the poor in the holiday season. And the prim woman who kept a good deal to herself refused to assist Becky in her preparations for the Christmas party.

The Yuletide spirit did not seem to have any beneficial effect on Becky's husband. Mark arrived home most nights as irascible as usual. He forever complained about her running of the household and when they made love it was a quick, cold act on Mark's part. He did not seem to care that she had not so far become pregnant. Or if he did, he made no mention of it.

Occasionally Bart Woods came to call on Mark after hours. At such times she inevitably had to act as hostess. And she was aware of the dark, handsome man's strong interest in her. His eyes followed her in an almost embarrassing fashion, and though he spoke little with her, he was always polite and quiet.

It was different when he was in duscussion with her husband. She had often heard Mark and the young man quarreling in the library. It was apparent that Bart Woods was gradually taking over more decisions at the shipyard, and Mark was often not in agreement with them.

The night of the party arrived. On Christmas Day Becky presented Mark with a copy of Dickens' new novel *Great Expectations*. Copies had been at a premium and hard to find, but she had a favorite bookseller who had found one for her. With it she presented him with a fine new gold chain for his watch.

Mark received the gifts with grudging appreciation, murmuring, "I wish my expectations could be called great!" And he presented her with a new shawl imported from India and a fine emerald locket, which opened to show small round cutouts of tintype likenesses of them.

Becky was delighted with her gifts and kissed Mark warmly. They both had gifts for his sister, Elizabeth. She received them casually and then dampened their day by going off to spend the entire day and evening at her mission. Buttoning the heavy coat she wore against the December weather, she informed them, "I find that the mission is my chief interest these days. So I will be happiest there!"

There was a light snowstorm in the afternoon, which made everything very picturesque and clean-looking. Lads came by offering to shovel the steps and sidewalks, and she gave them all coins. The household staff looked after such duties, but she did not wish to turn any of the urchins away. Mark sat in his study reading his book and drinking some fine brandy while she bustled about making the preparations for dinner.

The entire Kerr family appeared at five, with Bart Woods in tow. She could tell by Mark's cool greeting of the young man that he had not invited nor expected him. Woods looked as handsome as ever in a new dark suit of neat cut. Old Matthew Kerr still puffed as if out of breath all the time, and leaned on his cane until he found the first available chair.

James Kerr saucily kissed her under the mistle-toe in the hall. And Vera and her equally washed-out mother looked more alive than she have ever seen them. Alice Kerr had actually smiled at her when she wished her a Merry Christmas! And Vera was moving about as if she were a desired young beauty rather than a most woebegone, pale miss.

There was an exchange of presents while all sat to admire the Christmas tree with its many lighted candles, which gave a gala air to the parlor.

Mrs. Kerr asked, "But where is Elizabeth?"

"She is spending the day and evening at her mission. They plan to give food to a hundred or more," Becky said. "She was sorry not to be here."

"I should think so," Alice Kerr said with a mean look on her pale face. "This is the first time she's ever missed."

Mark looked angry as he said, "Well, this year we appear to have some missing and others present for the first time." He gave Bart Woods an unfriendly glance.

Anxious to cover up, Becky said quickly, "Yes. This is my first year as mistress of the house."

Mark glanced at her. "Time to serve the wine," he ordered.

The servants scurried in and out serving all the various delicacies, then they all sat down to a table groaning with its load of fine foods. Oysters were the first course, followed by turtle soup, and then the great Goose, which had been ordered specially. The feast ended with fruit cake, coffee, and brandy.

The men gathered at the table with cigars while the ladies retired to freshen up. Becky took a moment to congratulate the cook and the other servants below stairs and to give them further instructions. She felt the evening had been a reasonable success, though she worried a little about what would happen before their guests left.

Becky was due for a surprise. When everyone gathered in the parlor again in the soft glow of candles from the Christmas tree, old Matthew Kerr struggled to his feet and, clearing his throat, beamed at the assembled company.

"I have an important announcement to make," the old man said proudly. "I take great pleasure in announcing the engagement of my daughter, Vera, to a young man of great promise, Bart Woods."

It was a bombshell for Mark and Becky. There were not at all prepared for the news, though the others seemed to be. Vera demurely went over and allowed a smiling Mark to take her hand in his.

Mark finally said, "This is unexpected and pleasant news."

"Their marriage will follow shortly," old Matthew Kerr said happily. "I shall hope to have some grandchildren before I leave this world!"

"Don't count on me, father!" James said with meaning. And there was some laughter.

"I don't," his father told him. "Though I've no doubt I have a lot of nameless heirs about the town bestowed on by you on willing ladies."

Becky said, "We must have a toast to the happy couple!"

Wine was brought and the toast dutifully given. Then Bart and Vera exchanged happy glances and he addressed the room, saying, "As you may guess I'm more than happy to be offered a membership in the Kerr family. It will make my association with the firm all that much stronger."

"Hear! Hear!" said old Matthew Kerr, who had sat down again. "As my son-in-law, you will have control of Vera's share of my stock in the firm."

"Thank you, sir," Bart Woods said smiling and ignoring Mark's angry expression. "The firm has been having rough days of late. But I know that is going to change. And as a sign of what is in the wind, I'm happy to announce that the firm headed by Samuel Cunard has invited us to bid on their new iron ship, which will be constructed early in 1863."

"Good news!" James Kerr said with a roguish look on his young face as he turned to see Mark's reaction.

Mark's reaction was immediate and unpleasant. He took a step forward. With his square-face dark with anger, he demanded of Bart, "Have you made a bid on the construction of this iron ship?"

"Yes," the young man said in a firm voice. "I saw no harm in it."

Mark said, "We are not set up to build iron vessels."

"We need to change little," Bart Woods said. "I can show you."

"No need," Mark snapped. "If you should be so unfortunate as to be awarded the contract for building the new Cunard ship, you will have the shameful task of telling them that we cannot handle the project."

There was an unpleasant moment of silence. Becky felt she must do something. She exclaimed, "No more business! Let us all enjoy the season by joining in singing some Christmas carols!"

Old Matthew Kerr was quick to take her cue, saying, "A fine idea! I still have a good bass voice and I shall enrich the chorus with it!"

James Kerr was prevailed upon to select the carols and lead them and the others. Alice Kerr's thin soprano soared a trifle off-key while old Matthew's basso-profundo underlined all the others. James had a fine tenor, Bart was a pleasant baritone, and Vera sang so weakly she could not be heard at all. Becky joined lustily into the fun, but Mark stood back and didn't even attempt to join in.

When the carol singing became tiresome, their guests elected to leave. Mark joined her at the front door in seeing them out, but he deliberately refrained from speaking to Bart Woods. It was plain the two men were now adversaries.

Becky closed the door after them with a sigh. "How nice to have it all over and the house to ourselves," she said with a wan smile.

Mark said, "I shall never have that lot in this house again!"

"You and Matthew Kerr are old friends as well as partners," she pointed out. "You cannot behave in that manner."

"They can entertain and be entertained by their new member of the family," he said with sarcasm. "Let us hope his past doesn't catch up with him, and Vera doesn't celebrate her wedding with her bridegroom in prison!"

"How can you say that? You brought him into the firm!"

"A step which I now much regret!" Mark said angrily.

"You are hardly showing the Christmas spirit—and we are to be dinner guests of the Kerr's tomorrow," she reminded him.

"Not I," he said harshly. "I shall be indisposed. You and Elizabeth may attend in my absence."

"They'll know you're doing it deliberately; they'll be insulted," she told him.

"Let them be. There is no longer any friendship between us!"

"You can't go on in business with them taking that attitude," she said.

"While I remain managing director of the firm they will do as I say," he said grimly. "And I say we will have no part of iron ships. I'd rather close down the yard."

"Perhaps they are right," she said. "Almost everyone else I talk with believes in iron ships."

"Madam, I do not wish to hear more from you," Mark said coldly.

"You make me feel as if our first Christmas together has been a disaster," she said unhappily.

"You must admit it was!"

"Mark, I was not to blame. You make me feel as if you do not care for me or my feelings. I tried very hard."

"Im sure you did," he said coldly. "And I saw you and young James Kerr kissing fervently under the mistletoe."

She gasped. "That's merely a custom."

"You took good care to place yourself there at the right moment," Mark said. "It was not lost on me!"

She said impatiently, "You're hopeless!"

"I begin to sense that, madam," her husband said in a cutting tone. "I shall now proceed to my study to drink."

She stood wistfully among the Christmas decorations, not too surprised that this festive night had ended badly, as had most of the nights since their marriage.

CHAPTER 7

Early in January James Kerr left for America. Becky was relieved to see him go, since Mark had become so ridiculously jealous of the young man. She had been careful not to see him along again after that day they had lunched together, but this made no difference to her suspicious husband. She hoped that with James gone, the tension between them would ease.

Actually, it didn't. It became so noticeable that one morning before she left for work at the mission, his sister, Elizabeth, took time to sit with Becky in the parlor of the house and complain of the disintegration of her brother.

"You must realize that Mark is drinking far too much for his own good," Elizabeth said severely.

"I'm only too well aware of it."

"Surely you can do something about it."

"I have tried, but in vain," Becky told her. "He appears to want to destroy himself."

"He did not show this trait before his marriage to you," Elizabeth said as she sat with her thin lips compressed tightly.

Becky checked her urge to be angry and said, "I do not think that is true. I first met him when he was on a drunken binge. I understand he took such flings occasionally. Now he has become a steady drinker."

"Where did you meet him?" Elizabeth asked sharply.

She took a deep breath. "I've told lies enough. If you must know, I was a barmaid in a tavern where he appeared."

Elizabeth eyed her incredulously. "You were a common barmaid?"

"I prefer to think I was an uncommon one," was Becky's reply.

"That is disgusting!" her sister-in-law said. "And Mark married you! No wonder he is unhappy."

"I do not think my past has anything to do with it."

"I knew from the start you were not right for him," the older woman said angrily. "Now I understand why."

"Mark does not want my past known. That is why he invented the Birmingham story. You will do well not to let him know I've told you the truth."

Elizabeth sat there looking white and ill. "You would burden me with this!"

"I'm tired of pretense!"

The thin woman rose. "You should not have tricked my brother into marriage in the first place. Then there would have been no need for pretense."

"I didn't trick him," she replied hotly. "He pursued me and begged me to marry him!"

"Physical infatuation!" Elizabeth said with disgust. "It can make fools of the best of men!"

Also on her feet, Becky said, "I offer no apologies or excuses. Mark and I could be happy if he would allow it."

"He probably drinks because he hates himself for marrying you," Elizabeth told her. "And I do not blame him. You have brought shame to us. From now on I propose to speak with you only when I must. I shall remain under this roof solely to support my brother in his dire straits."

"I do not care if you remain or leave!"

"I'll remain," Elizabeth said. "And I shall keep your guilty secret for my brother's sake. Not for you!" And with that she marched out of the house.

Becky knew this was probably the beginning of a more tense situation in the fine house. Even if Elizabeth kept the information to herself, there would now be fresh acrimony between her and the spinster. And if Mark kept on with his drunken behaviour, life would be almost impossible for her.

She was in this mood when she went again to see private detective, Phineas Pennifeather. The old man sat droopily at his desk in a gray mood.

"I'm sorry, Mrs. Gregg," he said in his gravelly voice. "I have only found out one thing. As I suspected, your sister and this Alfie Bard returned to London a few months after they left here. He placed her in a well-known brothel. But she remained there only a month or two before he took her away. I have not been able to trace her from that point on."

She was encouraged. "At least you have found that much out. Did you learn anything about her? Her health or state of mind?"

"I talked with the woman who operates the place," the private detective said. "She told me that your sister was often in bad humor. That she and this Alfie had serious quarrels whenever he came to see her. She thinks that is why he took her away. He hoped to place her somewhere else where she would be happier."

Becky mourned, "I'm pained to know she was introduced to such a way of life."

"It was bound to happen once she placed herself in that fellow's hands," Phineas Pennifeather sighed.

"But she was in good health?"

"Yes, I think so," the old man said, but he seemed rather uncertain on the point.

"You will keep up the search," she begged.

"I will," he said. "But I believe they are no longer in London. I shall have to try the other large cities in England. That will take time and money."

"I'll find the money if you give the search your time," she said.

"Depend on me, ma'am," the private detective said. "I shall dedicate myself to finding your unfortunate sister."

When she left the detective's, she was in a strange mood. All her past seemed to come flooding back to her, and she had a great urge to see the tavern again, and talk with Mr. and Mrs. Crown. When she reached her carriage, she told the driver to take her to the tavern. He looked surprised but did not question her orders, and he showed the same discretion when they arrived in the narrow street where the tavern was located. She told him to wait for her.

She made her way into the tavern awkwardly and did not feel at ease until she saw the Crowns behind the bar. Then she rushed the rest of the way in. Mrs. Crown saw her and a smile spread over her wart-covered face as she came around to take her in her arms.

Hugging her, the big woman said, "I knew you'd come back one day!"

"She always claimed that," Luther Crown said, the thin face with the black eye patch bright with pleasure. "I said you were done with us."

"I shall never forget you or your kindness!" Becky declared.

"My, but you look the young lady," Mrs. Crown said with admiration. "And you speak and carry yourself so well!"

"I had training from a veteran actress," Becky said. "That's where I get me airs!" And she lapsed into her old nasal manner and then laughed heartily.

"The occasion calls for a whiskey all around," Luther said. "I never drink in the daylight. But this winter afternoon is a memorable one and shall be an exception."

They all three sat around a table near the blazing fireplace of the tavern, and Becky felt happier than she had in many a day. Then she had qualms about the driver and told Luther to take him out a drink.

Luther obeyed her and came back with the word," "He was most grateful to you for the drink. And he's put a blanket over the horse and he's sitting inside the carriage, cozy enough, until you're ready to leave."

Becky said, "I won't stay long."

"There are so many things you must have to tell us," Mrs. Crown said. "What is it like to be married to the fine Mr. Mark Gregg?"

"It isn't all sunlight," Becky told her.

"Nor would I expect it to be," Mrs. Crown said bleakly. "I could tell he has a temper from the way he acted when he came in here drunk."

Luther looked angry. "He's not been cruel to you, lass. If he has, he'll answer to me for one!"

"No," she said. "He doesn't mean to be cruel. The main trouble is his drinking and his basic nature. He has never truly been a happy man. And he's had labor troubles lately at the yard."

"We've heard about it," Luther said. "A lot of the men were laid off, and a few lost their jobs."

"He refuses to build any iron ships," Becky said. "It's a mad idea he has. And you know how stubborn he is."

"Aye," Luther said. "I can imagine."

Then Peg asked the question which had brought her there. "Have you seen Peg?"

The husband and wife exchanged glances and then Mrs. Crown said in a quiet voice, "Do you really want to know?"

"Yes," she said. "I must know!"

The buxom Mrs. Crown looked sad. "She came in here a few months ago."

"On her own," Luther put in. "Alfie doesn't dare come in that door. He knows I'd see to him if he did."

His wife said, "It was pitiful! Her face all painted and her clothes so cheap and gaudy. And she went about trying to sell herself to some of the customers."

"She did that!" Becky gasped.

"She had no shame at all," Mrs. Crown said grimly. "I expect Alfie beat all that out of her."

"What did you do?" she asked.

"I went to her," the older woman said. "And I told her we didn't allow that kind of thing in here. Then I asked her if she'd been in touch with you."

"And?" Becky said.

"She swore at me! Said something filthy! And then she turned and went out. She never came back again," the woman said.

Luther spoke up, "I heard later that Alfie left London because the police were on his trail for a robbery. The story is he went some place North and Peg with him."

"I have a private detective looking for her," Becky told them. "And that is just what he told me." She was relieved to have the private detective's information confirmed. At least it showed he was honest, though she hadn't really doubted this.

They continued talking for a few minutes, and then the door opened and another familiar figure came in. It was little Jimmy Davis, walking with crutches. He swung himself in and then shut the door and joined them in the main section of the tavern.

Becky ran and knelt before him and took him in her arms. "Jimmy! What luck that you should come here today!"

The bearded little man laughed. "I come here every day. It's not luck it's a chronic thirst that's responsible."

She stared at him. "Why are you using crutches?"

"You didn't hear?"

"No."

The little man looked bitter. "I was hurt in the strike. It's my back. I'll never work again, and I'm lucky to be able to get about."

"It happened in the strike?" she said.

"Yes," he said, leaning on his crutches. "One of the thugs hired by the company lifted me up and threw me down hard on my back. They thought I was going to die!"

"I didn't hear anything about it!" she gasped.

The little man said, "I was lucky. One man lost an arm, and three of the old workers lost their lives. It was a bad strike; nothing came of it. Thanks to Bart Woods, the company won."

"The law should do something about that!" she said angrily.

"The law seemed to be on the company's side," the little man said. "I don't even blame Bart Woods. He couldn't have come in if that Mark Gregg hadn't hired him!" And then the dwarf looked upset. "I'm sorry Becky. I forgot he's your husband."

"I'm not blind to his failings, even though we are married," Becky said.

"He's an evil man," Jimmy said. "You deserved better. If only Davy Jones hadn't been taken off as he was."

"I think of him often," she admitted.

She remained long enough to give Jimmy a drink and then left, explaining that she didn't wish to keep the carriage waiting out there any longer. The three were loath to see her go and made her promise to return. She left them with mixed feelings. The reunion had been a happy one for her, but some of the things she had heard worried her. Peg had become a prostitute, there were no longer doubts about that. And her husband had been responsible for even darker acts than she had guessed. She had not been told about the deaths and injuries resulting from the strike. And she had no doubts that if she faced him with this he would simply deny it.

The night became bitterly cold. Mark came in looking weary and blue from the chill of riding home in an unheated carriage. He at once asked her to bring him a whiskey. She obeyed him and gave it to him as he took a stand with his back to the excellent log blaze in the fireplace.

He downed half of the drink and with some relish said, "I fixed Woods today! Gave him a present for his wedding next week. I turned down the Cunard contract."

"His bid won?"

"Yes. But it did him no good. As managing director, I have the final say. Let he and the Kerrs fume as they like; I have the decision."

Becky said, "They are bound to try and find a way to get you out of your position of authority."

"They can try," he said, his eyes burning too brightly. "They'll find I'm not afraid of a fight."

"Do you have enough other work to keep the yard busy?"

"If we run out of work, we can close down for the rest of the winter," her husband replied downing the rest of his drink.

She frowned. "But what about the workers? They can ill afford to be idle in this terrible weather!"

He smiled nastily. "Let them do the same as me—live on their savings."

"Most of them have no savings," she said in despair. "No one knows that better than you!"

"There's always the workhouse," he said. "I suspect you've heard of it."

"I know about it full well," she said bitterly. "And I feel sad for those who must go there."

"What were you doing at the tavern this afternoon?" Mark asked with an abruptness that caught her off-guard.

She hesitated, "What do you mean?"

"Don't lie," he said harshly.

"The coachman who drove me home tonight went by the tavern on an errand and he saw our other coach, the one I have assigned to you, standing in that mean street. He mentioned it to me."

She listened in dismay. So the truth was out. She said defiantly, "All right. I did go back to see the Crowns today!"

"Water finds its own level," he said sarcastically.

"Perhaps it does," she said. "It's the first time I've been there since I left them for you. I do not think I did anything wrong. They were my good frineds."

Mark's square-jawed face showed anger. "I have put a great lot of money in you. You have been my big investment. And I think it may have all been in vain. You will be what you are in the end!"

"I'm proud to be myself," she said. "I only regret that I let you lie about me when I came here. And made me a partner to your lies."

Her husband said, "I should have let you go on the streets like your sister. Though judging from your performance in bed, I doubt if you'd have been a success!"

She stared at him for a long moment of rage. Then she raised her hand and hit him across the face as hard as she could. She heard the sound of her blow and saw the blood spurting where his teeth had penetrated his upper lip. Then she ran off sobbing.

From that night on she and Mark occupied separate rooms. She was well aware that Elizabeth knew that she and Mark were no longer living as man and wife, and she had an idea the spinster sister derived a sour satisfaction from this. Fifteen months went by without much happening. At least not to Becky.

The private detective still had not located Peg nor Alfie Bard, and Mark had continued with his suicidal drinking. He now looked like a man of seventy, and his hand trembled as if he were suffering from some disease. He spoke only infrequently to Becky, although he maintained a friendly conversation at the dinner table whenever his sister was present.

During the Holidays he refused to entertain the Kerrs or to be entertained by them and their new son-in-law, Bart Woods. In February Vera gave birth to a boy, whom she called Donald. Becky called on the colorless young woman and congratulated her. Vera received her with cool disdain, which was meant to discourage any further attempts at friendship.

March of 1863 was unusually mild after a rather bad winter. Becky was at home writing a letter one afternoon when she had a visitor. She went down to greet Bart Woods in the parlor, and she saw at once that he had not come with good news.

"What is wrong?" She asked impulsively.

"It's Mark," he said. "I'm sorry. He was stricken in the office. He's been taken to hospital."

"What is wrong?"

"He's had a stroke," the handsome, dark man said. "A bad one. If he lives through the next few days, he has a chance to recover."

She sat down, tears in her eyes. "So this is how it is going to end!"

The big man hovered over her. "I'm sorry," he said.

"Thank you," she replied in a low voice.

"I won't pretend that Mark and I got along; you know better. But I would never wish this on him."

"I know."

Bart sighed. "I'm afraid it is his own fault. His excessive drinking could not go on. You must have known that."

"I have," she said. "But there was nothing I could do about it. Mark and I have not been close for many months."

"I understand," he said. "What about his sister?"

"She is at the mission she founded," Becky said. "She must be sent word."

"Give me her address and I'll send a messenger," he said. "And I'll take you to the hospital."

She looked up at him. "I don't want to impose."

"I wish to do it," the handsome Bart said soberly. "And I want you to know that regardless of the differences between Mark and myself, you have a friend in me."

"Thank you," she said. "You must be happy in your marriage and proud of your new son."

"I'm proud of my son," he said, and she wondered if there were some significance in his making no reference to his marriage.

The Victoria Hospital was a new building with the latest in equipment. Following the Crimean War, a fine nursing staff had come into being and many of the best of the new group were working at the Victoria. Florence Nightingale herself had words of praise for the hospital and its staff.

Dr. Trevalyn was in charge of the case. He was a solemn young man with a balding head and a bushy red whiskers. He met Becky in the hallway and, after giving her a brief outline of Mark's condition, took her into his private room. She still found herself shocked at the sight and sound of her stricken husband. He was a ghastly gray in color, and his face seemed to have hollowed out so that he looked like a wizened old man. But his breathing was the worst, and his breath came in rattling gasps, each one of which seemed about to be his last.

After she had stood there staring at him with horror on her lovely face, the young Dr. Trevalyn gently guided her outside again.

He said, "You can do him no good by being there at this time. And seeing him like that has to be hard on you."

"Is he going to die?" she asked in a voice with a tremor.

"That is in God's hands more than ours," the doctor said. "We are doing all that we can. And in these cases, there is not all that much we can do."

"If he lives, is there any chance of a complete recovery?" she ventured. "He is the managing director of a shipyard."

Dr. Trevalyn shook his head. "Do not count on his resuming that position, even if he recovers. He cannot have as severe a stroke as he's had without suffering some permanent body or mind damage. In all likelihood, if he lives he'll be an invalid."

"When will we know, Doctor?"

"If he lasts the week, he'll live," the young doctor said. "Beyond that I cannot predict."

The prim Elizabeth came hurrying in while she and the doctor were still talking and demanded to see her brother. Dr. Trevalyn calmly studied the upset woman and came to a decision.

"I think it in your brother's best interests that he not be further intruded on," he said.

"I am his sister; I have a right to see him," the spinster said angrily.

"Do you want to help him?" the doctor asked.

"Of course!" Elizabeth said.

"Then do not go in there just now. He is unconscious and won't know you. But your presence, especially if you should break down, might do him some harm."

Becky told her, "The doctor thinks there is a good chance that he may live."

Elizabeth gave her a venomous glance. "Much you care! You are the one who drove him to this state!"

She gazed at the spinster's angry face with despair and turned and walked away down the corridor. She waited in the carriage until Elizabeth came out and joined her for the ride home. The spinster was now considerably calmer than she had been.

As she took her place in the carriage beside Becky she said, "The doctor talked to me. He explained that Mark was the one to blame for what has happened. I will not make any unfounded accusations again."

Becky said, "Thank you. It is best that we try to get along. If Mark recovers, he will need the loving care of us both, I'm sure."

• • •

Mark lived. But it was weeks before he could sit up or recognize anyone. His speech was badly slurred and his right side was paralyzed. Dr. Trevalyn offered hope that as time passed the stricken man might regain much of the use of his right side and also his speech.

Becky's first visit with him after he was able to recognize her was brief. She said, "You're going to get well, Mark. And Elizabeth and I will do all we can to help you."

He stared at her with glazed eyes and nodded. Then he waved for her to leave. He did not attempt to speak with her. But she learned from Elizabeth that he had managed to say a few words to her, and that he wanted to return home as soon as possible.

In mid-April he left the hospital, able to walk with the use of a cane. His speech was still hesitant but much better than when he'd first been stricken. He seemed to have withered into an old man, and his clothes were too large for him. At Dr. Trevalyn's suggestion a nurse was retained to care for him at home. He would still be convalescent for many months, so warm-hearted and stout Hazel Green accompanied him in the carriage as his private nurse.

He kept much to his own room after he returned home and refused to receive callers. He seemed to enjoy only the company of his jolly nurse and his sister, Elizabeth. He tolerated Becky for occasional visits but always gave signs of weariness that made her leave after a short while. The shocking thing was the change in his personality. He no longer grasped the simplest things quickly, and he had no interest in the business at all. He made no enquiries about it and seemed to have forgotten he held so responsible a post.

Old Matthew Kerr had been forced back to the office to show new interest in the affairs of the shipyard. His return to activity seemed to have improved his health in both mind and body. He was far more alert. Though he still used a cane, he did not lean on it as he had in the past. One day in late April he called Becky to the red brick building, which served as the headquarters for the shipyard.

He greeted her in his private office next to the one now occupied by Bart Woods, which had once been Mark's quarters. The old man saw her comfortably seated across the desk from him before he began to talk.

"How is Mark?" he began.

"The same," she said. "He takes a walk outdoors with his nurse occasionally. But he does not talk or read much. And he shows no interest in the world around him or in the business."

Matthew Kerr looked troubled. "I'm sure we are sorry for it all. It would seem that his mind has not the clarity of old."

"He is only a shadow of his old self," she agreed.

"Bart has asked me to talk to you about a matter of great import," the old man said. "We are at the end of our tether and must make a change, or wind up the business."

"I see," she said.

"We have a chance to get contracts for some iron ships—I feel we must take them."

"You and Bart are running the business now," she said.

"But the bank insists we get Mark's approval on a change before they advance us the money we'll need to refit the yard."

"Don't they know that Mark is not normal mentally?" she asked.

The old man looked embarrassed. "I'm afraid not. We don't dare tell them. These bankers are a conservative lot. They trusted Mark implicitly, but they do not have the same faith in Bart or myself."

"So?"

"If we divulged that Mark is too ill to take any interest in the business they might wait for months before deciding to give us the loan we need. By that time we'd have lost the contracts. But if we could get Mark to sign a paper, saying he approved. Or even if you would sign a statement as representing his wishes, I'm sure we could get the bankers to give us immediate backing."

She sat back in her chair. "You're asking a lot."

"I know."

"Mark is not going to approve if he understands. And if I had him sign something he didn't understand, I would feel guilty, just as I would feel guilty acting in his name against his wishes."

"He owns a large share of the firm," Matthew Kerr reminded her. "His personal fortune could vanish if the firm collapsed. We could all be ruined. You might find yourself facing a penniless widowhood."

Becky said, "You are asking me to betray Mark and save the firm."

"Since he isn't in a mental state to make judgements, you should undertake to make judgements for him," the old senior partner said. "It is more than a wife's prerogative and duty."

She felt herself trapped in a desperate situation. Was she to compromise herself once again? She gave the old man a pleading look. "I want to help."

"I'm sure you do," Matthew Kerr said. "And Bart felt you would not let us fall without attempting to help."

"The firm is on the brink of bankruptcy?"

"Thanks to Mark, it is," the old man said.

"Can I have a few days more to give this thought?" she asked.

"Only a few days," the old man warned. "I must have your answer within the week. Things are that bad."

"I will do everything possible," she promised him.

He rose with a smile on his round, old face. "I have always liked you, Rebecca. I think the best thing Mark ever did was marry you. But I know he has not tried to make his marriage a success, anymore than he tried to improve the business. In these last years he seems to have had a wish to destroy himself and all around him."

"I know," she said quietly.

"I will expect to have word from you," the old man said.

She left with a heavy heart. At home she tried to talk to Mark about the firm's troubles, but he simply sat there staring at her in a dazed state and made some comment about the garden blooming late. She could not reach him though she was sure he partially understood what she had told him. Perhaps he was merely weary of it all. It was too much for his sick mind to cope with.

Two days later a message arrived for her from private detective Phineas Pennifeather. In his scrawling hand was written, "Come to me at my office immediately. Urgent!—Phineas Pennifeather."

She quickly dressed for going out and summoned the carriage. Within the hour she was climbing the rickety stairs to the third floor office and facing the sad-faced old man.

"Do sit down," he urged her. "Those stairs are difficult."

She sat and breathlessly asked, "What have you found out?"

He paused dramatically and then informed her, "I have found your sister!"

"Heaven be praised!" she said. "Can I go to her?"

"Yes," the private detective said sadly. "But I doubt she will know you."

Fear stabbed her. "She won't know me?"

"I fear not," the old man said. "She is suffering from a loathsome social disease. Because of it or utter despair she seems to have lost her mind."

"No! It can't be!" she said with a sob.

"I cannot hide the truth from you," Phineas Pennifeather said. "She is dying in a hovel near the docks. Alfie Bard is dead. He was stabbed by another pimp in a quarrel over a bawd's earnings. So there is to be no bringing him to justice. He died as he lived."

"Surely Peg can be saved! When she sees me, she'll have hope! I'll breathe new strength into her. I'll have the best available doctors look after her."

The private detective stood up. "She is lucky to have a forgiving sister like you," he said. "I will take you to her."

They went down to the carriage, and the old man told the driver the address. It was indeed a hovel near the worst section of the dockyard slums. It was a warm day, and everything seemed foul and smelly in the narrow back street. The detective helped Becky from the carriage and led her up a fetid, dark alley which never saw the sun.

Becky swayed a little. "I'm fearful I may faint," she said in a low voice.

"Courage, Mrs. Gregg," the private detective said as he rapped on the faded wooden door with broken panels.

After a moment the door was opened slowly and an ugly harridan in a dirty gray dress glared at them suspiciously. "What do you want?" she challenged them.

"We have come to see Peg Lee," the detective said.

The woman eyed him disgustedly. "Too late. She died this morning. Her body is already gone. And good riddance!" She spat and slammed the door in their faces.

Becky turned to the private detective and then fainted.

CHAPTER 8

Becky was stunned by the shock of Peg's death. But Phineas Pennifeather proved himself even more competent than she had quessed. Not only did he revive her and get her safely back to the carriage, but he found out from the slattern where the body had been sent for a pauper's burial. Then he went and claimed the body but would not allow Becky to see the dead Peg.

"You have gone through enough," the old man said sternly. "You must remember her as she was. Not in the sorry state she is in now. The casket must be closed on her."

"Very well," Becky said, her eyes still brimming with tears, but realizing the sense of his suggestion. "But I want her to have a proper funeral in a proper grave. I want a service over her with mourners. And when it is all done, I want a fine little stone erected above her."

"I can manage all these things," the old man assured her. "You needn't trouble yourself with the details except the paying of the bills."

"The money does not matter," she said. And this was true. Since Mark's stroke she had been in full charge of his accounts and his bank balance. She knew it was more than ample for both their lifetimes.

"And I shall need the names of those you wish at the service," the private detective said. "Shall we make it for ten tomorrow morning?"

"If you can manage it all by that time," she said.

"I'm sure I can," Phineas Pennifeather said. "I shall send you a message this afternoon telling you where the service will be held. In the meanwhile I'll see you home, and you must promise to rest and not grieve too much. This is perhaps the best way it could have ended."

"I wanted to rescue her," she said brokenly.

"Peg was a wilful girl from all you say," the old man reminded her. "She might not have taken well to the idea of being rescued. She might have gone on being a cause of heartbreak to you. Death comes to us all. It has mercifully come to her a little earlier than for you or I. But in the passage of time it is only a trifle of years."

His wisdom helped her. But when she was back in the great mansion, she felt completely deserted. Not that there weren't others in the house. There were Elizabeth, Mark, and Mark's jolly nurse, but she could not share her burden with any of them. Not with Mark because of his illness, not with the nurse because she was a stranger, and not with Elizabeth because the spinster already thought her a low person. Knowing she had a sister who was a prostitute would only make her disgust increase.

The April evening was mild, and she went out in the garden to walk and think. After a little she heard footsteps in the gravel path and turned to see that it was Bart Woods who had come to join her.

He said, "You have not let Matthew know your decision?"

"No," she said.

The handsome dark man eyed her sharply. "You look most unwell. Is Mark worse?"

She kept her head bent, staring at the ground. "No."

"What is it then?"

And without ever being able to understand why she did it, she raised her eyes to meet his and said, "My sister was a prostitute. She died this morning—a terrible death. I'm burying her tomorrow."

He looked at her in utter amazement. "Do Mark and his sister know about this?"

"No."

"But you've chosen to tell me?"

"Yes," she said, somewhat shocked by what she'd done. "I guess I needed to tell someone."

The dark man said, "So that is why we haven't heard from you."

"Partly," she said. "My mind has been on other things beside the business."

"That is reasonable," he said. "First, let me say I'm sorry."

"Why should you be?"

He gazed at her unflinchingly. "You should know why. I've been in love with you since the first time I set eyes on you."

"I don't believe it!"

"I have no reason to lie."

"You want me to help you win Mark's permission to change the company policy."

"I'm not telling you this because of the business," he said with impatience.

"No?" Her grief helped her to be cynical.

"No," he said earnestly. "I do really care for you."

"You're a married man with a wife and an infant son," she said.

"Vera hates being married," Bart said grimly. "I might have known. It was fortunate she became pregnant early. She won't let me touch her now. She's as frigid as her mother!"

She stared at him. "You are telling me you and Vera are not living as man and wife?"

"Not for months," he said with some anger. "She bleats about her frail health and her general dislike of the entire business between man and wife!"

"Can't you have her mother talk to her?"

"Her mother encourages her. They are as alike as peas in a pod. Only Matthew is of any worth. And James does nothing but send for money to keep him in style in America."

She stared at his troubled face. "I can believe you," she said. "It seems it is a night for confessions."

The big man said, "We might gain a good deal from being honest. I take it Mark is no longer a husband to you in the full sense of the word."

"Not in the full sense of the word," she said grimly. "Not for a long time. I was a bar maid when he married me. I worked in the dock slums in a tavern operated by a man named Crown."

"I know it," Bart Woods said. "I have been there. I thought I was the only lowly-born living here in style. I'm happy to have a comrade."

"I was happy as a bar maid," she mused. "I had such wonderful dreams for the future. So did Peg for that matter. None of our dreams came true!"

"Like myself you have risen in life," the handsome Bart said. "We can be grateful for that. We should not know poverty for the rest of our lives. Unless the shipyard collapses."

She eyed him sadly. "Has money bought you any more happiness than it has me?"

"I don't care about money," he said with disgust. "I like power! Power is all that counts! I have that now if I play the game right. And I have a son!"

"Yes. At least Vera was more generous with you than Mark has been with me. I'm quite alone."

"You have my love," he said.

"I wonder."

"I would like to attend your sister's funeral in the morning."

She was startled. "Why?"

"I'd like to pay my respects, for your sake and for her. I knew many prostitutes along the docks. Most of them had good qualities."

"So you'd pay homage to those earlier conquests by paying honor to my poor sister?"

"Yes, if you wish to see it that way."

She hesitated, then said, "Trinity Church. The cemetery in the rear. Ten o'clock. If you're not there, I will not be hurt. I don't really expect you to attend."

"Ten o'clock at Trinity churchyard," he repeated after her. "I shall be there. Do try to rest tonight."

"I doubt that I shall sleep."

"Try," he said. "You will need your strength to see you through tomorrow. Do you want me to take you to the cemetery?"

"No. I couldn't risk that. I have a friend whom I'm meeting," she said.

He nodded. "Then, goodnight!" he said awkwardly.

"Goodnight," she said in a low voice and turned away.

When she looked around again he had vanished. And she found it hard to believe that the meeting between them had taken place, and that they had said the things she remembered them saying. So Bart Woods was in love with her? She supposed she should be pleased. But she was not in the mood for romantic thoughts. Yet she had turned to him in her despair, and he had not failed her. She should not forget that.

•••

The morning was thick with fog and drizzle. And it was colder than it had been. She stood between Phineas Pennifeather and Luther Crown as the young clergyman read the Anglican burial service. It was simple, meaningful, and short. Mrs. Crown sobbed aloud on the other side of the grave, with little Jimmy Davis standing sorrowfully beside her on his crutches. The clergyman had come to the final words of the service when Bart came to stand by the grave. He respectfully removed his hat.

The clergyman came to Becky and said, "You must be thankful your sister is at rest. And when the stone is ready, let our sexton know; we will see that it is properly placed above her grave."

She thanked him. When he left, she spent some minutes with the Crowns and little Jimmy. These three went on their way together after she'd promised she would keep in touch with them.

There was now only Phineas Pennifeather and Bart Woods left at the cemetery, aside from the grave diggers busy filling in the grave.

Phineas and Bart had introduced themselves and were talking in quiet tones when she joined them after bidding the others goodbye.

She gave Bart a grateful look. "You did come."

"I said I was going to," he replied.

"I had no intention of holding you to it," she said.

"I know," he said. "You'll be returning home in the company of Mr. Pennifeather?"

"Yes," she said.

"Very well," Bart said. "Then I shall see you later."

"Yes, later," she repeated, the finality of it all now striking her. She would never see Peg again. It was over. Just the grave and silence.

Bart said goodbye to Mr. Pennifeather and left. Then she and the private detective returned to her carriage. The old man continued to be sympathetic and helpful.

He told her, "You must not brood on this. Find some new interest. Keep busy. It is normal for you to sorrow for a time. After a while the grief will pass, though a touch of sadness about this will always remain with you. But it will be bearable."

"I picked well when I sought you out to help me," she said.

"You have always paid me my fee," he said as the carriage rolled through the foggy streets. "I owed you my best."

"And you have given it," she said. "I shall always think of you as a friend."

"I'm flattered," the old man said. "And if you should ever need me again as a detective or as a friend, do not hesitate to come to me."

"I shan't," she said, meaning it.

The rest of the day and night were an ordeal for her. She wandered about the house like a lost soul. Elizabeth always went up to bed early. And since his illness Mark also slept long and was never seen after dinner, His nurse occupied the room next to his and matched her sleeping time to that of her patient. So once the servants had retired to their quarters downstairs, Becky found herself alone in the big house.

She could not settle down but moved restlessly about. The fog was still thick. She went to the French Doors which overlooked the garden from the big living room, and saw that it was as gray and misty as ever. As she stood by the doors she saw someone outside in the drizzle. A moment later the figure came up to the patio, and she saw that it was Bart.

She opened one of the French Doors to let him enter. He stepped inside, his black hair damp from the mist. She said, "What were you doing out there?"

"Trying to get the nerve to come and speak with you."

She said, "You needed no special preparation for that. You are welcome. I'm alone in the house. The rest are all asleep."

The handsome Bart was wearing a fine blue frock coat and brown trousers and vest. He said, "How are you?"

"Not good."

"I was afraid of that."

"You want me to think you really care?" she said facing him, and speaking in a cynical fashion.

He frowned. "Must you always doubt me?"

"I know something of your past. How ruthless you are."

"I had to be."

"All cruel men say that," she told him.

"Have you found me cruel?"

"No."

"Then let us have an understanding. You take me as you find me, and I'll do the same with you."

She taunted him, "But you're madly in love with me? Isn't that bound to make you blind to my faults?"

"You think I'm lying," he said.

"Well?"

"I'm not," he said. "Whatever you wish to think."

"I'd say you want my help in twisting my insane husband into helping you rebuild the shipyard."

"I have a plan."

"Oh?"

"Yes. It will not involve you, except to keep silent. Or in the event of questioning, to tell a small lie."

"I might have known."

"Wait until I explain."

"Go on," she said.

"I have a paper here signed by Mark and giving me full authority to act for him."

"How did you get that?"

"I forged his name to the agreement," Bart said without any hint of apology.

She stared at him. "That sounds like you."

"All that you have to do is agree it's his signature if you are asked."

"He is not well enough to sign his name. Elizabeth and the nurse know that."

Bart said, "If they should question the document, you can tell them you often visit Mark's room after they are asleep, that occasionally you make love with him and that he seems most alert in the after midnight hours. It was during one of these secret sessions in which you had him sign the agreement."

"I marvel at you," she said. "You think of everything."

He said, "I do not expect you to be involved. I don't think the bank will question Mark's signature. They really want to go along with us. They stand to lose if we collapse, so it is in their interest to believe he has agreed to building iron ships." He waved the paper.

"This should save us all!" And he placed it in an inside pocket of his frock coat.

She sighed. "Since it will do nothing but good, I can't very well oppose you."

"Thank you, Becky," he said with sudden warmth. "It may be that out of all this misery there will come a great happiness for us."

Becky said, "After all that has happened I begin to question that there is any happiness in the world!"

Bart Woods was staring at her with great intensity. He said, "I love you, Becky, and I need you! And I believe you need someone like me!"

She stared up into his handsome face and saw that he was most earnest in what he'd said. Then he took her in his arms and kissed her with deep feeling. She did not know what she might have done under different circumstances, but in this moment when her spirits were at their lowest ebb she was hungry for love!

The warmth of being in his embrace helped ease the great ache she'd known since Peg's death. She felt that Bart Woods knew her and understood her. And she also felt she could depend on him for protection. So she responded ardently to his kisses and clung to him.

In the next moment he lifted her up in his arms and carried her like a child up the stairs to the bedroom on the second floor which she had occupied for so long. He closed and locked the door of the room and then removed his frock coat and vest.

So they became lovers! As they lay side by side in her bed she found herself comparing the handsome Bart's lovemaking with that of the other men she had known. Though not as meaningful as with her first love, Davy, nor as coldly brusque as the brief interludes she'd known with her husband, Mark, Bart offered her an unexpectedly gentle kind of lovemaking, which left no doubt that he truly cared for her.

Looking back, she would realize that the illicit passion between them made their otherwise difficult lives bearable. In the warmth of Bart's love she was able to overcome her grief for Peg and the melancholy frustration of her ruined marriage to Mark. She found herself in better spirits and had more tolerance for her ailing mate. And always she looked forward to those secret moments with Bart.

On certain nights he came to her place when all the others were safely asleep. Occasionally she would meet him in a flat belonging to a friend of his. And there were meetings for luncheons in the city, intriguing because they had always to be secretly planned and carried out.

Becky came to know much more about the handsome man. He still believed in power and violence when it was required to bring about his ends. He was the product of the London docks, where he'd spent his boyhood. Now he had accquired manners and could pass as a gentleman. But beneath the new facade there was still the ambitious and unscrupulous man who had once shanghaied drunken sailors and turned them over to captains of ships sailing far away for a price.

Often when they were together, he asked questions of her. And it turned out that as a lad he had met her father several times and admired him as a hard worker. Becky could not truly say she was deeply in love with the dark man, but she was surely fond of him. And he was supporting her emotionally at a time in her life when she desperately required such support.

She tried to spend more time with Mark, but he was so vague and disinterested she gave up. She left him with the jolly nurse most of the time. Nurse Hazel Green treated the sick man like a spoiled child and that was almost what he had become. Becky was a trifle uneasy about Elizabeth, worrying that the spinster might have guessed that she and Bart were lovers. But Elizabeth said nothing and was spending more and more time at her mission, which had been enlarged.

From all that she knew from her own observations and what Bart had told her, things at the Kerr house were much the same as they had been. Vera was more than normally devoted to her little boy, Donald, and Bart was a loving father. But they lived in separate rooms of the great mansion and were no longer all that one expected a husband and wife to be. Old Matthew Kerr relapsed to grow more feeble, leaving full management of the shipyard to Bart at a critical time. Alice Kerr devoted herself to her husband and her grandchild. Like Elizabeth, she also had numerous charities to which she gave both money and her own efforts.

There was talk that either Disraeli or Gladstone had prevailed upon Queen Victoria to give up her deep mourning for her dead Prince Consort. It was explained to her that her bleak mood had tainted the whole of her Empire, that out of consideration for her people she must show more interest in life and the desire to plunge forward and make new beginnings.

From the moment Bart changed the shipyard to the building of iron ships, all went well. Gregg & Kerr soon had more orders than they could fill. And the bank had never questioned Mark's forged signature.

The fact that the Kerrs and the Greggs no longer did any socializing made it easier for Becky and Bart to carry on their intrigue. Becky seldom saw old Matthew Kerr except at meetings of the company board. And she did not see Alice or Vera at all. Once she met Vera on a summer afternoon with her baby in a pram.

Becky had stopped and made much of the child, telling his prim mother, "What a healthy little lad Donald is. Just like his father!"

Vera's pale face had shown annoyance. "He is more a Kerr in manner."

Becky smiled at the other young woman, "Then there is something about him to please you both. That is how it ought to be."

"Yes," Vera said brusquely. "I must take him inside; it is past the hour for his afternoon nap." And she had hurried on with obvious relief at not having to make any other pleasantries.

Becky, somewhat hurt, for Vera had avoided her whenever possible, watched after the departing mother and pram and thought what a selfish, spoiled prig Vera had become—no doubt under her frigid mother's tutelage. Had she been a proper wife to Bart it was not likely that he would have turned elsewhere for love, since he had great pride in his marriage and son. Being linked to the Kerr family meant a good deal to him.

It was to be expected that sooner or later the lovers would be caught. And it happened quietly one night when Becky in nightgown and bathrobe was escorting a fully-dressed Bart from her bedroom to the french doors downstairs, which he regularly used to make his secret visits.

They were emerging from her bedroom, his arm around her, when suddenly Mark appeared in the hall in robe and pajamas. It was unheard of for him to be out of his room at this time of night. Becky could scarcely believe her eyes.

Leaving Bart, she took a step towards her husband and said, "Mark! You should be in bed!"

The prematurely-aged man who barely resembled the stern, square-jawed leader whom she'd married, stared at her in a vague, mournful fashion and said nothing. Then he turned and, leaning on his cane, limped back into the darkness at the end of the hall to vanish in his own room.

Bart stood frowning. "Shall I speak to him?"

"No," she said, turning to him. "I don't think he really took in the situation. It probably will seem only a bad dream to him."

"He seemed to know me," Bart worried.

"I saw no recognition," she said, realizing she was allowing her fervent wish to make her accept this as truth.

Bart gave a deep sigh. "I'm sorry."

"It will be all right," she said. "I'm sure."

Bart said, "Let me know. If you need me, I will come back at once."

"I will not need you," she said. "Now go on." And she urged him on his way.

Later, after Bart had gone, she went to the door of Mark's room and found it closed. She did not attempt to open it and go in for fear of waking him if he'd returned to sleep. Better to leave things as they were.

She slept restlessly that night. She knew this liaison between herself and Bart was wrong. But from another viewpoint, it had saved them both from the bleakest of lives. Now she had come to rely so much on Bart for understanding and comfort she could not give him up. If Mark had seen and understood and had been well enough to raise a fuss, she would have accepted his condemnation and would have urged him to divorce her. She had no doubt that Bart, despite his desire for the Kerr cloak of respectability, would have agreed to have Vera divorce him. Later, despite the scandal, they would have married.

She was in bed thinking about this the next morning when there was a knock on her door. She called out for whoever it was to enter, and Nurse Hazel Green came rushing into the room. The stout woman was sobbing.

"He's gone, Mrs. Gregg! He's gone!"

She sat up in bed. "Gone?" she echoed sharply.

"Dead, ma'am," the stout nurse said brokenly. "When I went to him a while ago, I thought he was sleeping. So I left him. Then I went back just now, and he's cold, ma'am! Cold in death!"

Becky threw back the clothes and reached for her dressing gown. "I'll go to him!" Becky followed her as she quickly made her way to Mark's room.

When she reached his bedside, his eyes were closed and his worn face was placid. It was easy to understand why the nurse had thought him asleep. It was clear he had died during the night. A stab of guilt went through her, and tears filled her eyes.

Nurse Green comforted her and placed an arm around her. "You must not feel badly, Mrs. Gregg. He passed quietly in his sleep, a wonderful way for a life to end."

"Yes," she said in a low voice. "I suppose so."

"He could not have lived much longer," the nurse went on. "Dr. Trevalyn said that only the other day. The doctor was afraid he'd have still another stroke and suffer more before he died. This way, God has been just!"

Becky nodded. "Have you told his sister?"

"Not yet."

"Better go upstairs to her room at once," she urged. "And break it to her gently as possible. We must keep our wits; there are many preparations to look after!"

"Yes, ma'am," the nurse said and went on out, leaving her alone in the room with her dead husband.

She gazed down at the worn face at last in repose. She whispered, "I'm sorry if I hurt you, Mark. Once there was something between us, just a small happiness for a short while. I shall treasure that memory and forget the cruel and ugly things that followed." And she bent and touched her lips to his cold forehead. It was odd, she knew, but she felt closer to him at this moment than she had for some years.

Elizabeth came into the room still in her nightcap and dressing gown. The thin woman was crying brokenly. She brushed by Becky and knelt by her dead brother. Her head bent on his folded hands, she continued to sob.

Becky said, "Perhaps it is a blessing,"

Elizabeth turned her thin, tear-stained face upwards to gaze at her with shocking hatred. Her sister-in-law said, "I'm sure it is for you!"

She gasped. "How dare you say that?"

"I hope you wind up in a bar where you came from," the thin woman said, her voice raised shrilly.

Becky sighed and turned to see Nurse Green standing there shocked by what she'd hear. Becky shrugged and went on out of the room. Elizabeth was so near collapse a doctor had to be fetched. Mark's sister was no help at all in the many preparations which had to be made. Becky went about everything with a determination not to let down Mark in his final hours before burial.

Word was sent next door. Old Matthew Kerr was the first to call on her. He had grown almost thin, and his voice had become quavering. Sadly he told her, "I expected to be the first to go because of my age."

"We can never tell about those things," she said.

"Mark was years my junior," the old man said with awe. "Well, the old guard will all soon vanish. You have my sympathy, my dear. The ladies will pay their respects in due time. And I'm sure Bart Woods will be by shortly. He had left for the shipyard before word reached us of this sad business."

"I'm sure he will come," Becky said.

And he did. He arrived in a carriage about an hour later. The undertaker was already busy preparing Mark's body for display in a fine coffin in the great living room. So Becky saw the handsome dark man in one of the rear parlors.

After she'd closed the door, she went to Bart's arms and he kissed her and held her close to him for a long time. She said, "He died peacefully in his sleep."

Bart frowned, "Do you think he saw us and understood?"

"He saw us, but there was no understanding," she said. "He probably didn't know who we were. He'd been so lost mentally of late. I think this urge to move about must have been a last restless exertion brought on by his approaching death."

"Then you feel he died without knowing?"

"I'm certain of it."

Bart looked relieved. "Thank God," he said. "I would not have wanted it to happen otherwise when I could not offer amends."

"You must not think about it," she said.

"How has Elizabeth taken it?"

"Badly. She suggested that I was happy he was dead!"

His eyebrows lifted. "Do you think?"

"That she suspects?"

"Yes."

"I'm afraid so. It could be she has spied on your comings and goings," Becky told him.

"I shall talk with her," Bart said firmly.

"No," Becky told him. "Better to say nothing. I doubt that she will want to darken the family name by bringing up such a scandal now."

"I will not let her make your life miserable."

"She won't," Becky said. "I do not propose to live on here. This house has too many bitter memories. There is a charming little brick house across the street that is for sale. I think I will buy it and move there. I'd like to live simply in a smaller place with only a single servant. This is Elizabeth's family house; she can remain here."

Bart showed interest. "You seem to have thought about this earlier. Before you knew Mark was going to die."

Her eyes met his. "Yes."

"What first gave you the idea?"

She said, "Because I'm going to have a child, Bart. Your child."

CHAPTER 9

An uneasy truce lasted between Mark's sister and Becky until after the funeral. A few days following the burial she confronted the thin spinster in the big living room where Mark had so recently rested in his coffin.

"I have decided to buy myself a smaller house," she told Elizabeth.

Her sister-in-law said coldly, "Perhaps that would be best. I do not wish to share this house with you."

Becky said, "I assumed that. The Lordley house is available nearby. I will need only a housekeeper-cook to run it. I think it will suit my needs."

"When will you be making the move?"

"As soon as possible," she said.

"That is satisfactory to me," Elizabeth said coldly.

"The will Mark left makes a generous provision for you as well as for me," Becky said. "So you will have no problem keeping up this place."

"It will do me for the rest of my days," the older woman said.

Becky rose and moved a step away. Then over her shoulder, she said, "There is one other thing."

"Indeed?"

"Yes. I'm going to have a baby."

Elizabeth looked outraged. "You are what?"

"I expect a baby in the early autumn," she said.

Elizabeth sprang to her feet, tiny patches of red on her pale cheeks. "His baby!" she cried.

"I plan to give it Mark's name," she said. "I do not think he would mind."

"Strumpet!" Elizabeth shrilled at her.

"I had to let you know," she said, careful to control her own emotions. "I did not wish you to hear it from anyone else."

"It is scandalous!"

"Not unless you make it so," Becky told her. "No one can say that Mark and I weren't active sexually, even though he was ill."

"I know better!"

"Could you swear it in court?" she asked. "Could you take an oath that while everyone else was sleeping Mark and I did not meet in his room?"

Elizabeth gasped. "You are evil!"

"I must be when it comes to protecting Mark's name," she said.

"You weren't concerned with his name when you entertained your fancy man almost every night!" the thin woman accused her.

"I will not try to explain my feelings to you. Nor the feelings of anyone else. You would not understand, in any case. I'll only say that if there is a scandal now, if the name of Gregg is soiled, it will be you who will be responsible. Think about that!"

Elizabeth stood there enraged, wordless, and defeated!

Becky purchased the smaller house and moved into it before the month ended. She took Mrs. Atkins with her. She was a pleasant middle-aged woman capable of any household duty and the servant Becky trusted most. After the confusion of settling into the smaller place was over, she found herself both happier and healthier than she'd been in a long while.

She had a tiny, brick-walled garden in the rear of the house, and she often entertained Bart out there. It was easier for them to meet now, without the fear of Elizabeth spying on them.

One late afternoon as Bart sat for tea with her in the garden area, he said, "I wish I were free."

"So do I," she said, staring at him across the table. "Have you talked to Vera about this?"

"Yes," he said, sighing. "She does not want a divorce. It seems her mother doesn't believe in divorces. Confound it, I can never be sure whether I'm married to her or her mother!"

"Alice Kerr is a dominant woman in her quiet way," she agreed.

"Old Matthew hardly gets out of his room now," Bart said.

"I thought he looked poorly at the time of Mark's funeral."

"He's worse now," Bart assured her. "I shall miss him. He makes living there more bearable."

"So you think you'll never get a divorce?"

"That is the way it looks at the moment," he said. "And I'm sorry. Especially under the circumstances."

"It simply means your child will have Mark's name."

"That worries me," he said. "And I'm concerned for you."

"Gregg is a good name for the child," she said. "And I shall manage. I have all the money I need thanks to Mark's will and the prosperity of the business."

"The firm is having an excellent year," Bart said. "Brunei has agreed to design some advanced screw propellors for our firm alone. This will give us an edge on our competitors."

"Iron steamships are sweeping sailing vessels from the sea, just as you predicted," she said.

Bart smiled. "It is our era."

"What of the future?"

"I can see no great changes. Improvements perhaps. That is all."

"I wonder," she said. "Things do seem to continually change."

"Don't worry about the business," the big man told her. "Let us concentrate on our own affairs."

"I'm enjoying this house," she said.

Bart nodded. "I'm beginning to look on it as my true home."

She smiled wanly. "We are a strange, lost pair. What would have happened to us if we hadn't found each other?"

"I hate to think what my life would have been," Bart said. "Meaningless, except for my son."

"How is young Donald?"

"Growing more like me every day," Bart smiled. "But I hate to think of him being brought up by Vera and her mother."

"You know the danger," she said. "Exert your influences on him from the start. Make yourself an important figure to him."

"I'm planning on that."

"Then it should be all right."

"And your child?"

She smiled. "I have a premonition it will be a girl. Would you mind?"

"I'd be delighted," Bart said, reaching out and taking her hand in his. Their eyes met fondly as he added, "especially if she resembles you."

Matthew Kerr died a month later. When Becky went to pay her respects, she was greeted rather icily by the dark-veiled wife and daughter. After the funeral she had no communication with them again. Nor did she ever speak with Elizabeth. She occasionally saw her leaving for the mission or returning in her carriage, but she never had occasion to talk with her. She knew her sister-in-law wished to avoid her, and this suited her very well.

When she used a carriage these days, she either rented one or Bart sent one for her. Since his youth on the docks he had a great liking for music hall entertainment. He enjoyed nothing better than to sit and watch a good performance by a troupe of vaudeville artists. There were a number of these music halls scattered about the city, and she and Bart often attended one of them, conspicious in an audience composed largely of working class people. Bart laughed as loudly as any of them and pounded his fist in the palm of his other hand when some especially good turn amused him.

As autumn drew near and her condition became noticeable, she spent most of her time at home. Bart came to see her more frequently. They had their meals together in the small dining room of the modest house.

One night when they were well along with their meal, she asked him, "Have you heard your wife and mother-in-law discussing my condition?"

He smiled grimly. "They were both properly appalled."

"I expected they'd make the most of it."

"Vera made quite a scene and accused me directly," he went on with a sigh.

"What did you answer?"

"I told her I had a right to be with you or anyone else, since she had long denied me my husbandly privileges!"

"Well said!"

"That shut her up," Bart said. "Now the two of them go about the house with outraged looks on their thin faces. Thank goodness my son resembles me rather than that dried-up two!"

"I'm having Dr. Trevalyn," she said. "He was Mark's doctor."

"He seemed a competent man."

"I have faith in him," she said.

"Then that is what matters," Bart told her. "Spare no expense. I want you to have the best. Our child must come into this world with every advantage."

"You hadn't many advantages, and you've survived and done well," she reminded him.

Bart's handsome face became grave. "I have scars I wouldn't want any child of mine to have."

Becky's premonition proved right. She gave birth to a lovely young daughter on October 15, 1865. She called her Peggy Anne. Even as a small infant, she showed a hint of Bart's handsome features along with her own eyes and nose. She was blissfully happy!

In 1881, the *Servia,* a merchant vessel crossed the Atlantic in seven days. It was constructed of a new metal made from blending certain other minerals and ores with iron; it was known as steel.

In April 1884 Donald Woods finished his studies at Oxford and joined his father in the family firm. He was a tall, elegant young man with his mother's slim build and his father's manly good looks, and sandy-colored hair. Almost the first thing he did was call on Becky, whom he called *Aunt* Becky.

But Becky was not deceived that the young man's affection was for her alone. She knew that Donald had developed a warm liking for her daugher, Anne. Thus far there had been no reason to discourage this, but now she began to be concerned for very sound reasons.

She had discussed this with Bart, but with his usual assurance, he'd told her, "There is no need to worry! It is right they should be good friends! They've grown up together!"

She looked at him very straight and asked, "What if they should fall in love and wish to marry?"

"Never!" Bart said. "They'll find other mates." But he sounded a trifle concerned.

At this moment Donald and Anne were out strolling in the garden, hand in hand, as he told her about his plans for joining the business. It seemed innocent enough, and she did not wish to take a stand against the two young people seeing each other, yet she was under constant fear of what might ensue if they should announce their affection and ask permission to marry.

She had made sure that Anne met many other young men while Donald was away at Oxford. So her daughter was not without a great many beaux. She did not know how many young ladies Doanld had courted, but she hoped that he had many of them on the string, with Vera so repressive and his grandmother still alive and whining about the unhappy changes which were taking place in the Victorian age. Old Alice Kerr was even shocked by the rumored romance between the widowed Queen Victoria and her Scot's farm manager, John Brown.

Bart quoted his mother-in-law as grieving, "The Queen has changed along with everything else. Who would have expected it of her?"

She and Bart had enjoyed a hearty laugh at this. The years had been kind to them. They had the same warm affection for each other as the usual man and wife. Vera had accepted the situation and no longer even spoke of it. Becky was sure that both Donald and her daughter knew that Bart and she were lovers. She believed they were rather thrilled by the longtime romance. The physical excitement had paled, and now it was merely a matter of sound friendship between she and Bart. It seemed nothing would ever upset them, until this small cloud of the future of the two young people came upon them.

As the two young people continued to stroll in the garden she halted before the oval, gold-framed mirror on the living room wall and gazed at herself in it. She was actually forty-two years old! As a girl she had thought this to be bordering on the elderly!

But she didn't look old! Her face was a little rounder and there were a few lines at her eyes and mouth, but her skin was still fresh and her eyes had a sparkle. She was often taken for a woman much younger, and this could not help but give her confidence. Best of all there was no gray in her hair, except perhaps a few strands which she was careful to conceal.

She could not equal Anne in beauty! Her daughter had a stronger face and an almost electric quality about her. She was continually vivacious and her youthful gaiety filled the house with warmth and laughter.

Donald was almost a male counterpart of Anne; he was attractive and pleasant. But he had a serious streak which was perhaps missing in Anne. Yet they got along exceptionally well—too well for Becky's liking.

She had barely turned from the mirror when the two came in with conspiratorial smiles. She asked, "You two look as if you were up to something! What is it now?"

"I want to take Anne out to dinner to celebrate my becoming a member of the firm," Donald said. "Father has given me his permission, and we now wish yours. I promise I shall have her back by nine."

"Please, mama!" Anne entreated her, looking too lovely to be refused.

Becky hesitated. Then said, "If your father agreed to this, Donald, I suppose I must also give my permission. Where are you planning to dine?"

"The Strand!" Anne exclaimed, her eyes sparkling. "They have an orchestra and there is waltzing at dinner!" To demonstrate this, she did a graceful waltz step for them.

"The Strand it shall be," Donald said, laughing. "I'll call for you at six. Wear that pink gown I liked the other night. And be on time!"

Becky was amused. She said, "You sound like an echo of your father!"

Donald looked pleased. "That wouldn't be so bad. But I'm truly much my own man. Father will find that out when I join the firm. I'm very interested in steel."

"Steel?" she said.

"You must have heard of it," he insisted. "It is coming into use both here and in America. Great bridges are being built of it because it is light and strong. And steel ships are already setting records crossing the ocean."

Becky was interested, she had vaguely read about this new metal, but it had not interested her much. She said, "Your father has done well enough with iron ships. I expect he'll know what to do about steel when the time comes."

"The time is now," Donald said. "I've tried to make him see that. But he insists on sticking with the old ways."

She smiled, "Again you sound like your father. He had the same sort of argument with my late husband, only it was over the yard making wooden ships as opposed to iron. Bart won out!"

"I'm glad to hear that," the young man said. "I hope I win out now. Gregg & Kerr should be starting to build steel ships."

He left. Finding herself alone with Anne, she said, "Donald has become very much the assured young man since his return from Oxford."

Anne, with her hair drawn straight back and tied in a pony tail and wearing a pale yellow dress which matched her blonde good looks, smiled and said, "Yes. He's terribly ambitious."

Becky was seated on the end of a divan, and Anne sat across from her on the arm of an overstuffed chair. Becky studied her daughter's happy face. "What were you talking about?"

Anne smiled knowingly. "He was telling me about the changes he's planning for the firm."

"His father may have something to say about that."

"I think his father will listen to him. Don't you?"

"Bart is hard to understand," Becky said. "He has been my friend for many years, and I'm never completely sure of him."

"You and Bart," her daughter said wistfully. "I think it rather sad!"

She raised her eyebrows. "What is sad?"

"That you and poor old Bart can't get married. I think Vera is mean to stand in your way. So does Donald!"

"Really!" Becky gasped. "I don't think you two children should be discussing such things!"

"We are not children!"

Becky said, "Well, whatever you are, you are also much too presumptuous."

Anne teased her. "You two are in love. Don't deny it!"

"We are good friends. We used to live in houses side by side," she said lamely. "Your father and Bart were partners."

"But I'll wager they were not friends!"

"Why would you think such a thing?"

"Because I'm sure Bart must have been in love with you before father died. How could he possibly feel friendly to a man who stood in his way?"

"You are talking wickedly," Becky said, blushing.

"And your face is crimson," Anne laughed.

"No wonder. You speak so frankly as to be almost indecent."

"I want to be frank. Donald likes that in me!"

"Does he?" she said. "And I supposed that is terribly important to you."

"It is. I value Donald's opinions."

Becky eyed her daughter worriedly. "I think it is time you stopped giving Donald so much of your time and thoughts. It is all very well for you to have been friends growing up, but now you should begin to lead your own lives. You keep on sharing everything with him."

"He is my best friend. Maybe my only friend," Anne said.

"Nonsense," she protested. "You have lots of beaux. You ought to be judging them, deciding which one you care the most for and whom you might one day marry."

Her daughter sighed. "That's a tiresome thought!"

Becky continued, "And Donald should be doing the same thing with other girls. You both should find someone nice to marry. You can still be friends. That will likely last all your lives. But the next few years will be critical for you both, the time for selecting your mates."

Anne gave her an odd look. "Why go to all that bother?" she asked. "Couldn't we marry each other? Donald would make such a fine husband, and I'd try to be a worthy wife to him."

She gasped. The worst was out. She'd suspected this had long been in her daughter's mind, and perhaps Donald felt the same way, in which case trouble loomed for all of them.

Becky recovered enough to say, "It is stupid to marry a boy you grew up with! Stupid for Donald as well! You'd both do better to seek out strangers, enjoy the thrill of discovering new loves, and marrying them."

"Can't we decide that for ourselves?"

"Of course you must," Becky said seriously. "But I'm fond of Donald, and you are my daughter. I don't want to see either of you cheated!"

"We won't be."

Becky stood up and crossed to the girl, touching her shapely shoulder. "You and Donald haven't discussed this seriously, have you?"

"No. We don't talk about it. But maybe we are taking each other for granted."

"That could be tragic!"

"Why?" Anne said staring at her.

"There are many reasons," Becky said wearily. "I've told you the most important one. You ought to know many men before you decide to marry. Marry Donald, and you'd both be unhappy in a few years and flirting with other wives and husbands."

"Mother!" she said, shocked.

"That goes on!" Becky warned her. "And it's mostly among couples who have married too early without giving their marriage proper thought."

"You sound like dreary old Aunt Elizabeth before she died," Anne told her.

"Why do you say that?"

"Whenever Aunt Elizabeth saw me with Donald she'd become angry and tell me he was like his father. Not to be trusted and I shouldn't play with him."

She listened to her daughter patiently. "I'm sure she only meant to give you good advice."

"It was silly."

"Aunt Elizabeth was a strange woman. But when she died, she left you her fortune. You must never forget that. She must have cared for you."

Anne looked down at her hands. "I suppose so. She could be nice. And I liked her when she wasn't mean. She always smelled of lilac."

"I'm glad you were friendly with her in her last years," she said. "Elizabeth lived and died a lonely woman."

"Why did she never want to see you?" Anne asked.

"I've told you before," Becky sighed. "She and I had a foolish quarrel about my moving here. She never forgave me for it."

"She would never talk about it. Just changed the subject whenever I mentioned your name."

"That was best."

"I almost felt she hated you," Anne said. "And I couldn't understand why. She seemed to be so fond of my father."

Becky said, "That is why she hated me. I think she resented my coming to the house. She would have hated anyone who married her beloved brother. In her eyes no one was good enough for him."

"I see," Anne said. "She would have preferred that he remain unmarried as she did."

"Yes."

Anne smiled and kissed her on the cheed. "I'm glad he did marry, or I wouldn't exist and I wouldn't have a wickedly, pretty mother like you!"

"You're buttering me up," Becky chided her. "I'm a woman of middle-age. I'll soon be old."

"You're still most attractive," Anne said. "Donald thinks so." And with a sly smile, she added, "And I don't have to tell you Uncle Bart thinks you're beautiful!"

She pretended annoyance. "Brat! You had to get that in!"

Anne ran away from her to go upstairs. "I must bathe and dress if I'm to be ready at six," she said.

Becky called after her, "Remember what I said. Think of other young men when it comes to marriage." But she was almost sure Anne was no longer listening to her.

When Donald came to pick Anne up at six, Becky felt her blonde daughter had never looked more glorious! In a tiny pink evening bonnet, dark cape, and pink gown she presented a fetching picture. She kissed Becky hastily and then hurried off with Donald to the waiting carriage.

Becky watched after her sadly. And she was still in a somewhat melancholy mood some hours later when she and Bart lay together in bed after making love. Their rounds of love were not so frequent these days, but then Bart would come to her almost in a stage of frantic need, as he had tonight.

She glanced at him fondly as he lay with his eyes closed, his head on the pillow beside her. His hair was completely gray with white predominant at the temples, and he had put on a great deal of weight. He had a double chin and his youthful dash was replaced by a heavy look. He was still handsome but in a weary, mature way. He had lately suffered from arthritis and at times suffered much pain. He would not use a walking stick, nor take his doctor's orders to give himself more rest.

Softly, she said, "Dear Bart!"

He opened his eyes and turned to smile at her. "I needed you tonight."

"I always have a need of you," she told him.

"Things have been difficult at the yard," he said. "We are actually slack after years of prosperity. I think the whole country is having bad times. I blame it on the government."

"You shouldn't worry. You could retire."

He frowned. "Not yet! My son is just coming to take his place with the firm. I want it in good shape for him."

"Perhaps he could take over with the help of the men you have trained."

"Too rash in his ideas."

"Are you thinking about his conviction that steel is the coming things for ships?"

Bart gazed at her across the pillow in surprise. "How do you know that?"

"He told me."

He sighed. "I forgot. He spends most of his free time over here. It vexes Vera and her whining old mother!"

"It worries me as well."

Bart stared at her again. "Why? Don't you like the boy?"

"I like him far too well," she said. "And so, I'm afraid, does Anne."

"Well, why shouldn't they be friends? They always have been since they were children!"

"Yes," she said quietly. "And there's a danger in that now they've come to the time to find marriage partners."

Bart raised himself on an elbow and looked down at ther worriedly. "You're not telling me those two foolish children have fallen in love?"

"I'm not sure," she said. "I think Anne has, and perhaps Donald is close to it!"

"Good God!" Bart gasped.

"I pain for them," she said. "And I feel this may be our punishment."

Bart brushed this aside, "That is nonsense talk."

"I wonder."

"You should have mentioned this before, if you'd seen it happening."

She said, "Donald was at Oxford until now. I hoped in the meanwhile they'd both find loves."

"And?"

"It hasn't happened," she said unhappily. "Donald has come straight back to her, and she has attached herself to him like a magnet. They're so happy together—it is pitiful."

"Damn!"

"What's to be done?"

"Have you talked to Anne?" Bart asked. Anne was his special joy. He never looked more happy than when she called him Uncle Bart. He had been dangerously close to spoiling her with attention and gifts.

"Yes," she said. "I've told her the mistake it is to marry someone you've known from childhood without giving other young men a chance."

"Did you convince her?"

"I don't think so."

The man beside her in bed gave a deep sigh. "A new problem!"

"I'm sorry," she said. "I've always had secret fears that one day something like this might happen."

He stared at her. "You didn't tell me."

"I didn't want to upset you."

"Well, we must face it now."

"Yes."

"I always thought of the four of us as family," Bart said. "It is normal for a family to be close. That is why I never had any worries about Donald and Anne liking each other."

"We are a family," she said. "That is precisely the trouble."

He thought a moment. "There is one thing in our favor."

"What?"

"Donald entering the business. He'll have plenty to do in the next year or so. If he ever mentions marriage to me, I'll make it plain I think he should give at least two or three years to prove himself in the business before taking on the distraction of a wife and the family to follow."

She smiled her approval. "That sounds logical. You have always been smarter than me."

"It is true; that's the best part of it," Bart said. "And because Donald is just as ambitious in his own way as I was, I think he will listen to me."

"I hope so."

"In the meanwhile you must try to see that Anne spends time with other young men."

"I have been trying, but I'll go on with it."

"It will be all right," Bart said. "I'm sure. I know Vera is always nervous when Anne comes to visit. I guess I can understand why."

"She will see it as our sin falling upon them."

Bart shook his head. "It is not a sin to love. And I have faithfully loved you for more than twenty years!"

Becky smiled and reached up and drew him to her so their lips met. Then she said, "I have never regretted it, Bart."

"Nor have I," he said in a gentle voice.

"And now we must dress," she said. "The children already believe we are lovers. But I refuse to allow them to find us naked in bed together!"

CHAPTER 10

Charles Dickens had been dead for fourteen years and his body had been given an honored burial in Westminister Abbey. Prince Edward and his lovely Danish Princess Alexandra were at the height of their popularity, though it was whispered around London that the Prince was much more a ladies' man than his stern Queen mother liked. Tall tales of his infidelity were repeated in low voices in many of the London private clubs. And it was occasionally the ladies of the gentlemen who repeated the tales with relish who were the ones involved!

The London stage was flourishing and enjoying the patronage of the popular Prince and his Princess. One of the great idols was Henry Irving, whom Victoria would knight in a few years. He had taken over the Lyceum Theatre and, with the delightful Ellen Terry as his leading lady, was thrilling audiences with such plays as *Othello* and *The Bells*.

Bart Woods had come to love the theatre as well as the music halls. He often took Becky and Anne to see the great theatre productions. His wife, Vera, peevishly refused to attend any theatrical offerings, on the grounds that her aged mother considered the theatre a sinful place.

So when Gilbert and Sullivan took London by storm, one of their first devotees was Bart Woods. He had faithfully attended the productions of *The Pirates of Penzance*, *H.M.S. Pinafore*, and *Iolanthe*. Now the new musical satire of the D'Oyly Carte Company at The Savoy Theatre was scheduled. It was Gilbert and Sullivan's *Princess Ida*. So it was quite natural that he purchased tickets for the opening for himself, Becky, Anne, and Donald.

Becky had been relieved when Bart told her that he had given his son a serious lecture about his responsibility to the firm.

According to him, Donald had accepted the advice in a most agreeable fashion. He had admitted that entering the business and marriage at the same time might prove a problem. He had promised to defer any wedding for two or more years.

Becky had then asked Bart, "Did you ask him to make the same reservation about becoming engaged?"

Bart showed surprise. "That didn't occur to me."

She smiled wearily. "I fear you overlooked a most important point."

"You think so?"

"I do," she said. "What if he insists on giving Anne a ring and becoming engaged to her."

"We must try to stop that," Bart agreed.

"It may be difficult," she warned him.

So she was especially pleased when on the opening night of *Princess Ida* an almost ideal solution to their difficult problem presented itself. They were mingling in the foyer with the other affluent first-nighters during the intermission. It was a gala affair, with much of London society represented and all dressed formally in their best.

Out of the crowd a diminutive dark-haired girl suddenly came rushing over to Anne. The dark girl was wearing a stunning blue gown with white ruffled trim. Her hair was done in the latest style; she was very much the elegant young lady.

Kissing Anne on the cheek, she exclaimed, "I haven't seen you since finishing school!"

"That is so," Anne said. "And we were such dear friends!"

"Inseparable," the girl smiled.

Anne introduced her to everyone as Susan Gray, the daughter of a wealthy importer. Susan seemed to be intelligent but somewhat given to talking on and on rapidly. She offered opinions on the play, talked about her father's health, which was apparently on the decline, and announced that she was going to Paris for six months to perfect her French.

"A terribly smart school," Susan said happily. "And operated by women with great social background. My mother says every lady should know a second language."

"I dare say she is right," Bart Woods said.

Susan turned to Anne and asked her, "Why don't you join me? We would have such fun together exploring Paris and meeting French society people!"

Anne said, "It would be fun. But I think not."

Becky spoke up quickly, "Why couldn't you take the course? I think Susan's mother is right. French is an excellent second tongue."

Anne stared at her mother in wonder. "You don't speak any other language but our own."

"And I regret it," Becky said. "It would only take six months. And I could come over once or twice to make sure you were doing well."

Susan implored, "Please, Anne! Tell me you'll join me!"

Anne was blushing. "I don't know! I'll have to think about it." And she turned to Donald to ask, "What do you think I should do?"

Donald said, "The decision must be yours. But it does seem a good opportunity to broaden your knowledge and experience. And I shall be very busy getting familiar with my work at the yards for the next six or more months."

Bart now said his piece, declaring, "I vow I wish I had the same chance. Paris is a great city."

"You see," Susan told Anne. "Everyone wants you to go."

Anne said, "I'll have to give it more thought."

"You!" Susan pouted appealingly. "Well, I shall be in touch with you in a few days. You may expect to hear from me!"

Just then, the bell sounded for the second half, and they all returned to their seats in the theatre. Becky was in a better mood now to enjoy the performance, for she was almost sure she could persuade Anne to go to Paris with her friend. They all went to The Strand Restaurant for a late supper after the show, and she noted that Anne and Donald spent quite a lot of time discussing the six month trip.

A few days later Anne decided to accompany Susan. Becky sent the two girls off on a shopping trip while she prepared to get enough clothes ready to send. She chose a good-sized trunk and brought it down to Anne's bedroom to begin packing it. Choosing all the items to be included would take several days. Not until Anne was ready to leave would the trunk be locked and sent to the railway for transport to the channel boat.

She was busy with the trunk when her elderly housekeeper came in to inform her she had a visitor. When she went out to the parlor, she was surprised to see Vera Woods primly standing there.

She was startled to see how Vera had aged. Her face was almost as withered as Becky remembered her mother's had been. She made a brave show of hiding her confusion by asking the thin woman in an unfashionable black suit, "Do sit down!"

Vera said, "I can only stay a few minutes."

She smiled. "Still we may as well be comfortable."

They sat in chairs facing each other. Vera on the very edge of hers looking most unhappy. The thin woman asked, "Is your daughter at home?"

"No. She is out shopping with a friend."

"Very good," Vera said, hunching a little in the chair. "I had hoped never to enter your house."

"You are most welcome. We were all good friends once."

"As my dear mother often says, times have changed a good deal."

"How is your mother?" Becky asked politely.

"Poorly," Vera said. "Very poorly. She cannot live long."

"I'm sorry to hear that."

"Then I shall be quite alone," Vera said.

She lifted her eyebrows. "You have a fine son and a husband."

Vera eyed her viciously. "My son will be leaving home in a short while. And you have taken posession of my husband!"

Becky was shocked. "I?"

"Better to understand each other from the start," the withered Vera said. "It is a fact and we both know it. Bart is a coarse, cruel man with a nature different from mine. My mother warned me against marrying him, but I would not listen."

Becky said, "I remember. You did it because I had married Mark Gregg, with whom you were infatuated."

"I loved Mark," the other woman burst out. "I shall always cherish his memory until I die!"

"You are welcome to do so," she said. "I remember Mark as a good deal less than a saint. If you think Bart coarse and cruel, I can promise that you would have found Mark worse. He was most unfeeling where women were concerned."

"How dare you say that! You who betrayed him!"

"It is true."

Vera glared at her. "You will not change my memory of him. Nothing you can say will do that!"

"Then I shall say no more. Only this, had you tried harder to be a proper wife to Bart he would never have turned to me, just as I turned to him when Mark treated me with extreme cruelty. I mean—before his last illness."

"Excuses!" Vera said with derision.

"I suppose we all seem very weak and sinful to you and your mother."

"Do not bring my dear mother into this," Vera said. "We all know that Anne is your bastard child by Bart."

"Strong words from a genteel lady."

"It's the truth. And now it would seem you are encouraging my son, Donald who, thanks to his father, pays no attention to me, to be overly friendly with your daughter, although you know full well that the two have a common father."

"I would rather not discuss this with you," she said.

"I insist," the withered Vera said. "That is my reason for being here."

"Very well," Becky said in a tired voice.

"What are you going to do to prevent this tragedy?"

"It has already been done," she said. "I'm sending Anne to France for six months to study French. This will remove her from the London scene. I feel reasonably sure that both she and Donald will meet someone else to their liking during this time."

Vera's pale face turned scarlet. She said, "So I did not need to make this call."

"No."

The thin woman rose angrily. "I might have known you and Bart would arrange it in your own way. That is what you have done since the start. I have continually been left out. At least it is not a new experience."

Becky escorted her to the door and as she opened it, she said, "I'm sorry you feel so strongly about me. I wish I could somehow make things easier for you."

"I despise you!" Vera said with a venomous glance. Then she went out into the street.

It had been a rather shattering experience, and Becky followed it with two glasses of sherry. By that time her nerves had calmed and she had decided that Vera had merely been playing the familiar role of being her own worst enemy. She was thankful she had arranged for Anne's trip and hoped the six months grace might offer a small miracle.

Anne left for Paris the following week. They all went to the train with her, and Bart and Becky exchanged troubled glances as they saw the ardent kisses between Donald and Anne as he put her aboard the train. Anne waved as the train started and Donald shouted to her that he would write a letter every second day—a sign that they had only delayed a crisis, but had not solved it.

Becky was lonely without her daughter. But Donald made it a practice to come by almost daily. It was as if being in Anne's home and talking with her mother somehow made him feel closer to the lovely blonde girl. Becky worried about his calling, but was almost grateful for his coming by since it helped her at a difficult time.

Almost every day Donald had some new complaints about the way the shipyard was being operated. Pacing up and down before her, he worried, "Father is just plain too old-fashioned!"

She smiled. "He used to say that about Anne's father. I can't imagine that he has lost so much ground."

"You're a major shareholder in the company, and you should be concerned," the young man said. "All around us the other yards are converting gradually to the construction of steel ships. While father is busy making a new long-term committment with an iron factory."

"Don't you think his experience counts?" she asked.

"I think he is not well; and he has lost interest in any expansion," Donald said.

"That could be. His arthritis has given him much trouble. I've even suggested he should retire."

"I wish he would retire," Donald said worriedly. "Then I and the other young men heading the firm could put Gregg & Kerr in step with the modern shipbuilding scene."

She was thinking of long ago and that forged letter. How Bart had risked both their reputations by forging Mark's name to a letter of agreement for the banks. He had badly wanted to save the company then.

She said, "Do not make any mistake. Your father fought hard to modernize the yard years ago. He risked everything. I can understand that he is weary now."

"Then ask him to let go of the reins," Donald begged her. "He will listen to you."

"I'll talk to him," she promised. "Your father has a background on the waterfront. He was very poor and worked his way up in the world. He wasn't always that careful about what he did. Some of it was criminal. But he left that behind when he came into the firm and eventually married your mother. He became as respectable as any Kerr. But there is still much of that early savagery left in him. He won't give up easily. Be sure of that!"

"His marriage to my mother was wrong!"

"I agree, but it is too late to correct that now."

Donald looked at her with admiration in the handsome face so like his father's. "I'm glad he has you. Otherwise, his life would be meaningless."

"Thank you," she said quietly. "Perhaps that is why I'm against Anne making too hasty a decision about marriage."

His smile was grim. "You mean about marrying me!"

"All right," she said. "Since you say so."

"Why?"

"Because I'm older. I've seen too many hasty marriages turn out unhappily. I love you both, and I don't want to see either of you hurt."

"I love Anne," he said.

"I know that."

"And she loves me."

"That is all too likely," she agreed. "You've been so close since you were children. But I beg you to at least try a flirtation with some other young woman before you ask Anne to marry you."

He stared at her. "You think I will find someone else I like better?"

"I think you should try."

"I never will."

"Try!" she urged him.

He knelt before her and took her hands in his. What is wrong with me? Don't you want me for a son-in-law?"

"It is because I like you so much I'm frightened for you. You must believe that," she said.

He stared at her. "I think you honestly mean that."

"I do," she said.

He smiled sadly. "It's a subject on which we aren't apt to agree. I think we'd better drop it."

"Perhaps," she said. "I had no letter from Anne this week. What about you?"

"I had three," he said proudly.

"Now I know why I haven't heard from her," Becky said with a resigned smile.

In her loneliness she found herself hiring a carriage one day and going to the cemetery where Peg was buried. The past was almost closer to her than the present. The Crowns had long ago given up their tavern and gone to live with a nephew in the country somewhere in their old age. Poor Jimmy Davis had died before the tavern closed. The Crowns had let her know, and she had attended his funeral. The sight of him in a child-sized coffin had brought her to tears. So much heart in such a tiny body!

She had the carriage wait and walked in past the gray stone church to the cemetery. It was a fine, sunny day, not at all like that gloomy, wet morning on which Peg had been buried. She stepped carefully between the crowded gravestones until she came to the small one she'd had Phineas Pennifeather erect over her sister's grave.

It was somewhat stained by leaves falling against it, but the lettering was there, clear enough for anyone to read. She knelt and touched the lettering, following each letter with her finger, tracing out the words *Peg Lee*. She felt love for her younger sister who had so unhappily let herself be destroyed. She had been hungry for the good things of life long denied her, so she had stumbled into a life of degradation and died before her time!

She remained there, thinking about her childhood with Peg and how happy they had been until her father's accidental death. She could lay some blame to Mark for that! Mark who had tried to bargain with her for her father's life with a few gold coins ! She had never truly forgiven him for that. But so much had happened since.

So many dead. Peg, Davy Brown, and Jimmy Davis, to name only those who had been closest to her. Then Mark, old Matthew Kerr, and Elizabeth, the spinster sister of Mark who had come to love Anne as if she had been Mark's true child, and had relented on her deathbed and left her fortune to Anne. Becky knew she could not think badly of the lonely spinster, not after that.

She thought about Phineas Pennifeather and what a strong support he had given her when she badly needed it. The old man had been frail then, his body had been bent prematurely. Was it possible the venerable private detective was still alive? On an impulse, she left the cemetery and returned to the carriage to give him the address she remembered from long ago.

The stairs were just as dark and rickety as ever. And she was even more breathless than she'd been twenty years earlier as she reached the third landing. She went to the door which had led to the private detective's office and found it locked.

"Who are you looking for?" asked an elderly man who'd emerged from another office.

"Phineas Pennifeather," she said. "A private detective."

The old man in the long black apron and wearing an eye-shade stared at her with his faded gray eyes. "I knew him," he said.

"I hoped I might find him," she said.

The old man chuckled. "Not here, you won't. You can try the Green Road cemetery."

She sighed. "He's dead."

"Yes. Not so long ago either. His business went to pot, but he still kept coming here. Habit I guess! How he climbed the stairs those last years is beyond me."

"When did he die?"

"Only about three years ago. The office hasn't been rented since. They'll soon be tearing this building down."

She nodded. "I see. I'm sorry I didn't think about it sooner. I would have liked to talk with him."

"Could tell a story or two, he could," the old man said with a nod. "Claimed to have been employed by royalty at one time. But until the end his hearing was bad and his eyesight was almost gone."

"I'm sorry to hear that."

"He didn't turn up one morning, so I knew he must be dead. I went around to where he had a room, and sure enough he'd died in the night. His landlady had called on a cousin to look after his burial."

"I'm glad there was someone. He was a kind man."

"Yes. I'd say that," the old man with the eye shade said. "You don't want anything in the line of printing? I have a small press and do fine work."

"Not now," she said. "But I will keep you in mind. I promise."

"Well, I won't be here long. Just till the building goes," he said sadly. "Nothing lasts too long! Not even us!"

"All too true," she agreed. And she made her way back down the stairs to the carriage. In a short time she was back home.

She did not tell Bart about Vera's visit. He was in such pain from his arthritis of late that she hated to bother him about anything. Often when he came to spend the evening with her he would suddenly drop off to sleep. When this continued she knew he was weary beyond just ordinary tiredness. And she once again suggested he turn the business over to Donald.

"Not yet," he said firmly. "I'm not ready yet."

Henry Irving had revived *The Bells*. This play about the Polish Jew who committed murder and was afterwards haunted by the bells of the sleigh in which his victim had been travelling was a favorite of Bart's. So he suggested that they attend one of the first performances. She never turned down these requests because she enjoyed getting out.

He picked her up in his carriage and on the way to the theatre told her, "Vera's mother is in the hospital. Her heart. I don't think she'll last the week."

"She must be very old."

"Well over eighty," he said grimly. "No one will miss her but Vera. I had Donald go to the hospital tonight with his mother."

"You should have cancelled the evening at the theatre if you felt you should be there," she said.

"Not I," he said angrily. "I'm not a hypocrite. That old woman has been my enemy since the day I married Vera. I can't pretend liking her because she's dying."

Becky suggested, "Perhaps it will be better after she's gone. Vera may be easier to live with, not having her mother to dominate her."

"No hope for her now," he said darkly. "She is cast in her mother's mold for all time. It will be like the evil old woman living on."

"I'm sorry," she said.

"Have you heard from Anne?" he asked.

"Yes. I finally had a letter. She's having a wonderful time."

"Met any young men?"

"I doubt it," she said. "The only young man she mentioned in her letter was Donald and she's been writing him three times a week."

"I know," Bart growled. "Confound it, what is that old saying about absence making the heart fonder? I think that is what is happening."

"I still have hopes," she said.

They reached the theatre and Bart told the driver of the carriage when to return. The bright gas lights of the theatre district and the milling, excited crowds on the street always thrilled Becky and made her forget her cares. Hansom cabs forged their way through the busy streets with difficulty and let out their elegant passengers in front of the various theatres.

Bart guided her towards the Lyceum. She smiled up at him and was shocked by the lines on his handsome face and the look of pain which had become almost a mask.

"Is your arthritis bad tonight?" she asked.

"I will forget about it when the play is on," he promised. "I always do."

She worried. "Perhaps we should not go out to supper afterwards. You'd best go straight home."

"No," he said. "Having supper is part of the evening. I'm not an invalid yet."

She argued with him no more. He had made up his mind and was adamant. Irving gave his usual magnificent performance and she secretly glanced at Bart and saw the interested look on his face; she knew he was getting his usual enjoyment from the play.

But during the last act she suddenly felt the pressure of his arm against hers. She turned quickly and was shocked to see that he had fallen asleep and was slouched against her, breathing deeply. She felt sure it was only sleep and not a sudden illness, but she was worried about him.

Then there was a round of applause as the company took their curtain calls. Bart at once came awake and sat up as if nothing had happened. He joined in the applause and rose to his feet and shouted "Bravo!" when Irving appeared alone to take a final bow. She was relieved to know that he was all right but deeply concerned about his health.

They had supper at the Strand, but he seemed listless. She was sure that once again he almost fell asleep at the table. She was glad when they were able to leave and get in the carriage to be driven home.

She linked her arm in his and said, "You are working too hard."

He stared ahead of him at the shadows of the gloomy interior of the carriage. "It is the pain," he said. "And the struggle. They're all opposed to me!"

"Why don't you give up?"

"I never have!"

"The time may have come," she said. "I'm afraid for your health. I don't want to lose you. I don't think I can face life alone."

"You're still lovely," he said. "And not that old. Someone will come along."

"No" she said, her throat tight with emotion.

"Come now, be sensible," he said. "I'm by no means dead yet. Nor do I intend to be soon."

The next morning she learned of the death of Vera's mother. She sent a wreath of flowers and a letter of sympathy, but she did not attend the funeral. She missed seeing both Bart and Donald for a few days. But in the interim she did receive a letter from Anne full of exciting news.

"Dearest Mother," Anne had written. "I have had the most amazing experience. At a party given by the school I met a count! And he's young and attractive! He is paying me court, and I must say I'm enjoying it! I feel guilty about Donald, but I have decided to be honest and tell him all about it. After all, it is a flirtation. Nothing serious!"

The letter had gone on to tell of the Count André Lemont taking her to a famous restaurant for dinner, and on a later afternoon having her meet his mother for afternoon tea. Becky read the letter over several times with happy tears in her eyes. It sounded promising.

Then Donald reappeared and called on her in the late afternoon, as was his usual custom. He seemed edgy and not at all in a happy frame of mind.

He asked her, "Has Anne written you?"

She nodded. "You mean about the Count? Yes."

"Blast the Count!" he said with anger.

"You mustn't blame her. She's young and attractive. Having beaux is part of every girl's right."

"What about me?"

"I've already told you to seek out some nice girls and pay the same attention to them. Flirting is good for young people of both genders."

Donald frowned. "She had the nerve to write me and tell me all about it!"

"She's merely being honest. And why not? You're not married or engaged!"

"I feel we have an understanding."

"Thank goodness she doesn't seem to share your views," Becky said. "Be sensible and keep yourself busy with some other girl. I'd be willing to venture that Anne will tire of this Count in a week or two."

He brightened. "You think so?"

"I hope so," she said. "I don't want her serious about him, any more than I wish her to be serious about you."

"You want her to be a heartless flirt!"

"I think every girl should try it for a little. I did!"

The young man looked astounded. "You are the most faithful of women. You and father have been true to each other for many years."

She smiled ruefully. "I'm getting to be an old woman. We change with the years."

"You're not old," he teased her. "You're terribly beautiful, and if I weren't in love with Anne I'd try to steal you from my father!"

"Donald!" she protested, but with a smile.

He kissed her and left.

It was later in the evening when Bart arrived. And because there was a chill in the air she had a good log fire blazing in the fireplace and saw that Bart sat before it.

He relaxed in the easy chair and smiled. "That feels so good."

"I'm glad," she said. "Donald was in to see me." And she told him all about it.

He heard her through the account and then asked, "Do you think Anne might be serious about this titled Frenchman?"

"If he's a suitable man, I hope she is," Becky said. "But I'd first like to meet him and know something about him before I give my approval."

"At least it's a healthy sign that she and Donald might drift apart."

"Not if he can help it," she said.

"He's stubborn," Bart said. "One day he may have to know the truth if he persists in wanting to marry Anne. We can spare her, but one of them will have to be told."

She gave Bart a frightened look. "He would never understand. He would hate us!"

"Do we have any choice?" Bart asked grimly.

CHAPTER 11

A week later Becky received another letter from Paris. Trembling a little with excitement, she opened it and sat down to read her daughter's latest account of life in Paris. It began ordinarily enough with Anne's description of a visit to a famous restaurant and her belief that the French truly did outdo the British when it came to good food.

This was followed by her difficulties in getting some proper dress materials for her Paris dressmaker, and a request that Becky find some suitable silver buttons the size of a penny to send to her. She also mentioned that she was becoming quite proficient in speaking French, though Susan had a better grasp of the writing of it.

But it was at the very end of the letter that she revealed her most important news, she said, "Dear, mama, I find myself in a predicament, the like of which I have never known before. My charming André has actually made me an offer of marriage! I can be Countess Lemont if I wish and live near Paris on a beautiful estate. He is anxious to meet you and discuss this with you. I have not given him any real encouragement, though I do like him. But there is Donald. So you see, you must help me!"

Becky sat back with a sigh of relief, the letter still in her lap. So the miracle she had prayed for was at last happening. There was someone else to rival Donald and marry her daughter. She could tell by the letter, in spite of its cautious tone, that Anne was more than a little in love with this young Frenchman. And that was very good!

She could only try to encourage the romance without seeming to be interfering too much. Bart would be as relieved as she was. Of course, when Donald heard the news, he would be upset but he would get over it. With all this in mind she decided she should write a reply letter at once.

Seated at the tiny desk in her bedroom she began a letter to Anne, saying, "My darling Anne, I shall go to that little button shop on Gray Street tomorrow and try and find the silver buttons you've requested. Your restaurant experiences sound fascinating and make me hungry, even at this distance. I have always felt British food lacking in some departments.

"The last paragraph of your letter is, naturally, the one which offers me the most excitement. I think your romance with André most appropriate and delightful. And it would seem he is serious in his intentions. I think you should judge him on his own merits and not feel you have to compare him with Donald. You know that Donald has an advantage, in that you and he grew up together. But that very thing makes him a more dubious choice for a life mate. Think about this. I will be happy to meet and talk with your Count. Let me know when you'd like me to join you in Paris for a week or two, and I shall make all the arrangements."

When she'd finished the letter she read it over and it seemed all right. She sealed it. and addressed it and placed it on her desk to take out and mail. Bart generally came by to see her on Wednesday nights, and she hoped that he would come this week so she could share the good news with him.

She was on her way to discuss dinner with the cook when the doorbell rang. She answered it herself and discovered a troubled elderly man in a black stovepipe hat and long black coat standing on the steps.

"Yes?" she said.

"Beggin' your pardon, ma'am," the man said respectfully. " I'm Mr. Bart's coachman."

She smiled. "Of course. I recognize you now."

"Yes, ma'am," he said nervously. "Mr. Donald sent me to fetch you. His father has met with a bad accident, and he is at the Charing Cross Hospital."

"Bart met with an accident?" she asked tautly.

"Yes, ma'am, Mr. Woods is in the hospital in bad shape."

"What happened?"

"I can't rightly tell you," the old man said. "I only know you're supposed to come to the hospital at once."

"I shall," she said. "Wait until I get my coat and hat and speak to my cook."

The drive through the busy London streets to the hospital was an ordeal for her. She kept imagining the worst sort of things. Perhaps Bart had been personally inspecting one of the ships under construction in the yard and had fallen.

Donald was waiting for her in the hospital entrance. He kissed her and said, "I knew you would come."

"What happened?" she asked, with a questioning look.

His handsome young face was grim. "It's very strange, to be truthful, my father isn't being all that helpful."

"Did he fall?"

"No."

"What then?"

Donald grimaced. "I find it hard to believe. Father left the office alone. Before he could reach his carriage, he was intercepted by a burly man in a black coat and a broad-brimmed black hat such as people on the Continent wear. According to the coachman, who was the only eye witness of the happenings, this man spoke angrily to father. My father raised a hand, as if to strike him. Then, without warning the stranger attacked my father and gave him a most terrible beating about the face and head."

"Horrible!" she gasped.

"Incredible," Donald agreed. "The coachman tried to stop the fight but was himself thrown to the ground. My father fought back as well as he could, but with his arthritis he was no match for this fellow. Eventually he was knocked down also. Then the stranger strode away and escaped before anyone could charge him with the attack!"

"It has to be the act of some madman!" she said in fury.

"I agree," Donald said worriedly. "Otherwise, there is no explanation for it. At least I can't think of any."

Becky said, "Perhaps in the old days it could have happened. Your father made many enemies when he was a strikebreaker. You must have heard him talk about those times."

"He prefers not to dwell on them."

"There was much violence then," she said. "Both on his part and on the part of those who opposed him."

The young man frowned. "Nothing like that goes on now. We have a union shop and they are extremely loyal."

"But was this someone outside the firm who made the attack on Bart?"

"It had to be," the young man frowned.

"How is he?"

"Badly shaken up. His face is cut and bruised. I had him brought here, because I feared he might have body or head injuries."

"He's resilent," she said.

Donald took her arm and nodded "He needs to be to survive this."

Bart lay bandaged in a private room. One eye was covered with the bandage, and he gazed up at her with his unhurt eye in a dazed fashion.

"Becky!" he manage hoarsely.

"Are you in pain?" she asked.

"Donald had them give me some stiff brandies. I'm better."

She said, "You should have fled as soon as you realized he was a madman!"

His son chimed in, "I agree."

Bart spoke with difficulty, "Thought I knew him."

"Did you know him?" she asked, but Bart made no reply. After a moment, she tried another question, "What did he look like?"

"Hard to say," Bart replied. "It all happened quickly. He was about my age and size."

"A large man," she said. "And I hear he wore a broad-brimmed black hat and cloak."

"That's what the coachman told me," Donald said.

"The hat served to hide his features," Bart said. "I shall be all right. Donald ought not to have brought me here."

"I had no alternative," Donald told him. "You were still unconscious when you were carried in here."

"I'll be all right," Bart murmured and closed his good eye.

Becky whispered to Donald, "He wants to rest. We should go."

"Yes. The doctor said not to bother him," his son agreed.

They left the room and Donald talked with the doctor in charge for a moment. Then he returned to her to escort her to the waiting carriage.

As they left the lobby with its smell of disinfectant which pervaded the entire structure he said, "The doctor says there are no major injuries. He was simply badly beaten. He should be able to leave the hospital tomorrow and spend the rest of his time recovering at home."

"Does your mother know?" she asked.

"Not yet," he said as he helped her into the carriage and then took a seat beside her.

"You'll tell her when you get home?"

"Yes," he said dispiritedly as the carriage started on its way. "Not that she will care too much. I think she hates him. She'll enjoy hearing this happened."

"She couldn't be that cold!"

"You underestimate her," Donald said with bitterness. "And she has little time for either father or me these days. She's taken up with this spiritualism circle, and she spends a lot of time with them!"

"I didn't know!"

"Some Mrs. Haddam," Donald went on angrily. "She claims to get messages through some girl who died years ago. They hold meetings at the medium's house, and sometimes they visit the houses of members for special sessions. They were at our place once, and I can promise you they're an odd lot."

She said, "How did Vera become mixed up with them?"

"After grandmother's death," Donald said. "She was under the domination of that dreadful old woman all her life, and now she's looking for guidance from her from the other side."

"Sad!"

"Worse than that most of these spirit mediums like Mrs. Haddam are fakers! It all is staged with assistants playing the ghost voices and creating the effects. How any intelligent person could be influenced I don't know. The whole point is to take as much money as possible from the gullible."

Becky gazed out the carriage window at the dark London Street. She said, "I've never paid any attention to such people. I feel we ought to let the dead rest."

"Not my mother!" the young man said. "So you can be sure what happened to father tonight will be only a minor interest to her."

She glanced at him again. "I still feel there's something very strange about it all."

"The attack?"

"Yes."

"I agree," Donald said.

She wrinkled her brow. "I had the feeling that Bart wasn't completely truthful with us. That he wasn't telling all that he could."

Donald showed amazement. "I was about to say the same thing to you. What could it mean?"

She sat silent for a moment, then said, "It can only be something to do with the past."

"When father was himself involved in violence?"

"Yes."

"That was so long ago."

"It might seem so to us, but not to anyone else," she said. "Let us just suppose that someone was badly hurt by your father. Perhaps sent to prison. Today he was free after some long prison term, and the first thing he did was seek out your father and attack him."

"I suppose something of that sort could happen. But father would surely recognize the man. Why is he so silent about him?"

"That is the mystery," she said. "And I doubt if we will know the truth unless your father helps in revealing it."

Donald scowled. "I'll question him tomorrow."

"No."

"Why not?"

"I think you should wait. He will talk eventually when he is ready."

The young man nodded. "Perhaps that would be wisest."

"One other thing," she said

"Yes?"

"From now on he should never go about without some sort of bodyguard. At least not until we know who his attacker was. If some madman is at large stalking him, he must be protected."

"True," Donald agreed. "I hadn't thought of that."

"He will be safe enough during his recovery period. He'll be at home. But when he returns to the office, he must be guarded."

"I'll see to it," Donald said.

They reached her place, and he saw her to her door. Only then did he ask, "Have you heard from Anne?"

She felt it a poor time to broach the subject. So she said, "I'm sure I'll soon have a letter."

Donald's handsome face showed concern. "She has missed writing me for a week! That's never happened before."

Becky smiled. "You mustn't be too hard on her. I imagine she has made many friends, and life in Paris is much busier than it was when she first went there."

"I suppose so," the young man said unhappily. "Thank you for going to see father."

She said, "You were right in sending the coachman for me. I have to go out and do some errands in the morning. I shall make it a point to stop at the hospital early and see Bart before you come to take him home. It will be awkward for me to visit him then."

"I understand," Donald said. "I'll keep you in touch with his recovery."

"I count on you," she said, bestowing a light kiss to his cheek.

He looked pleased. "I still insist you're more charming than any girl I know! Including Anne!"

She laughed and went inside warmed by the compliment. She was concerned about Anne's startling letter from Paris and its implications now that this new bizarre and worrisome business of the attack on Bart had been thrust on her. He had for so long lived a lawful existence that his doings of the old days had been forgotten by her.

Actually, by the time she met him, he was beginning his determined climb to respectability. But there could well be others who still saw him in the light of a villain, perhaps someone who had been harmed or sent to prison through Bart's dealings. And this person might be back looking for revenge.

The battered condition in which Bart had been left should have been revenge enough. But she worried that there might be other unpleasant developments. And she felt Bart was holding back the truth about it all.

Becky kept her word. The next morning she went to visit Bart at the hospital before starting on her round of errands. She was amazed to find him dressed to leave and seated in a chair in his private room. His head and eye were still bandaged, and he looked unfit to leave the hospital.

She went to him and kissed him and asked, "May I ask what you are up to?"

"A carriage is coming for me shortly," he said with a slight air of defiance.

Becky scolded him. "You ought to remain here for a day or two longer. You don't look well enough to go home!"

He waved a hand impatiently. "This is no place to remain because of a few bruises!"

"What about your cut head? And your injured eye?"

"The head cut is minor, and my eye is no more than properly blackened," he argued. "The doctor covered it, since he felt it would get better more quickly if I didn't strain it."

Becky shook her head. "You're impossible!"

Bart Woods smiled bleakly. "I'm not going to die. It's too soon for my enemies to rejoice."

She said, "Speaking of enemies, have you been able to recall anything more about your attacker?"

"No."

She stared at him. "I don't believe you."

"Well," he said, and then with a touch of anger, "That son of mine has complicated matters by reporting the attack to the police!"

"I think he did right," Becky said.

"I didn't want all that fuss made of it. The police were here this morning questioning me."

"Were you helpful to them?"

"I could tell them no more than I've told you."

She said reprovingly, "I know you as well as anyone, Bart. And I know you're not being truthful. You are fully aware of who attacked you and why. It has to do With the past. Because you may think the attack was justified, you do not wish to see the man punished."

Bart stared at her with his good eye. "You have it all neatly worked out."

"And I'm right!"

"If that's what you wish to think, so be it!" Bart grumbled sitting back in the chair.

"So the man will never be found?"

"Probably not," he agreed.

"And that is the way you want it?"

Bart smiled pathetically. "Don't plague me about it. I'm going home to recuperate under Vera's watchful eyes—that will be punishment enough."

"Poor Bart!" And then she remembered she hadn't mentioned Anne's letter, so she went on to tell him about it. She finished with, "It would seem time for me to go over there and try and encourage the romance."

"Just don't try to push it," he said. "Ann can be stubborn. She still cares deeply for Donald; a decision will be hard for her and should be her own."

"I agree," she said, "It must be handled discreetly."

"Does Donald know about this other fellow?"

"He doesn't think it is serious."

"Don't tell him or he'll be rushing over there to try and interfere between the two," Bart worried.

"I'll say nothing. It will depend on Anne. She may possibly write him about it herself. In fact, I expect she will."

"Then let them work it out on their own," the man in the chair advised.

She kissed him and left him doggedly waiting for the coach to come and get him. She was impressed by his courage, but she worried about it all. Whoever was responsible for his condition would not be revealed by him. Bart must have some truly good reasons for keeping the news to himself.

It was two evenings later that Donald came to see her once again. She had just sent a letter to Anne. As he began to pace restlessly in her parlor, she asked him, "What about your father?"

"Improving daily," Donald said. "He threatens to return to the office the first of the week. I wish he wouldn't. I've been going over some figures on steel construction, and I don't want him to find the staff engaged in checking them."

"You still are determined that steel is the material for new ships?"

"Shipping itself is proving that," Donald said with some disgust. "Every day I hear word of steel merchant vessels making record crossings."

She smiled. "I cannot argue shipping with you!"

"Just vote on my side when the board meets," he said. "And I have another matter to discuss with you, madam!"

"How formal you are today!" she teased him.

"This is a personal matter and serious," Donald assured her. "And I have an idea you may know more about it than you have been willing to reveal to me."

"Go on," she said, guessing that Anne must have at last written him about her count.

"Does the name Count André Lemont mean anything to you?" he demanded.

She gazed up into the stern face of the upset young man and thought how much he resembled Bart when he was angry. She said, "Yes, Donald, I have heard about him."

"And you did not warn me?"

"No," she said. "I felt it a personal thing. Something between you two. I have no wish to interfere."

He frowned. "I thought you were on my side, that you would defend my case with Anne."

"That wouldn't be fair. She is torn between you and this count, it seems. I say, let her own heart be the deciding factor."

"And I say, her head is turned at the thought of becoming a countess," Donald said unhappily.

"Not my Anne!" she reproached him.

He made an apologetic gesture. "Well," he said, "she seems to be in love with the fellow. Or at least she thinks she is."

"Oh?"

"She hasn't decided for him," Donald went on. "She has made that clear. But he has asked her to marry him, and she is thinking about it and felt I ought to know."

"I call that fair."

"It comes of her going to Paris," the young man said angrily. "I was never in favor of it. And now she is in this trouble. And worst of all, I can't leave England because of the critical state of the company and father's poor health."

"If Anne really feels she should marry you, she will decide in your favor," she said.

"Cold comfort!" Donald said. "I understand you are going to visit her?"

"Yes, she said.

"That makes me feel better," the young man said, not knowing that it was the Count's suit she must favor.

There were further exchanges of letters, and soon Becky found herself packing for her visit to Paris. It was her first excursion outside England in years, and she looked forward to it. She also looked forward to meeting the charming young man whom Anne wrote increasingly about. But before she could get away she was involved in a situation more dramatic than any she might have read in a popular novel, or seen in one of the plays on the London stage.

A visitor arrived at her house one afternoon. And she almost fainted at the sight of him, for he wore a black wide-brimmed hat and a long black cloak and his face, though somewhat altered by the passing years and heavier of jowl, was that of a man she had supposed dead, Davy Brown!

"You recognize me!" Davy said with delight. "And you have changed only a little. I have taken some time to seek out Becky Lee and find her in the person of Mrs. Mark Gregg, widow!"

"Davy!" she said, as they faced each other in her small parlor. "I was certain you were dead!"

"Almost, but not quite," the big man said, removing his hat to show a bronzed older version of that good-looking man who had been her first love.

She went to him and he took her in his arms and kissed her so warmly that she felt embarrassed and afraid. She pulled away. "Please! you have taken me by surprise! I must have time to accustom myself to your being alive!"

He took it in good humor. "I know of no better way to convince you than with a rousing kiss!"

"Do sit down," she told him, bringing forward an easy chair. "You must tell me what happened and how you have managed to come back from the dead!"

He sat down across from her and asked, "Do you have a bit of good whiskey in the house? I'd like to wet my parched throat before I begin!"

Becky laughed and stood up. "I shall be a barmaid again and fetch your drink, just as I did at Crown's Tavern!"

A look of sadness crossed the big man's bronzed face. "I went there! It isn't a tavern any longer, but a bake shop, and the Crowns are long gone."

"I know," she said, bringing him back a bottle of whiskey and a glass. "You can help yourself," she said, seating herself again.

"You remembered," he smiled, "I drink it straight."

"I remember so many things," she said, staring at him with fond eyes. "I have never forgotten you!"

"Nor I, you," he replied and downed a good-size drink. Then he sat back and smiled at her. "You knew I was shanghaied and thought to be dead?"

"Yes, Crown found out that much for me. You were sold to the Captain of a ship bound for Australia."

"Aye," Davy agreed. "When the Captain first looked at me, he thought I was dead and he was in a temper. Then he found I was alive and too weak to be a crew member, and he was in a rage all over again. As soon as the ship docked in Australia, he put me on the dock and told me to look after myself."

"You must have been dreadfully beaten up when you were shanghaied!"

"They were not tender! Not those wolves!" he said, his face darkening. "Well, I wandered about Sydney until I found a doctor willing to care for me. All I needed was proper care. In a month I was myself again."

"But you didn't write me or come back?" she said.

Davy nodded. "I should have," he said. "But what had I to offer you if I did come back? I decided it would be best if you thought me dead. I also made up my mind to make a fortune in that new land."

"I see," she said.

His eyes met hers. "And you did do well. You married Mr. Mark Gregg, the famous shipbuilder, and I have been told you have a lovely daughter by him!"

"Yes," she said quietly.

"What of your sister, Peg?"

"Dead," she said. "She ran off with Alfie, and he destroyed her. I would rather not think about it."

"I'm sorry," he said, obviously touched by the news. "I did not know, though I remember that villain, Alfie, well enough, along with some others."

"Tell me more about Australia," she said.

Looking somewhat sheepish he said, "The doctor who cared for me had a daughter, a fine-looking, high-spirited girl who took a fancy to me. I saw her as far above me, but she encouraged me to try and make my fortune."

"And?"

"As I result, I set out for the gold fields. And for a change, everything began to come my way. I fell in with an old miner who knew all about searching for gold. He taught me everything he'd learned over the years. He'd been in California when the big strike was made there and then had shipped out to Australia. Until we joined up as partners, he'd never had any luck."

She smiled, "I'm sure you changed that."

"I did," Davy said proudly. "And within eighteen months we struck a rich vein. I went back to Sydney and married the doctor's daughter and then returned to the mining town to build my fortune larger."

"And you were successful?"

"Beyond my dreams," Davy Brown said. "I'm a very wealthy man today. My partner recently died and left all his shares to me. So I shall never worry about money again."

Becky said, "I'm so happy for you. What about your wife? I want to meet her. Is she in England?

Davy looked sad again. "No," he said. "She is buried back there in Australia."

"I'm sorry!"

"The mining towns were hard on women, even though we had all the money we could use," he said. "She contacted a fever. In a week she was gone."

Becky said, "What a tragedy."

"It was," the man seated across from her said as he poured himself another whiskey and downed it. Then he looked more cheerful as he informed her, "But she left behind a great treasure."

"Did she?" Becky said politely.

"Yes," Davy said. "And I know you'll agree. My daughter, Julia is named after her dear mother. She is here in London with me."

"Wonderful!"

"A grown young lady with a convent and classical education," Davy Brown said with pride. "I have a mature female companion for her, a lady of genteel background to show her the city and help her adapt to England, since this will be our home."

"You plan to live in London?"

"Yes," Davy said. "I have come to that decision. Though I first returned here to settle a debt and leave for America. I have had my revenge, and now I'm going to stay here."

"Your revenge?" she said, tautly.

He nodded. "Yes. Against the man who so cruelly shanghaied me years ago. That dark scoundrel, Bart Woods!"

CHAPTER 12

"So it was you!" she cried.

The man in black looked surprised. "You know about the incident?"

"How could I help but know! Bart Woods has long been the managing director of Gregg & Kerr. He married Vera Gregg, and he was my husband's business partner and is now mine!"

Davy Brown stared at her. "I should have realized. At the moment I attacked him I had just arrived in London. I could not rest until I faced him and whipped him! He recognized me and asked my pardon. I pardoned him with some heavy blows!"

"You hurt him badly," she said. "He is not well."

"Is he recovering?"

"Yes," she said. "But you might well have killed him. I trust you have no intentions of revenging yourself on him further?"

"None," the big man said staring at his hands. "I'm sorry I did what I did. But he was a villain, and he did send many poor seamen to ships for blood money!"

"I realize that," she said. "I can understand your outrage. But I beg you now to forget about it."

"You have my word."

Becky said, "To Bart's credit he protected you. Even though he recognized you, he would not tell the police or any of us who you were. So that must be said in his favor."

Davy stared at her. "You speak of him as if he were your friend?"

Becky knew she was blushing. She said, "Yes. We have become close friends over the years. I have admired him for putting his black past behind him and making an honest man of himself."

"I find it harder to forget that past," Davy murmured.

"But you must be fair. You have changed greatly, so have I, and so has he. You must allow for the passage of time. The years have not been as kind to Bart Woods as they have been to you. The shipyard is doing badly, his marriage to Vera has been an unhappy one, and about the only thing he has to take pride in is his son, Donald."

"And his friendship with you."

"I have tried to be his friend," she said. "I feel the friendship has not been wasted."

Davy Brown said, "Perhaps you are right. I cannot quarrel with your choice of friends, since you have no control over mine. Nor can I blame you for marrying Mark Gregg. May I ask if that was a happy marriage?"

"Not as good as yours, by all accounts," she said. "But we did have good moments. It was bad in the end when he was very ill. But I do have a lovely daughter, Anne, who is in Paris at the moment."

Davy said, "I wish you had a son. I've often dreamed of coming back here and finding you and my daughter marrying your son!"

She smiled. "Such things happen in novels, but rarely in real life."

Davy was studying her fondly. "You must meet Julia soon," he said. "It is strange! I vow she is more like you than she is like her late mother."

"You probably only imagine that."

"No. It is true," he said. "She has your liveliness and she loves the outdoors. She has been a fantastic horsewoman since her childhood."

"Wonderful!"

"I have bought an estate on the edge of London," Davy said. "A find old castle with a good piece of land, including a bridle path. You must visit us for a few days and get to know my girl. You will approve of her."

"I'm sure I will," she said. "And what are you going to do? Live the life of a retired gentleman?"

"Hardly!" the big man said. "I have bought me a steel mill situated on the Thames. We are in the midst of perfecting a new process which will be cheaper and stronger than most types now offered. We plan to build bridges, machines, and steamships of it."

"That's strange!

"What?"

"That you should be the owner of a steel manufacturing plant. Donald, who is Bart's son, is angry with his father for staying with iron plates. He claims steel is the metal of the future."

"So it is," Davy said.

"And Donald can't persuade his father of this. That is why the shipyard is on the verge of ruin."

Davy smiled grimly. "Bart Woods will surely die a pauper if he stays with iron ships."

"My daughter and I will also be impoverished," she reminded the big man. "Our fortune is invested in the shipyard. If Bart takes it down to ruin, he will ruin all of us."

Davy frowned. "The man must be a fool!"

"No. Stubborn and perhaps behind the times because of his bad health. The future of the firm depends on Donald, his son. I would like you to meet him."

"He sounds like a good enough lad," Davy said.

She nodded. "Perhaps he could discuss the possibility of your producing the steel plates for vessels the shipyard would construct. Or even arrange a merger between your business and ours."

"Not too fast," Davy said, raising a hand. "I can't say that I would like the idea of being a business partner of Bart Woods or his son!"

"Why not? You are looking for an outlet for your steel! And Donald is young and filled with enthusiastic ideas about building steel ships. The only catch is that his father won't agree."

Davy said, "I am just not sure."

"Bart is not well," she said. "He may not be active in the firm long. That is why you and Donald should meet."

"Would he want to talk to me if he knew what I did to his father?" Davy wondered.

"No one need know that," she said. "Except myself and Bart. And he has shown he doesn't intend to mention you."

Davy helped himself to another drink and smiled bleakly. "So I'm to discuss business with the son of my old enemy."

"Donald bears no blame for what his father did."

"I know that."

"And you might well be saving the fortunes of all of us," she said.

Davy looked at her. "We've spent too much time talking about business and not enough about each other."

"We've told each other about our past lives," she said. "What more?"

He leaned forward and said, "I'll tell you what more. I think I'd like to see a link between us before I go in for any business partnerships. I say let us go through with the plan we had all those years ago. Let us marry! And as soon as we can!"

She'd been afraid it might end like this. That he would try to revive the old love between them. And while she still cared for the bronzed man, she had given her allegiance to Bart Woods. And come what may, she could not desert the ailing Bart at this moment, when things were turning against him.

She offered Davy a gentle smile and said, "I know you will not be angry with me. But while your offer flatters me and makes me happy, I'm not able to accept it. I have found a way of life, and a husband would not fit in with it. Perhaps after my daughter is settled in marriage, I might think of it again. But by then, I'm sure no one will want me!"

Davy said, "I will want you any time you make the decision! And I'm willing to wait until you make it, having been patient all these years."

She said, "I'm grateful wealth hasn't changed you. You are as kind and understanding as you ever were."

"With you, Becky," he said. "Perhaps not with others. Now when will you visit me?"

"I don't know," she said. "I'm leaving to visit my daughter in Paris late next week."

"Then come this weekend before you leave," Davy suggested. "I will send a carriage to bring you and then return you here on Monday morning. You must meet my Julia and we still have many things to talk about."

Becky smiled, "Very well," she said. "I'll accept your invitation and be your house guest for the weekend. And while I am visiting you I may have Donald Woods drop by."

Davy shook his head. "You drive a hard bargain. Very well, if the price of your joining us is that I should meet Donald Woods, I'll agree."

"Good. You may send the carriage for me Friday afternoon at four."

He rose. "It shall be here on the dot."

She also stood up to see him on his way. And with a knowing smile, she suggested, "I recommend that you buy yourself a new hat and another cloak."

The big man looked grimly amused. "I might be well advised to do just that!"

He kissed her on the cheek as he left, and she watched him leave and get into his richly decorated carriage. He waved back to her from the window. Davy Brown had come a long way.

At once she sent Donald a message inviting him to join her for dinner at the Holborn Restaurant the following day. She told him she would be waiting at the entrance of the large eating place at twelve-thirty and said it was urgent that he be there. She had no doubt that he would come, thinking it had to do with Anne.

That night she had some strange dreams. She found herself back in the tavern serving drinks. All the familiar faces of that day were there. Peg, Jimmy Davis, Davy as a young man, the one eyed Crown, and his kind-hearted wife. And also old Phineas Pennifeather and the sinister Alfie Bard. She awoke perspiring. And she was filled with a melancholy. She lay staring up into the darkness and tried to think it all out.

She must fight against living in the past. She was still not truly old. Life might have much for her yet. She must talk with Bart and try to make him give in to his son about the change to steel ships. She must also try and comfort him when he was recovered. Just now she could not see him. It was Vera's house, and she would not enter it, though in most ways she had been a better wife to the handsome Bart than his frigid wife had been. Her sole contribution had been Donald, and she had never given Bart the opportunity of having another child by her.

Becky smiled to herself in the gathering light of dawn. At least she'd given Bart another child, a daughter. And even though the unforeseen romance between half-brother and half-sister was causing some problems now, she did not regret Anne. She could never do that. And she could only try hard to work things out for them all.

She was standing in the foyer of the busy restaurant when a tweed-suited and derby-hatted Donald entered to join her. She was wearing a new woollen coat over a late-style taffeta dress. The morning had been cold and rainy.

Donald said, "What is it you want to tell me?"

She smiled at him. "Nothing that can't wait until we are at our table."

He was embarrassed at his breech of etiquette and apologized, "I'm sorry. I'm so concerned about Anne I've completely forgotten my manners."

Anne is all right," she said. "I have something else to discuss with you."

Relieved, he sought out the head waiter and they were shown to a table not far from the door. After they ordered, she briefly told the young man about Davy Brown, without revealing that he was the man who had whipped his father so badly.

She said, "Davy Brown is now extremely wealthy and the owner of a steel mill. He's looking for an alliance with a suitable shipyard. I think we should try to interest him in Gregg & Kerr."

"It's an excellent idea," the young man agreed. "But my father's health is better, and he'll be well enough to return to the office on Monday. He'll not listen to any such idea."

"You feel sure of that?"

"Yes," Donald said grimly. "If we don't get a few steel ships to build, we'll be bankrupt within the year!"

She gasped. "We can't let that happen."

"I'm thinking of going to America," Donald said with a sigh. "I mean to talk to Anne about it if she ever returns from Paris."

"Anne would not want to leave London, not as long as I'm alive," she protested.

Donald said, "You could come to America with us. Your own fortune will be lost if the yard collapses."

"I don't mean to have that happen," Becky said with a hint of the brave barmaid who had fought her way so long. "I haven't come this far to give way weakly."

"Father is stubborn on the point. What can we do?"

"We can force his hand," Becky said. "Don't forget I own a major share of the company. You have some in your own right which you inherited from your grandfather. If we placed our shares together, we could outvote your father."

Donald looked shocked. "He'd never forgive us."

"I think he would if he found we could save the shipyard," She said. "And whether he forgives us or not would be up to him."

The young man stared at her in amazement. "You would put him out of power at the yard! You and he are lovers!"

"Yes," she said quietly. "That is true. We have been lovers a long while. And I shall always be faithful to him unless he turns against me."

He looked at her in silence and then said, "You are a strange but wonderful woman!"

"No," she said lightly. "Practical would be a better word. Now I'm to spend the weekend with Davey Brown at his estate south of London. I want you to come by and spend Saturday afternoon with us. Come for luncheon and stay until late in the afternoon. I want you and he to have a good talk."

Donald was excited. "It's too good a chance to turn down! And maybe if we put over this steel proposal, Anne will be so impressed she'll forget all about her Count."

"Who knows? she asked.

"My father will be angry at us both."

"Let us hope he gets over it," she said.

"Yes. It is for his own good in the long run."

"I'm sure he'll eventually see that," Becky said. "So you will not fail me on Saturday. I shall be there to introduce you. I'll write down the address for you before we leave after lunch."

"I'll be there," he promised.

"Oh, by the way," she said. "Brown has a daughter, Julia. He sets great store on her because he's a widower. I don't know what sort of girl she is, but for his sake we must be pleasant with her."

Donald nodded without showing interest. "Yes, of course."

It was a pleasant, sunny Friday afternoon and Becky had just arrived at Tenby Hall. Davy Brown was showin her about the gardens, after she'd been safely installed in a large guest room. She came downstairs in a red linen dress with a white lace trim at collar and cuffs, and with a modest bustle. The chic red bonnet she wore had a white facing as well. She wanted to look her best, as she wanted Davy in good humor.

Davy was apparently put in his best temper just by having her at his newly purchased estate. He took her by the arm and led her through the gardens. At one point he paused to pick several yellow roses and give them to her.

"Make a deuced good contrast to your dress," he said.

"Thank you," she said. "I hesitated to wear crimson, since some might not think it fitting at my age."

He halted and stared at her. "Your age, Madam? You are not yet forty, if I'm not muddled in my figures."

She laughed lightly. "You are a trifle muddled, but by only a small margin."

"Then let it be," he insisted. "You have a beauty many women half your age would envy."

"I fear you praise me too highly."

"I do not," he said. "And I'm not one of your London gallants, only a rough gold miner from Australia."

They emerged from the garden to the back yard of the house in time to see a pretty, darkhaired girl in grey riding habit ride up. She dismounted lightly, patted the face of her brown horse, and turned it over to a waiting stableman. As the man led the horse away the girl pulled off her gloves and came gracefully towards them.

Her eyes bright, a mischievous smile on her pert, oval face, the girl held out a hand to Becky and said, "You must be Becky! I can tell by the way father radiates happiness beside you."

They exchanged kisses and Becky said, "Davy told me he had a lovely daughter, and I must confess I wasn't much impressed. Meeting you is much different. You are a beauty!"

Julia smiled. "And I hear you have a daughter of my age who is presently in Paris."

"Yes," she said.

"Lucky girl," Julia said. "I loved Paris during the short time I was there. I should like to return."

"Why don't you?" she asked.

"Not for a while," the girl in the riding habit said with a sly smile for her beaming father. "I have to wait until this father of mine gets his new business in hand."

"Of course," Becky said. "It is so kind of you to have me here."

"I've wanted to meet you," Julia said. "All my life I've heard about you."

Becky was impressed with the attractive, witty girl. And she was more than impressed by life at Tenby Hall. She had become used to a luxurious way of life, but the wealthy Davy and his daughter lived in what could only be called royal style. A myriad of servants took care of the house and grounds, and everything was of the best quality.

She was tired that night and went to her room early. She had only been there for a little when there was a light tap on her door. She went and opened it to find Julia standing there in an attractive dressing gown of yellow silk.

"May I come in for a moment?" she asked.

"Of course," Becky said. "I always knit or read a little before I go to bed."

Julia smiled at her. "I'm so happy to have you here. There's been such a change in my father."

"Really?"

"Yes. He became strange when we first returned to London. He was almost dour. I know he had many business matters to bother him, but there was more to it than that. He was also searching for you."

They were sitting on the edge of her canopied bed, side by side. Becky said, "I thought him dead long ago."

"I know," Julia said. "He was so delighted when he found you."

"It has been good," she said.

Julia gave her a shy glance. "Has he asked you to marry him?"

She was amused by the girl's question. She said, "As a matter of fact, he did. Would you disapprove?"

"Not at all!" she said. "I would like to see him marry! But he seems to think he must wait until he finds someone for me."

"You're not engaged?"

"No."

"A wealthy and attractive girl like you. I think you must have had many suitors," Becky said.

"I have," she admitted. "But never the right one. I think you know when the right man comes along."

"You do," she said with a sigh. "I'm sure of that."

"Was Mark Gregg the right man for you?"

"No," she said sadly. "He brought me wealth and position. He saw that I was taught to be a lady. But he could not give me true love. I suppose that was the reason our marriage ended tragically."

"I know nothing about it."

She gave the girl a gentle smile. "It was all long ago. Let us say Mark loved me in his way. He was a man hardly capable of love. Ambition ruled him. And then I met someone else. The father of the young man who is coming here tomorrow to see your father."

Julia said, "Mr. Donald Woods."

"Yes."

"What is he like?"

"He looks very much like his father. So he is handsome. But he is different in nature. His father had a streak of wildness, but Donald is a fine, young man."

"But you fell in love with his father in spite of his wildness?"

Becky sighed. "I'll admit that to you, my dear. I have hardly admitted it to myself. It began with my admiring his determination to make something of his life. Then I became sorry for him because he was treated badly by his wife. Before we knew it, we had become dependent on one another. We are like a married couple, even though Bart and his wife have never divorced. He had not lived with her in a man and wife relationship since before we became lovers."

"You've had such an interesting life!" Julia said with rapt interest.

"I sometimes feel very old!"

"You look and seem young to me!"

Becky said, "But I know how old I am. I can't pretend with myself. One think I must warn you. Your father does not know that Bart Woods and I are lovers. I hope you will not tell him."

Julia looked solemn. "I won't betray your trust. But what about father? He asked you to marry him. What did you say?"

"I had to refuse him because of Bart. And it wasn't easy, since Davy was my first love and perhaps the only man I have loved completely."

The pretty dark girl said, "Could you not turn away from this Bart and marry my father?"

"I could," she said quietly. "The temptation is great. But Bart is in failing health and unhappy. Would *you* desert him?"

The black-eyed Julia considered a moment, then she said, "No, I don't think I would."

"You see?" Becky said. "I had the feeling from the time I met you that we are much alike."

"And I at once found someone I liked in you," the girl said. "Father has placed so many of his hopes on you. I trust that you will at least be his good friend."

She smiled. "Be sure of that. And there is even a good chance we shall be business partners. It depends on how much your father and Donald Woods like each other after their meeting tomorrow."

Julis said, "I shall be anxious to meet that young man. He sounds interesting."

Julia remained with her a little longer, then kissed her goodnight and went on to her room. Becky was much impressed with the girl. Davy had done a remarkable job in raising her. But he'd had the money to hire good people to care for her. She hoped that when Donald arrived he would meet Julia and take to her.

But Donald arrived too late for lunch the next day. Becky was feeling much at home at Tenby Hall. She and Davy were exchanging reminiscences in the great living room when Donald was shown in. He wore a black frock coat and gray trousers and looked very much the sedate, young business man. When introductions had been made, she sat for a while in general discussion of the shipyard's problems and the introduction of steel ships.

"Steel is the metal of the future," Donald said earnestly. "At least until some new development comes along."

"Exactly my feelings," Davy Brown agreed. "I gather your father is not so impressed, Mr. Woods."

Donald smiled bitterly as he sat across from the older man. "Like most young firebrands, my father in his old age is strongly conservative in his opinions."

"That is so," Becky agreed. "Bart Woods fought to have the year turn to iron ships. And he was right. But now he can't seem to realize that day has passed."

Davy Brown was smoking a large cigar and he studied the glowing tip of it. He asked Donald, "Are you able to dictate the policy of the shipyard. Even if your father disagrees?"

Donald gave her a look and then turned to the huge Davy again and said, "Yes. But only with the help of Mrs. Gregg. We have enough shares together to outvote my father."

Davy looked grimly amused. "What do you say, Becky?"

"In this I shall have to back up Donald," she said.

The big man puffed thoughtfully on his cigar. "I shall speak to my manager at the steel mill on Monday. I will ask him to draw up a proposal for a merger with your shipyard to be presented to your company board in due time, the object being the joint production of steel ships."

Donald smiled his gratitude. "Thank you, sir. The moment the proposal reaches me I shall act on it."

Davy Brown said, "I should like to see the project go through, since I understand Mrs. Gregg's fortune is threatened by your father's stubborn position."

"That is true, sir," Donald said.

"You have my word on this," the burly Davy said. "And now let me show you around the grounds. I won't hide the fact I'm proud of this place."

Davy Brown conducted the young man and Becky through the place and then out to inspect the gardens. They were there when Julia returned from her afternoon ride and came to join them still in her riding habit. She looked as lovely as on the day before, and tiny touches of red showed in her cheeks as she was introduced to Donald.

She studied him with her lovely black eyes and said, "I've been hearing a great deal about you, Mr. Woods."

"Donald, please!" he begged her. And Becky could see that he was finding her far more attractive than he'd expected.

"Very well, Donald," she said mischievously. "But I haven't found out whether you are interested in horses or not."

"I had my own horse a few years ago," Donald said. "I used to ride a good deal. But lately I've given it up."

There was an impish light in her eyes. "What a Pity!"

"I agree," he said. "And especially since you are obviously a horsewoman."

"I believe I can find you some riding things. We usually have some extra clothing for guests in the room over the stables. Would you like to join me in a canter through the grounds?"

Donald smiled. "I will be clumsy in my seat, I promise you."

"That doesn't matter," she said, weighing her riding crop in her hands. "It will give you a chance to see all this lovely place and for us to get to know each other better."

Donald turned to Becky and Davy to ask, "Do you wish to talk with me further?"

"No," the older man said warmly. "Go on with Julia! She wants to test you on a horse. That's the way she judges people—by how well they ride!"

"Father!" she said in amused protest.

"It's more than half true," Davy insisted.

"In that case I shall try to prove my worth," Donald said with good humor. "Lead me to the stables, Julia."

Becky watched after them as they walked towards the stables talking animatedly. Then she turned to Davy and smiled, "What a lovely thing youth is!"

"Aye," he said. There was a wistfulness in his voice. "I well remember the first I saw of you—pert and pleasing and asking for a job in a tavern. Your father had just been killed in an accident in the very yard you now practically own."

"Who would have believed it?"

"I know," Davy said. "If Bart Woods hadn't set his thugs on me and sold me to a ship Australia-bound, I'd have gone on working in the yards and eventually we'd have been married and had children. But I would never have become rich, nor would you. But are we any the happier for it?"

"I hope we are," she said. "So many people would wish to be in our places."

"True," he agreed. "But we lost each other as man and wife."

"We are friends, dear friends," she said. "Surely we can be satisfied with that. We have so much else."

"Perhaps," he said.

"Do you like Donald?" she asked.

Davy Brown gave her a wry smile. "I was afraid that would come up. He looks remarkably like his father. But he's an improvement on him in most every way. I like him."

Becky's eyes met his. "I'd say that Julia also was favorably impressed by him."

"Aye," Davy said grimly. "I hope he does badly on his horse. That will put her off."

CHAPTER 13

An hour later Julia burst happily into the living room where Becky and Davy were enjoying a sherry and informed them, "Donald is a fine horseman! We had a lovely time!"

"Good!" Becky said. She smiled at her, then she gave Davy a teasing look.

The big man said, "There has to be a lot more about a man than being able to ride a horse!"

"Donald has all those attributes as well," Julia said with a mischievous twinkle in her lovely eyes. "I'm going up to change now. Donald is changing at the stable." And she hurried out and upstairs.

Davy sighed. "I might have known we could be in trouble. That young man has a lot of charm."

"Why worry about them?"

His eyebrows raised. "My daughter wed a son of Bart Woods? The very thought of it angers me!"

"He is in no way to blame for his father's actions," she said.

"Maybe not. But I could not stand for Bart Woods to be linked with my family. I'm sorry, Becky. I'll go into business with him and his son, but I draw the line at encouraging any romance between Donald and Julia."

"What if they fall in love?"

"I can always take Julia back to Australia," he said. "And I will if anything like that happens."

Becky had no doubt that he would do as he threatened. This depressed her somewhat, since she sensed the two young people liked each other. If a romance developed between them, it would end the problem of Donald wanting to marry her Anne. But it seemed that Davy would interfere, even if Donald and his daughter should fall in love.

She would have to depend on Count André in Paris to sweep Anne off her feet. This appeared to be the best hope. And from all that Anne had written her, this romance was in full strength. The Count had formally proposed to her!

Julia proved herself to be her father's daughter, in that she persuaded Donald to stay for dinner and the night. "You and Becky can return to London together tomorrow," she told him. "It will be ideal to give Becky company."

Donald did not need a lot of persuading, and the two young people seemed to have a wonderful time all evening. Davy showed colored lantern slides of Australia, which were most interesting to all. And Becky noted that at one point Julia and Donald were sitting in the darkened room holding hands. She hoped that Davy was too preoccupied at the lantern to notice this.

The weekend came to a close for her and Donald after breakfast on Sunday morning. Donald told Davy that he would await the proposal for the merger from him. And Julia and Donald parted with mutual promises to see each other again. On the surface all were in the best of humor, though Becky knew that Davy was not pleased about his daughter's sudden interest in the son of his ancient enemy. It was a complicated situation, but she hoped it might work out.

In the carriage returning to London she questioned the young man. "What do you think of the Browns?"

"Mr. Brown is a remarkable person," Donald said. "Vigorous for his age. I wish father had half his health."

She sighed. "True. Your father has failed a good deal of late."

"Mr. Brown is also much more forward looking," Donald went on. "If he offers to merge his steel mill with us I'll fight for the deal."

"And you shall have my support," she assured him.

"Julia is also a most interesting girl."

"You like her?"

"I do," he said enthusiastically. "Frankly, if I didn't consider your daughter and I to be engaged, I would find myself much taken with that dark-haired beauty."

She smiled. "I could see you two got along well."

"Fabulously," he said.

"But you aren't truly engaged to my Anne," she pointed out. "You shouldn't feel bound not to pay attention to any other attractive girl who comes your way."

"But I do," he insisted.

"You shouldn't," she said. "Anne is at least dating Count André. I can see no harm in your seeing the Brown girl or taking her out occasionally."

The idea seemed appealing to him. He gave her a questioning glance. "You think it would be all right?"

"I'm sure it would be, and Anne would be bound to agree with me."

Donald sat back with a relieved look on his handsome young face. "Well, it might be fun to take her around a little and show her some of London."

"I would consider it thoughtful of you."

"And her father might appreciate it," Donald pointed out. "And I do hope to do business with him."

"Whether he appreciates it or not, I'd take her out. It is the girl you'll be entertaining. Think of her and what she'd like."

By the time they reached London she was reasonably sure that Donald would make an attempt to see Julia Brown again. This pleased her. The hard feelings between their fathers would have to be dealt with later. Enough for the present!

Two nights before she was to leave for Paris she had her first visit from Bart Woods following his fairly long period of convalescence. She was worried by his loss or weight and the increased toll his arthritis was taking. He walked with a cane now and said it was for protection against another attack, but she was sure it was because he couldn't manage without it.

He seemed in a badly depressed mood. He complained of unrest in the shipyard over lack of work, Donald's arguing with him about turning to steel construction, and Vera's near madness in pursuing her new fad of spiritualism.

She tried to comfort him and told him, "I think Anne has continued seeing that young count in France. And now Donald is showing interest in the daughter of a friend of mine." She was careful not to name Davy.

Bart assumed it was some woman friend, and she did not bother to correct him. He said, "Then that is all to the good. Let us pray that something comes of both romances. Vera had long threatened to inform Donald that your Anne is his half-sister."

This upset Becky. "She wouldn't!"

"She is capable of it. But if she has no excuse, she'll likely keep silent on the matter."

"No matter what," Becky said, "I wouldn't hurt them that way. We could find some other means of separating them."

"I would hope so," he said with a sigh. "We now have another problem on the horizon."

"Another?" she gasped. "I would say we had enough!"

"You will remember that Vera had a brother, James," Bart said grimly.

"Yes. He went to America."

"He is still there, but he threatens to return."

"Oh?"

"Years ago, Vera's father paid for his shares of the business. Now he is threatening to come back to sue for his rights. By the terms of the will, he doesn't have any!"

"James was always a wastrel," she agreed. "That could well spell trouble."

"I think it will," Bart said bleakly. "He has written hinting that I seized control of the company unfairly. That Mark Gregg was ill and could not have signed any agreement, and that he couldn't have fathered Anne."

She gasped. "He is already blackmailing you by letter."

"Yes. I have refused him everything. Now he says he is returning to England and hiring a lawyer to represent him and press a suit against the company."

"Oh no!"

"If he resorts to the courts, it could be a dirty case," Bart said unhappily. "He would smear me as a possible forger, bring out that we were lovers, and reveal that Anne is our love child!"

"That must not happen!"

"I shall do all in my power to stop it from happening," he promised.

"You must," she begged him. "It could be our ruin. You did forge Mark's name, though your saved his fortune in doing so.

He frowned. "I had little choice, or the yard would have gone then."

She shrugged. "And Anne is our love child. Surely for the honor of the family James will not stir up such a mess."

"I understand he has run through with his inheritance and now is looking for another one. Perhaps his threat is idle. He may never return. But should he come back, I wanted you to be prepared."

She sighed. "It seems the past is to go on haunting us."

"Haunting me!" he said. "I thought I had escaped it. No more! I know now that I was often violent and wrong in those distant days. Now I pay."

Tactfully she asked, "Have they ever been able to track down your attacker?"

He gave her a suspicious look. Then he said, "No. I don't expect they will."

"Don't you want them to?"

"Donald made a great fuss about it!"

"He is worried for you."

Bart said, "I think it should be dropped."

"I see," she said quietly. "Do you want to tell me about it?"

The weary Bart shook his head. "No," he said. "I want you in my arms!"

Two days later she left for Paris. Anne received her with delight. And in a short time she was whisked off into a wild round of socializing. There seemed to be parties for her on every side, and Anne appeared to have made friends with most of the charming people of the great city.

Becky had always considered Paris more lively than London. She loved its food, its exciting theatre and dance, and the air of romance which the great city of France always held for her. What more suitable place for her daughter to fall in love?

Count André Lemont became a successful architect. He had designed a number of fine buildings, and he was also the heir to a title and vast wealth. His widowed mother, Countess Maria, was frail but highly intelligent. She favored the match between Anne and her son.

Becky sat with her daughter in the small apartment she had rented within sight of the Eiffel Tower and listened over the breakfast table as her daughter told her all these things.

Becky sipped her tea and asked, "Then all is right here!"

"No!" Anne shook her head. "It's all wrong! I have no right to be in love with André. Donald trusts me! You should read his letters!"

"Donald may be in the process of finding someone else whom he cares for," she said carefully.

Anne's eyes widened. "You think so?"

"It's possible," she told her daughter. I can't say definitely. But I have to believe he is paying court to a girl from Australia. But he is held back in giving her his full attention because he feels he must be loyal to you."

"You think he might fall in love with this other girl if I weren't available. If we hadn't our agreement?"

Becky said, "I don't know what agreement you have. But it must be a foolish and easily-put-aside one. Your happiness and his are what is most important. You shouldn't feel locked in by past promises."

"Donald has always been like a brother to me," Anne said tautly. "I can't hurt him!"

"Let him remain a friend and sort of brother."

"He wouldn't," Anne said unhappily. "If I turn him down, for André, he'll hate me."

"He might be upset for a little, but he'd get over it before too much time passed."

Anne stared down at her empty teacup. "Susan would give everything to win André'."

"But he loves you."

"Yes."

"And you care for him?"

Anne looked at her mother. "Yes. He is exciting.

And life here is so different and thrilling. I have never been happier in all my life!"

Becky said gravely, "And you have not seen Donald since you came here."

"No."

"And his letters have only worried you."

"Yes. But that is my own selfish fault. I want to desert him, and he resents it."

Becky said, "I think there is some selfishness on his part also. He will not accept that it is possible you have fallen in love with another man!"

Anne considered this. "I hadn't thought of it that way."

Her daughter came around the table and threw her arms around her as she sobbed, "Oh, mother, what shall I do?"

"Follow your heart."

"I love André in a way I've never loved anyone before."

"Then marry him."

Anne sighed and let go of her and stood touching a hankie to her eyes. "No. I can't do that. Not until I return to England and talk to Donald."

At once Becky knew the old fear. She said," I say that is the worst thing you can do."

"Why?"

"Donald will try to urge you into marrying him and putting André out of your life."

Anne said, "He can't force me to unless I agree."

"He'll work on your sympathy, and you will agree. You'll be married, and in a short time you'll feel restless and frustrated. You'll never forget André, and you'll come to hate your marriage."

"Hate Donald? Never."

"You think not now," her mother said. "But I'm older than you, and I've seen such things happen."

"I will have to risk it," her daughter said. "André has promised to wait until I can go to England and work this out. If I am meant to marry him, I'm sure I shall return."

Her daughter's decision worried Becky, not only for the obvious reason that Donald and Anne could never marry, but also because Count André Lemont was such a fine prospect for a son-in-law.

At a garden party held at his mother's house the next day, she and the young Frenchman stood together by a lovely fountain. Fragrance of the flowers in the surrounding gardens filled the air.

André was copper-haired with rather thick, sensual lips and an even-featured pleasant face. His eyes were brown and alert. And he had a wry, ready smile which he was quick to use.

He smiled now as he told Becky, "I have to be worried."

"You do?" she said, pretending not to understand him.

The Count said, "Yes. Anne is determined to return to London and discuss her plans with that young man she grew up with."

"Oh, that!"

"I do not like it."

"Nor do I," she smiled. "From all she has told me she is clearly in love with you. And you have asked her to marry you. She should accept."

"Thank you, madame," the Count said. "My mother is of the same opinion. But Anne will not decide."

"I have talked to her."

"So have I. Endlessly," he said. "It has been of no use. I love your daughter. But I do not always understand her."

"I must admit to the same thing," Becky smiled. "Her father's character was a strong one. She seems to have inherited it."

"What shall I do?" André asked in despair.

"Be patient."

"I have been."

"When she returns to England, you come with her. Then you will at least be able to hold your own in this contest for her."

The Count brightened. "I had not thought of that."

"But if she protests?"

"Come anyway," Becky said. "I will entertain you."

"Excellent," the young man said with one of his quick smiles. "You are a most understanding mother!"

"I'm concerned for my daughter's happiness," she said quietly.

And she was. A few days later she returned to London. Anne would complete her Paris studies within the month, and then planned to come back to talk with Donald. No matter what Becky said, she could not make Anne change her plans. So that was how things now stood.

Becky was exhausted by the time she reached her house in London. She found several messages waiting for her there, including one from Bart Woods which said, "James Kerr back in London! Watch out!"

She'd barely had a warm tub and changed to a suitable robe for the house when her housekeeper informed her she had a visitor. Thinking it must be Donald or even Bart, she went downstairs to find someone else, someone whom she thought to be a stranger for a moment. Then she recognized him and gasped, "James Kerr!"

"The same," he said, with a courtly bow from the hips. His hair was white, and his face was bloated. His eyes, which had once held a merry expression, could now only be called shifty. He was dressed elaborately in a pale blue coat and black and white checkered pants. A glowing diamond stickpin decorated his purple cravat. He looked prematurely old and unhealthy.

She said, "You've returned to England."

James Kerr laughed mockingly. "Surely that is obvious. I would expect something better than that from a smart girl like you, Becky."

Upset, she said, "I'm sorry. You did surprise me."

"I'm rather strong on surprise," the prodigal said. "I will now make a prediction. You are going to offer me a strong whiskey, or better still a glass and bottle so I can help myself, and an easy chair in which to rest my poor body."

She said, "I'm also weary. I've just returned from Paris."

"I know," he said.

"Oh," she said. And she went for the whiskey, wondering who might have told him.

He took the glass and bottle from her when she returned. Seating himself with feet sprawled out he bade her to sit in the chair across from him. "Sit down where I can see you," he said.

"I had planned on retiring early," she said as she sat down.

"I won't keep you long."

"I'll be grateful if you don't."

He poured a drink and downed half of it. "You don't seem happy to see me."

"We were not all that close."

"More your fault than mine," he rebuked her. "I was very much taken with you at one time. But you were out to marry Mark Gregg and you did."

"That's all over with," she protested.

"Not as I see it," he replied. And he finished off the whiskey in the glass and poured himself another. Then he asked, "Where was I?"

"You mentioned that I married Mark."

He laughed. "So I did. Quite a match for a barmaid whose sister became a prostitute and who might have been one herself!"

She jumped up, enraged. "How dare you say that?"

"I have a certain lady friend," he mocked her. "Somewhat the worse for wear I will admit. But in her sober moments she recalls a Becky and Peg Lee. And she can tell a few stories of Peg working side by side with her in Alfie Bard's stable of girls!"

"Get out of here!" she demanded.

"Not yet," he said, calmly finishing his drink. "I can prove what I've said. And I also know that Mark Gregg was duped by you and Bart Woods after his stroke. Mark was not able to sign any documents, and he certainly could not have fathered your girl!"

"You can prove none of that!"

"I don't need to," he sneered. "I have only to say it abroad and in court. I was wrongly robbed of my share of the shipyard, and I mean to get it back!"

"You were paid off by your father!"

"And cheated—though I mean to get mine!" He coughed and all at once bent his head as if in pain. Then he reached into his inner coat pocket and yelled at her, "Fetch me some water!"

Terrified at his sudden attack, she hurriedly fetched a glass and a pitcher of water. She filled the glass and put it on the table by his chair. He brought out a bottle with white pellets in it. He took out one and put it on his tongue. Then he drank some water and sat back in the chair staring until the attack passed.

She watched him closely and after a little the glazed look of pain left his eyes. His face, which had gone paper white now became reddish again. He seemed to breathe easier. He picked up the bottle of white pellets and replaced them in his pocket.

He smiled and said, "Wonder pellets! Supplied to me by a doctor friend in New York. I brought a supply here with me. I must have them constantly at my side, or my life is in danger."

She was standing. "You are better now?"

"Yes," he said. He looked up at her. "You hate me, don't you?"

"What do you expect after the things you've said?"

"All of them are true."

"You twist everything to suit yourself."

"I'm willing to argue that in court," James said. "I'm going to plead that Bart and you, being lovers and ambitious, persuaded my senile father I was worthless and had him pay me off with a paltry sum!"

She said, "I have heard a different story. I heard that you were well paid."

"From Bart Woods?"

"It doesn't matter."

"Well, I'm back," James Kerr told her. "And if Bart does not come up with a goodly sum, all that I've told you will be public knowledge."

"Why do you wish to ruin us?"

He smiled coldly and rose. "I have no such wish. I'm only interested in my rightful inheritance. If you wish to bring ruin on yourselves by denying me, then I cannot do anything to stop it."

"Unless you get your way, you will do all this," she said. "And Bart cannot give you a lot of money, even if he wished. The business is in bad shape."

"I would say that is his concern and yours, not mine," the dandy said. "I'm living at the house at the request of my sister, Vera, though I must admit I've been coolly treated by both Bart and his son. How like his father he is !" James gave her a leer. "I should like to meet your daughter."

"You will please me best by leaving and never returning," she said coldly.

He picked up his hat and fashionable walking-stick. "Have no fear," he said. "You are bound to hear from me again." And he left her.

She was in a state. She paced up and down without any thought of rest. And she was actually glad when the doorbell later sounded. She opened the door and a tense Donald entered.

Donald said, "I just learned you had returned. Dear Uncle James kindly told me!"

"That creature!" she exclaimed.

"I know!"

"Despicable," she said. "He was never a nice person, and now he's thoroughly rotten!"

"I couldn't agree more," Donald said. "And as soon as Father heard he'd been here he asked me to come over. Father was worried about you."

"I'm all right," she said. "He did upset me. That's all."

Donald frowned. "What are all these threats about? Father won't tell me. And James only goes on about revealing certain family secrets if he's not properly treated. What is he talking about?"

"There's a great deal of bluff to it," she said, slumping down into a chair by the fireplace.

"My mother looks terrified, and she has even had several sessions with father in his study. They usually never talk over anything, but he has driven them to consulting each other. Mother seems to believe her brother can cause trouble."

Becky sighed. "He can slander us all and cause a nasty scandal. He claims he was cheated out of his share of the firm."

"Father says there are papers he signed to accept that he was being paid off. My grandfather showed them to him—they are in the safe at the office. So he doesn't have a true claim that it's a case of blackmail!"

"Without doubt!"

"We'll have to wait and see," she said wearily. "He is a sick man. He had a bad attack of some sort while he was here."

"Did he?"

"Yes. I was terrified. He took some pellet and seemed better."

"His wonder drug," Donald said sarcastically. "It's his heart. He's had several attacks at the house since his return. But he keeps the tablets by him always, and as soon as he takes one he improves."

"I saw that," she said. "I wonder that a man clearly so near death would wish to do so many people harm!"

"He's vicious," Donald said. "I've had a bad time since you left—trying to keep the merger plan from my father, having to deal with this unpleasant Uncle James, and worrying about Anne! She only writes me every ten days or so, only a short note with little in it. What is she doing?

"She's finishing her studies and enjoying the city," Becky said.

"She's not being fair!"

"I understand she is coming back to London soon to talk with you. She's not making any plans until she does."

He sighed. "At least I've been able to get that much sense in her. When she returns, she'll see this other romance is wrong and marry me."

"That's what you want?"

"It is what is right for both of us."

"I wonder," she said.

"How can you have any doubts?" he protested.

"I thought you and Julia Brown made a nice couple," she told him." What about Julia?"

"She's all right."

"Have you seen her?"

"You told me to see her!"

She smiled. "Don't be so aggressive. I'm not accusing you of anything. I'm simply interested. Her father is a dear friend; perhaps he will be our business associate. I'd like to know how you and his daughter have made out."

Donald paced up and down. "She's a fine girl. You know I think that. I've seen her several times. In fact, I'll be taking her to dinner and the theatre tomorrow night."

"Ah!" she said. "That sounds as if you've been truly kind to her."

He shrugged. "It wasn't completely altruistic on my part. She's jolly good company. I never tire of being with her."

"I can imagine she's delightful."

"She is!" He said almost enthusiastically. Then he looked at her strangely. "Why should you be lauding her so?"

"I'm only saying what I think to be true."

"You're Anne's mother. You should be anxious for me to marry her!"

Becky said, "Only if I'm sure you are better suited for each other than to anyone else. And I'm not that sure!"

He shook his head. "I think you had me meet Julia just to confuse me!"

"You had to meet her if you're going to be a business partner of her father's." She paused and said knowingly. "And if you are confused, it means you must care more than you'd like to admit!"

"I'm going!" Donald said. "I'll tell father you are all right."

CHAPTER 14

The next morning she received an unusual message from Bart, an invitation to join him for a ride in his carriage that afternoon. She could only surmise that he wished to speak with her about something concerning James, and that it was of such a private nature he thought they had best meet and talk in the carriage. She put on a brown taffeta dress she'd purchased in Paris, and one of the wider-brimmed bonnets which were popular over there. Then she waited by the window overlooking the street until his carriage arrived.

London was slowly changing and becoming larger and more populous. Elgar Street was no longer a quiet residential area, as it had been twenty years ago. Business places had located at either end of the street, many new houses had been built, and its cobblestone surface was the route for several horse-drawn bus lines. As she watched, a two decker came by with the driver perched high at the upper level and four horses moving it along at a good rate. The upper section was open to all sorts of weather, but the lower seats were protected. The front wheels were smaller than the rear, and there were advertisements of many kinds painted along the red sides of the bus in gold letters.

A bicycle rider went by on the latest model with its two giant wheels, a hawker of fish and chips halted to shout his wares and move on, and then the elegant carriage of Bart Woods pulled up before her door. She at once hurried out; the driver helped her inside.

Bart was sitting in a corner of the shadowed interior with a blanket pulled up over his arthritis legs. In his stove-pipe hat and drab grey suit he looked nothing like the daring man she had once known. He was a tired, dejected figure, yet there was immense strength in his face.

She leaned forward and kissed him. "How nice of you to think of this."

"I needed to talk with you," he said. "And we can do a bit of sight-seeing at the same time."

"A delightful idea," she said, settling close beside him with a smile.

As the carriage started away, he asked her, "How did it go in Paris?"

"I'm hopeful."

"Just hopeful?"

She gave him a knowing look. "I fear Anne inherited your strong character. She refuses to break with Donald until she returns and talks it all out with him."

"Damn!" he said. "That means we may be faced with telling them the truth. It seems nothing short of that will make them change their minds."

"It may not be as bad as you fear," she said. "Donald has been seeing a fine young woman. And I have reason to assume that he is more than a little fond of her."

He frowned. "I have gathered that. But he has been most mysterious about it. Refuses to tell me anything about her."

"That is often the case with young men in love."

"You think he may actually be in love?"

Becky nodded. "He has admitted to being confused. I find that promising."

Bart looked out the window and sighed. "I would not count too much on it. Things could hardly be worse. I sent Donald to you last night to warn you about James."

"He came to see me, you know," she said. "I mean James."

Bart turned with anger showing on his worn face. "The Devil he did! What did he say?"

"Exactly what he must have said to you. He wasn't at all careful to hold anything back. In fact he even called me to task for having been a prostitute, which you know to be a lie."

"He's loaded with lies," Bart said, clenching his hands as they rested on the blanket. "He's given me a deadline of three days to make a settlement. Then if nothing happens, he will tell his stories to the scandal sheets and the courts."

"I think the yellow press is more likely to listen to him than any court!"

"The very fact he makes his accusations will be enough. He need not prove them. We will be ruined by what he implies. People enjoy scandal and are always ready to accept the worst."

She reached out and took his hand in hers. "We have faced many things together."

"And we can face this," he agreed. "But I'm not worried about us. I'm thinking of the children."

"Donald and Anne are hardly children."

"They are young, with most of their lives ahead of them. I do not wish their names to be tainted with scandal."

"So?"

He sighed. "I shall have to deal with James. I have not yet decided how."

Becky said, "If you could make him wait a little, with his bad heart he is apt to die at any time."

"He has those cursed pellets to help him," Bart said.

"He had an attack at my place. I was shocked!" she said.

"We can hardly depend on his heart ridding us of him," Bart said. "It may be that I may have to scrounge up a number of pounds more on the firm's credit and pay him off."

"The firm doesn't have the money."

"No," he said grimly. "And the banks are into us deeply. We have little interest left." They crossed the bridge and drove to a more familiar area, the East End dock section where she had grown up and where the shipyard was located. It was also changing, and not for the better. More houses were crowded into the narrow, crooked streets, and everywhere there was filth on the cobblestones. She could not believe that it had been this bad in her day.

They passed a bakery shop whose exterior looked familiar, and Bart pointed to it and said, "Used to be Crowns' Tavern."

"Of course !" she exclaimed, leaning to have a final look out the window as they passed it by. "I should have known it at once!"

"I'm taking you to the docks," he said. "I want you to see a small wooden schooner we've just finished. She's still on the stays, as graceful and beautiful a craft as you're ever likely to cast eyes upon."

"A wooden boat? Aren't they usually built by the smaller yards?"

Bart looked down at his hands. "They are. But we had no work for our men. Better take a small job than have none at all."

"I see," she said.

"I know your thinking," he said. "You side with Donald. You'd like us to go into steel ships."

"Then I need say no more," she said. "I don't wish to plague you. You have enough other worries."

He was looking straight ahead now. "Do you know who is to have the largest steel mill in the London area?"

She felt her throat tighten. How much did he know? She said, "I wonder who it might be."

"A man called Davy Brown," Bart said grimly. "I had him shanghaied years ago. He was just a sailor on the street to me. His head brought me a bounty. He went to Australia and made a fortune. And he is the man who thrashed me and sent me to the hospital."

"It's a strange story," she said.

"A bitter one for me," Bart said. "I wouldn't have recognized him. But he told me who he was and what I had done to him. Then he beat me unmercifully."

"That was hardly justified after all those years."

"I think perhaps it was," the man at her side said. "That is why I didn't name him. He had his revenge, and I paid the price for my evil."

Becky felt a little easier after hearing his reaction. She said, "Then it is at an end. You need think no more about it."

Bart said, "I don't think Brown is quite finished with me. He has bragged to his banker, who in turn gossiped with mine, that he intends to take over Gregg & Kerr and build steel ships."

"These idle rumors often have no basis in fact," she tried to placate him.

Bart said, "I think this one may have. I'm sure Brown wants to ruin me and will never be content until he takes over my business."

She dared not tell him that it was she and his son who had approached Davy Brown with the idea, that he was proceeding with it on the assumption that he would have their support. She asked, "It might be the only way you can keep the yard operating?"

"Then I'll let it close," he said grimly.

"All the men out of work, and our investment in it lost!"

Bart said, "You must have enough put aside without being dependent on the yard's income. I have."

"We shall be much poorer if it goes."

"I can endure that, but I cannot change my beliefs," the ailing Bart said in his old, weary voice.

They reached the docks overlooking the yard, and he insisted on getting out and her joining him. His legs were so stiff both she and the coachmen had to help him. But after he moved about for a little, he was easier able to walk with his cane.

Using his cane as a pointer, he indicated the small, trim craft on stays at the end of the yard. It was, as he'd said, a fine example of wooden construction.

Staring at it with pride, he said, "When ships like that ruled the sea, a passing craft was a graceful sight. Now its naught but metal plates and wads of black smoke rolling up into the air!"

"It is a lovely vessel," she said. "What is she to be called?"

He turned to her with a smile. "I had only one name for such a lovely vessel. That's why I wanted you to see her. She's to be the *Rebecca!*"

She looked up at him with shining eyes. "That is a truly lovely compliment!"

"There are few ways left I can express my love for you,", he said. "This is one of them. She'll keep your name alive over the seas as long as she sails."

He took her back home again, and she could tell that he was exhausted. It had been a strange afternoon, with her learning some new facts. Oddest of all was that he had found out that Davy Brown was anxious to take over the yard. He still did not know that she and Davy had once been lovers and were still staunch friends.

Nor did he guess that attractive girl whom Donald was seeing was Brown's daughter. If he did find out, there would be a row between the father and son. The feud between Bart and Davy continued.

That evening it was Davy Brown who came to see her. He had heard of her return from Donald. And since Donald and Julia had gone out for dinner and the Theatre, he was on his own.

He told her. "Those two are at the theatre tonight."

"I know," she said.

"That young man is winning her gradually," he said with a stern look on his bronzed face. "I may have to send her back to Australia."

"She might refuse to go."

"She'd better not," he said hotly.

"People in love are difficult to reason with."

"Puppy love!" he scoffed. "I didn't think anything would come of it, or I'd have discouraged him at once."

She said, "They seem to get along so well together. And I can't say anything against Bart's son. He and my daughter have been very close."

"Then let him marry your daughter!"

"I think Anne is in love with a Frenchman."

Davy Brown looked frustrated. "Well, I can't abide the thought of being linked with a Woods!"

"That's nonsense. You might go far and not find as suitable a prospective husband for Julia as Donald."

"I have the proposition ready for consideration by your people," he said. "Now its up to you and Donald."

"I know."

He eyed her with a gleam in his sharp eyes. "We'll see what happens then."

"You mean what Bart does then?"

"He's opposed to it. I know that much."

"And it would give you satisfaction to break him?" she said. "Tell the truth."

"It'll be your decision and his son's," Davy said.

After he left she thought about it all. How cleverly he had worked it out. Bart was bound to lose, and not only was he doomed to be defeated but he would also be defeated by his son and the woman he loved. How could she go along with it? Yet, if she didn't, they would all be impoverished for the sake of his stubborn refusal to face progress. It was a dilemma.

She was up early the next morning expecting to hear from Donald about the offer arriving from Davy Brown's office. But she didn't hear from Donald; she heard from Bart Woods. Her bell rang, and when she answered the door Bart was standing there looking almost as weary as when she had left him the previous afternoon.

"Bart, What is it?" she exclaimed.

"I'll come in for a moment," he said. And when he was inside, he suggested, "Let us go to your sewing room I do not wish to be overheard."

She led the way and he followed, his cane in hand. When they were in the room and the door closed, she faced him anxiously to ask, "What is wrong, Bart?" She couldn't help wonder if he hadn't already heard of the plot to take the business from his hands.

He looked at her with a strange gleam in his eyes. And in an even voice, he said "James Kerr is dead!"

"Dead!" she gasped.

"Yes. One of the servants found him stretched out on the floor of his room this morning. He came in late last night. Very drunk."

She was beginning to sense the unusual calm in him. Almost a mad calm. Fear made her taut. She repeated. "He was drunk, you say! You saw him come in?"

"I happened to be in the hallway by his door when he came stumbling up the stairs," Bart said. "Crippled as I am, I was able to help him into his room and put him on the bed. I made no attempt to make him more comfortable. I thought I had done my duty."

"You had," she agreed, still bothered and not knowing quite why.

In that unnatural, even tone he said, "The next thing I knew they found him on the floor this morning."

Becky said, "He must have had one of his spells in the night and had been trying, in his still drunken state, to find his bottle of pellets."

"Pellets?" his tone was blank.

Her eyes windened. "You know what I mean. The pellets he brought from America with him. He used them whenever he had a seizure. He took one here, and it brought him back fairly quickly."

"You must be confused," Bart said stonily.

"What?"

"I know of no pellets."

"But you told me about them," she insisted. "I remember!"

Bart Woods shook his head. "You're making a mistake. There were no pellets. None were found on him or in his room."

She gasped again. "So!"

"I thought you should know."

She caught him by the arm and in a urgent voice, said, "Bart! What are you telling me?"

"That there never were any pellets!"

She was near hysteria. "Bart, he came in drunk last night. You helped him onto the bed where he collapsed. Then you searched him and took that vial of pellets he always carried on him. After that you searched the room and located whatever other cache he had of them and took them. After that you left him!"

"You have a fine sense of melodrama," Bart said, "You're almost the equal of Dickens!"

"This is a dreadful business, Bart! You had no right!"

"James will tell no tales," he said. "That worry at least is ended."

She closed her eyes for a moment, trying to somehow reconcile it all in her mind. Then she said, "I wish you had let him talk. Anything but this! You left him there to die!"

He behaved as if he had not heard her, saying, "Vera is looking after all the funeral arrangements. It will be a private affair. You will not be expected to attend."

"Thank you," she said, in a near whisper.

Bart's eyes were cold. "I wanted to bring this news to you myself."

"Yes, Bart."

"I will go now."

"Yes, Bart," she repeated, almost under her breath. She was still standing there in a numbed state as he let himself out and went back to his carriage.

She could not deny that she was relieved to know that James was dead and that he would not blackmail them any longer. But to mar any good feelings about that, there was her certain knowledge that Bart had committed a murder to save them. For it was surely the next thing to murder to strip this ailing man of the medicine that kept him alive.

Bart had done this, counting on James having another heart seizure sometime before morning. And it had worked out that way. She could picture the dead man's last tormented convulsions as he groped about desperately trying to locate the precious pellets which might save him. Villain that he was, she could not have wished him that sort of end.

Most horrifying of all, it meant that Bart had reverted to the violent methods of his beginnings. Somewhere under the cloak of the conservative business man of today there was still the criminal who had preyed on innocents like Davy Brown on the docks. And Bart had proven he felt guilt for his wrong-doing when he refused to give the authorities any hint of his attacker, even though he'd known it was Davy.

She was so upset she hired a carriage to take her to Tenby Hall. All during the long drive she sat not seeing or hearing anything, lost in her thoughts. A drizzle of rain was starting as she left the carriage and made her way to the door of the mansion.

She told the servant who answered that she wished to see Mr. Brown. She was shown into a small reception room and left there to wait his arrival. When he came into the room he frowned, "How dare they leave you out here!"

"It doesn't matter," she said rising.

"It matters to me how my friends are treated," he said. "And you are much more than an ordinary friend."

"Davy, let us go somewhere so we can talk privately without being overheard!"

The big man stared at her. "You're in a state!"

"Somewhat!"

Come along," he said, taking her arm. "We'll go to my study. That is quite safe."

When they were in the study he seated her and insisted she have a brandy before saying anything. Then he stood to listen to her story. "What is it brought you all the way across London?"

She sipped the burning brandy and summoned all her courage. Then she began a recital of James Kerr returning and all that had happened, including his death as a result of being denied the pellets.

Davy Brown rubbed his chin. "So Bart went back to his old criminal tricks."

"You might say that."

"Mind you, this James was in bad shape. The time would come when those pellets wouldn't help. That time could have been last night."

Distressed, she said, "But Bart had taken them."

"So he hadn't even the opportunity to see if they would benefit him. And at the same time he'd be in a worse panic knowing he couldn't find the pellets. That could increase the severity of his attack and make it more certain he'd die."

"Bart left little to chance."

"So we could say Bart Woods has committed another murder."

"Please!" she begged, tears in her eys.

Davy stared at her. "What puzzles me is why he came directly to you and confessed? How could he trust you?"

She took a deep breath. "Davy, there's something you should know if you haven't guessed it before."

"What?"

"Bart and I are lovers. We have been for years."

The big man sighed. "I did sort of suspect that. I thought there must be someone, and that is why you refused to marry me. I didn't know who it would be. So it is Bart!"

"Yes," she said, wryly. "Fate played a strange trick on me when it put me in the arms of the man responsible for my losing you."

"How long have you loved him?"

"Ever since Mark Gregg had his stroke." She paused. "You may as well know it all. What James Kerr was threatening to expose. My daughter, Anne, is not Mark's daughter, but Bart's. I lied to save my reputation and give Anne a name. I also meant to protect Bart's marriage, even though it was no longer a true marriage. They were merely living under the same roof."

"That is a shocker," Davy admitted as he sank down into a swivel chair by his desk and thought about it for a moment. Then he said, "This Donald, Bart's son, didn't you say he wanted to marry your Anne?"

"Yes," she said unhappily. "That is why Bart and I have been trying to break the romance!"

He said, "And that is why you have been such a matchmaker between my daughter and Donald Woods?"

"Not really! I honestly think Julia and Donald are ideally suited to each other."

"Under the circumstances, you would," the big man said grimly.

"Davy! You must hate me!"

"Why?"

"For holding back the truth and not telling you everything. I actually told Julia most of it. So she knows."

Davy Brown's handsome face showed a bemused look. "It seems to me I'm being twisted and turned at will by the women folk around me. I'm not sure that I like it!"

"Don't blame Julia for anything!"

"Life was more simple in Australia," the big man said looking at her sadly. "But I couldn't be satisfied until I had returned to London and to you."

"Now you're sorry!"

He got up, and with his hands clasped behind his back and his head bent he began to pace slowly back and forth. "My greatest concern is for Julia. She is dearer to me than anything else."

"I understand."

He shot her a glance." And yet you would be willing to see me let her marry the son of a murderer."

"Bart is not exactly that. And in any case Donald is in no way to blame for his father's behavior."

"His father is your lover; naturally it is easier for you to forgive him than it is for me."

She sighed. "Bart and I have talked about it many times. If the worst comes to the worst, we will bring the two young people together with us and tell them the truth."

"They'll surely hate you."

"I know," she said unhappily.

"And with reason."

"I'll grant you that. I won't deny it," she said. "I came to you because we were once in love. My first love."

"And mine," the big man said.

"I automatically thought of you," she said. "I'm sorry. It would have been better if I hadn't come here."

"Not at all," he said, going to her and placing one of his large hands on her shoulder. "Just give me time for the shock of all this to wear off."

She looked up at him. "I cannot expect you to think of me pleasantly again."

"I think of you pleasantly at this moment," he said. "Both of us have gone through a lot. There is nothing to gain by our holding grudges against each other."

Becky rose. "I should go now."

"No. You will stay here for a little." It was a command.

"I have burdened you with my troubles," she said. "I had no right to."

His arm was around her. "Your troubles will always be mine. I have a feeling for you which will never change."

"Not even when you know I'm Bart's mistress?"

"I can even forgive that," he said. "Just give me time."

On the third evening of Becky's stay at Tenby Hall Donald arrived. He had heard from her housekeeper that she was there and so was not surprised. Julia and he embraced like the best of friends. This did not go unnoticed as Davy gave Becky a wise look. They were all gathered in the living room for drinks before dinner.

She quietly asked Donald, "Did the funeral go well?"

Donald nodded. "Yes. It was private. I do not think any tears were shed except by my mother. And she's already promising to try and reach him wherever he is."

"So it is over," she said.

"Yes," Donald said. "And I'm glad with everything else coming up. Father seems very relieved. And I want him to be at his best when we put forward our proposition to him."

"That probably would be wise," Davy Brown agreed. "At that he may oppose."

Donald said, "Becky and I can outvote him. He hasn't a chance."

They soon went on to the great dining room, where servants in formal wear looked after their needs. It was another of the sumptous meals for which Tenby Hall had become famous. There had been appetizers of oysters and soups and pheasant was the main course.

She and Davy strolled back to the living room. She sat watching him as he went through the ritual of unwrapping and lighting a fine cigar.

After he'd taken a puff or two on it, he said, "I'm about to agree with you about Donald Woods."

"I'm glad!"

"Perhaps I can make myself forget Bart is his father. But what about Bart?"

"He should be delighted to get a daughter-in-law like Julia."

"My daughter!"

"What of it? He didn't betray you to the police. He felt he deserved the whipping."

"And I enjoyed giving it to him!"

"That was violent and brutal on your part," she said. "He is not a young man any longer, nor is he well."

"Neither am I young," Davy said, taking his cigar from his mouth.

"You are far more active than he is, and you know it," she said.

"If he's in such poor shape how do you think he'll stand up to you and his son taking control of the company from him?"

"I'm afraid to think about it," she admitted.

CHAPTER 15

At last the morning of the confrontation arrived!

The meeting was to be held in the board room of the Gregg & Kerr Shipbuilding Company on the third floor of the brick building overlooking the river and the shipyard to the left. It was a bright, sunny morning, and Donald and Becky entered the big room with its shining oak table and fifteen chairs.

Bart Woods was already seated at the head of the table. His head was in his hand as he studied a number of documents spread in front of him. When they came in, he lifted his head to greet them.

"Where are the others?" he asked.

Donald held a large file of papers under his arm. He told his father. "The lawyers for both sides and the president of the steel company are all on the way here."

"They should be on time. I dislike tardiness," Bart said sternly.

"Yes, father," Donald said. And pulling a chair out for her part way down the table, he suggested, "This might be a good place for you to sit."

"Thank you," she said with a tremulous smile and sat in the chair.

Bart glared at her, "I can't imagine why you felt you must be here, Rebecca."

She said, "I do have considerable stock in the company, Bart."

"Agreed," Bart said. He looked strained. He had not come to visit her since the death of James. That report the morning afterwards had marked the last time he'd set foot in her house.

Donald, seated on the right of his father, spoke up, "I think it is proper for Mrs. Gregg to protect her large shares in the company."

Bart eyed him with disdain. "How formal you've become, son? There are only we three here. Surely you might call her Rebecca or even Becky. I know you do that often."

His son blushed furiously. "I'm trying to preserve the spirit of the occasion, father. We are not here as family or individuals, but as officers of the company board. Being formal helps maintain that kind of atmosphere."

"I see," his father said dryly. "Having risen to this position from the streets, I do not have your suave manner of conducting these business matters."

Before Donald could make a reply, the others came filing into the room: Mr. Wilowby, attorney for the firm, and his young assistant, Mr. Sneck. Then there was the lawyer for the steel company, an elderly, bald man named Stockford, and he had his assiciate, a Mr. Yardley, to back him up. The last man to slowly enter the board room was Davy Brown. He bowed to Becky and nodded to the others.

Donald, on his feet, said, "If you would please sit at the end of the table opposite my father in the chairman's seat."

Davy Brown sat in the designated chair. At the same time Bart Woods raised his eyes to meet his. It was a tense moment. Then Davy nodded slightly to Bart, and Bart returned the nod. The lawyers for Davy sat on his right and left. And the legal people for the company sat at the head of the table near Bart.

Bart glared about him. "I move we begin the meeting."

Donald read the minutes of the previous meeting, and they were approved. Then various routine matters were brought up. After these were cleared away, Donald rose with some uneasiness and addressed the group.

"Gentlemen and our lady shareholder, this is both an urgent and important occasion for us. The moment has come when we can no longer put off the facing of our largest problem—loss of contracts for building ships. If we are to continue and prosper, we must expand our yards and move toward the construction of steel ships." He sat down.

There was a tense moment, and then Bart lifted his eyes from his papers and spoke, "I think the meeting this morning is a waste of all our time, unless we wish to briefly go over what the company has done and is doing."

There were rustlings of documents about the table and Donald, looking angry, rose again, "I say let us put aside all other business until the matter of conversion of the yards is settled!"

Becky spoke up, "I second the motion."

The motion was passed!

Bart glared at her and then said, "As the managing director of this company for more than a quarter of a century, I would like to settle this matter for once and all. Gregg & Kerr came to true greatness under my management and with the introduction of the building of iron ships. It is my belief that we should continue with the construction of iron ships and let others go in for this new fad of steel if they like."

Mr. Wilowby adjusted his pince-nez and cleared his throat. "Speaking for a minority share owner, I would like to ask how we can make a profit building iron ships, when fewer are being built each year and the competition for those few grows greater!"

Bart glared at the lawyer. "We have now in our dock and under construction for the Kent Line, one of the largest iron ships ever on our stays. I secured this order against competition from America and from Scotland. We won the bid, gentlemen, and if we launch this vessel successfully, there would be the ordering of many more from the same company."

Donald was on his feet quickly. "I would like to make some slight comments. Our bid was so low on this ship we are bound to lose money on its construction. The figures in so far bear me out. You need only consult them. Second, the Kent Line is itself in such poor financial shape that only a few firms around the world were willing to bid for their work."

Mr. Wilowby spoke up in his dry voice again, "In the words of another of the smaller shareholders, desperation is the word to cover our position."

Bart scowled at him. "Even if we are desperate, we cannot switch to steel construction. We have neither the capital nor the physical means for such a change."

From the end of the table Davy Brown spoke up in his deep voice, "I believe, Mr. Woods, that is where I come in. I personally own the steel company of which I speak. I am willing to exchange stock with your company and merge our two firms. I am further willing to advance needed working capital for the changes required in the shipyard, and I will be content to have the company continue under its present management, which includes Mr. Donald Woods."

Mr. Wilowby's wrinkled face took on a brighter look as he said, "You are so certain of the success of the project, sir?"

"I am," Davy said firmly. "I will bring with me a number of contracts from Australian shipping companies with which I'm associated."

"I am not interested, Mr. Brown," Bart said cuttingly. "And so we may accept that the company is not interested."

Mr. Wilowby jumped up and lost his pince-nez and busily had to retrieve them. With them balanced on his thin nose, he said sharply, "Out of order! Speaking for the few shares I represent we are wholly for the merger."

Bart snapped, "The few shares you represent do not count. That makes you the one out of order!" Mr. Wilowby sat down with an angry exclamation.

Donald glanced nervously at his father and then at her. He rose and said, "I must take my stand. I have a certain lot of personal shares left me by my grandfather. I go on record as joining them with the minor shareholders." There was applause at the table from Mr. Wilowby and his assistant, and dead silence on the part of Bart.

As Donald sat down, Becky rose. She ignored the look of alarm on Bart's haggard face and the pleading in his eyes. She said, "I suppose it seems odd for a woman to express her opinion at such a meeting. But after all, our England is ruled over by a Queen!"

"Hear! Hear!" Mr. Wilowby said, still stinging from Bart's reproach.

Becky managed a small smile. "I have right to vote all the share owned by my late husband, Mark Gregg. I know how much he wished this company to prosper and grow. It was a matter dear to his heart. One might say his life was dedicated to it. But when the time came, he gave way to the opinions of Mr. Woods, who saw the value of iron plates for ships, and my late husband turned his voting stock over to Mr. Woods in a statement signed on his sick bed, knowing that he would die and wishing to assure that this firm would live."

She glanced for a moment at Bart and saw that his mouth had gaped open a little. She went on, "I now feel impelled to carry out the same action. This time against Mr. Woods and for his son Donald, and our new partner, Mr. Brown. I assign my voting stock to the cause of steel, and that leaves Mr. Bart Woods in a minority position."

She sat down to murmurs of approbation. Davy's eyes were shining with delight, and Mr. Wilowby leaned over and personally congratulated her. "A fine address, madam!"

"Thank you," she whispered.

There was silence and then Bart Woods spoke up bitterly. "I see how cleverly this was planned. And I admit to a minority position. So the firm of Gregg, Kerr, and Brown will come into being. My name has never been on the masthead of our notepaper, nor on the building. But I believe, nevertheless, that I have made a mark in the shipbuilding history of my time."

"None will argue about that, sir," Mr. Wilowby said.

"Thank you," Bart said with sarcasm. "I will continue as managing-director until the Kent Line ship is off the stays. Then I will turn the office over tomy son, Donald Woods, whom I'm sure you will all support."

There was applause at this point, and then a motion that the meeting be adjourned. The formality of the meeting ended, and the lawyers chatted amoing themselves before preparing to leave.

Donald was in consultation with Mr. Wilowby and Davy Brown came straight to her. "You were a champion, lass. You have a firm head on those pretty shoulders."

"I'm sorry it had to come to this," she said, turning to where Bart still sat alone at the head of the table. He was staring at his papers, he was either too shocked or weary to move.

Davy Brown at once advanced to him and in what seemed a generous gesture said, "Let us shake hands! In a way, you were the one who started me on the road to power and wealth."

Bart looked up at him, his haggard face a grim mask of defeat. "That was not my intention, sir, so I cannot accept your hand."

Davy sighed and dropped his hand. "As you wish! But I hold you no ill will. The account is settled."

Bart nodded. "Yes. I would say you settled it today and well!"

Davy turned from him and came back to her. He said, "You heard him. There is no hope of any friendship."

"Give him time," she said quietly. "This had been a terrible reverse for him. This shipyard is his life, and you have taken it from him."

"His own fault," Davy said.

"True," she agreed. "But still hard for him to bear." She paused, then added, "I think it would be best if you and your lawyers went. He may have something to say to me."

Davy looked worried. "Don't let him flog you with harsh words, Becky. You only did what was right."

"I hope so," she said.

"Then I'll be going on," he said. "Me and my fine team of lawyers. They consider themselves the pride of the Victorian Industrial Revolution, and they can't put a candle up to you!"

Davy went on to say good day to Donald, and then he and all the lawyers left. Donald stood for a moment at the far end of the table and regarded his seated father and her uncertainly. She gave the young man a nod to go, and he nodded back. He left with the giant file of papers under his arm.

Now they were alone! The bright light shone mercilessly into the room! She advanced down the length of the table with uncertainty. She halted by him.

"I'm sorry, Bart," she said.

He raised his eyes to her. "Do you know why I didn't get up?"

"It doesn't matter."

"Had I done so, I'd have become sick. "That's the sort of shell of a man I've become!"

"You have a right to feel badly," she said. "But it is for the best."

"Yes," he said with a a deep sigh. "It is always for the best, isn't it? Whatever we really want to do!"

"I didn't want to go against you."

His eyes met hers and there was pain in them. "I didn't think you would, even when I saw you here. And you knowing all I have done! All I've been guilty of! I still had no thought you might betray me!"

"Why did you think I had come?"

"To observe. Perhaps, in my desperation, I fancied you would back me."

Softly, she said, "I wish I could have."

"I lost you today, Becky. I've really lost you!" He seemed to sob out the last words.

Tears blurred his eyes. "No, Bart. I love you. I told Davy Brown that. I will always be at your side!"

"Not after today," he said sadly. "You may think you feel love for me. What you feel is sympathy, and I don't deserve that!"

"Bart!" It was an agonized plea. She bent and put an arm around him and kissed him.

Patiently he pushed her away. "I want to be alone here for a little," he said. "It has been the scene of my greatest triumphs and now my most total disaster. I have many things to think about."

"Very well," she said. "You know where I am, and you know I will be waiting."

He said nothing, but the expression on his worn face told her that it was truly the end for them. To hide the tears that rushed to her eyes again she turned and ran from the room.

Donald met her downstairs and anxiously asked, "Are you all right?"

"Yes," she said. "I shall manage. I have my carriage."

"What about him?" he asked.

"He's at a low ebb."

"I know."

"Don't intrude on him," she said with a sigh. "Give him time to somehow come to terms with it all. Then he'll be all right. Whatever else he may have been, or is today, there is a wondrous strength in Bart."

Donald said, "I'll vouch for that. Depend on it. I'll not disturb him."

Becky's prediction proved correct. Once Bart Woods had recovered from the shock of the meeting, he went about his duties at the shipyard as usual. He worked hard for the completion of the last, great iron vessel the line would be building. He treated Donald like a business associate, but not like a son. He was polite, but in no way warm or understanding.

As for Becky, she found herself deserted by him. She knew this from the start. Bart Woods had a pride as large as his massive body. That pride had been badly punctured and he could not come to share his love with her ever again. She kept hoping that it would change, that one day his angry pride would pass and he would relent and make the journey to her door. But weeks went by and this didn't happen.

Then Donald and Julia came to see her one evening. They were both clearly ill at ease, so she gave them some sherry and sat them in her small parlor and waited for them to tell her what was troubling them.

Julia's lovely eyes were sad. She said, "Why don't you come and visit us? Father is so lonely."

Becky smiled. "I'm sorry. I'll place you at the top of my list when I begin visiting again."

"You must. It is stupid to shut yourself off from all of us, as you've been doing."

Becky said, "I've had a lot of thinking to do."

Donald frowned. "You've let that business at the office bother you too much. Father is better now. He's working just as he used to."

"Is he, really?" she said.

Donald looked uncomfortable. "Well, he's not truly the same. But he does do his work. It's at home he worries me most. He and mother rarely ever spoke. But now he mostly ignores me."

"He is still angry?" Becky said.

"I think so," he said. "I saw a letter on the desk in the hall, which was put out with the rest of the mail for the maid to take to the post office. In father's handwriting, there was a letter addressed to Anne in Paris."

Becky was surprised. "I've never known him to write her!"

"He asked me for her address one day," Donald said. "That made me wonder. It must have been so he could send the letter."

Quietly she said, "I suppose he feels Anne the only one who hasn't betrayed him. It's natural he should reach out for someone."

"I think it's sick and selfish that he should write to your daughter behind your back and probably try to turn her against you," Donald said. "And against me as well."

"I wouldn't be afraid of that," she told him. "I think you'll find the letter has little to say about us. Your father always had a special feeling for Anne, and I think he's sorely missed her lately."

Donald frowned. "I don't understand him. He's a strange man!"

"We are all a little difficult to understand," she said ruefully.

Julie complained, "Donald, you've talked about everything but why we are here!"

"I know," he said, frowning.

"Go on," the pretty dark girl urged him.

"I will," he said. Then turning to Becky he continued, "I guess you're not going to believe what we have to tell you."

She smiled. "I think I know what it is."

"What?" Julia asked.

"You and Donald are hoplessly in love and want to get married!" Becky said.

Julia blushed. "Is it so obvious?"

"I'm afraid so," Becky said. And she went to the girl and hugged her. "I'm so happy for you both!"

Donald said, "What about Anne? I feel like a heel!"

She went to Donald and kissed him. Patting him on the arm, she said, "Anne will survive this all right. She has her Count André. And he's really very nice. But you should write her a short note and tell her how you feel. Do it at once!"

"It's hard to do," Donald worried.

"It must be done," Becky said firmly. "Let Julia help you with it."

"If he likes," Julia said willingly.

Becky asked her, "How does your father feel about the match?"

"He's given us his blessing, but he doesn't expect Donald's father to show up at the wedding."

Becky said, "You never can tell."

As soon as Anne received Donald's letter, she sent one to her mother. It was brief and said, "All is well! I've accepted André! We're coming to see you next week. We must try and make England especially pleasant for him!"

Becky smiled and cried a little at the same time. So it was settled, and the two she loved so much need never know the truth. She wanted to have Bart with her so they could go over it all and laugh and talk. But there was no Bart. She was alone now.

According to Donald, his father had taken to long night walks. Sometimes he went as far as the docks. This was a dangerous practice with Bart in such a frail state, and the number of criminals prowling the docks. There were assault and robbery cases almost every night. But Bart subbornly had refused to listen to anyone and kept having these midnight strolls.

Becky had a frightening theory. She believed that he went out deliberately seeking danger, hoping to be attacked and perhaps killed. He was weary of life and so threw himself open to this needless danger.

Then Anne and her young count arrived. Becky was beside herself with joy at having two young people in the house for a while. She had been lonely, with only the occasional visit of Donald or Julia to cheer her up.

As soon as she and Anne had a moment to themselves, she asked her about Donald's letter. "What did he finally write to you?"

Anne laughed. "It was so apologetic and intense. And I really didn't care. I'd made up my mind to marry André."

"Good! He'll make a fine husband," Becky told her daugher in the privacy of their bedroom, where women's talk could be shared openly.

"I hope he is happy with Julia. She sounds nice," Anne said.

"You'll like her," Becky said. "Her father is a dear friend of mine. And he is going to be a partner in the new firm."

Anne's pretty face clouded. "Oh, that!" She gave her a troubled look. "That must have been really bad!"

She nodded. "It wasn't easy."

"You and Donald voted against poor Uncle Bart!"

"Yes. We betrayed him. But for his own good. He doesn't think so, of course."

Anne said, "He wrote me."

"Did he?"

"A long letter. It was touching," Anne said. "He spoke of his loving you and his pride in Donald. And then he said something that I found truly touching, he told me he'd always loved me as his own daughter. Wasn't that nice of him?"

"It was very nice."

"I wrote back," Anne said, smiling sadly. "And I told him that since I'd never known my father, he had always been a father figure to me. And that I also loved him dearly. I apologized for not marrying Donald and hoped it wouldn't make any difference."

"I'm sure it won't."

"I must see him soon." Anne said. "Poor old thing! You've all turned on him and neglected him."

Becky reminded her, "He can be terribly cruel and proud when he wishes."

"I know," Anne said gently. "But, mother, he's old and he's been badly hurt."

She rose quickly, not wanting to display tears on this first night of having her daugher home. She went to the door and said, "I'll check on André and see if he's comfortable in his room."

Anne laughed. "He will be. André can be comfortable anywhere!"

The pounding came on the front door in the middle of the night. Becky's housekeeper answered the door and then came to rouse her.

"What is it?" Becky asked, sitting up sleepily.

"It's a servant from Mr. Woods' house," the woman said, holding her robe close around her. "The shipyard is on fire!"

Anne had been awake. "The shipyard?"

"Yes. It is on fire," the housekeeper said.

"We must go down there," Becky said. And she told her housekeeper. "Thank the servant and ask him to get us a carriage to go down to the yard. We'll be ready in ten minutes!"

And almost exactly ten minutes later she, Anne, and a sleepy André were in the carriage on the way to the docks. The blaze could be seen long before they reached the water's edge. The flames rose high in the sky and could be viewed from many parts of London.

When she reached the wharf, Becky was the first one out of the carriage. She ran through the crowds which had gathered in search of Donald. She finally found him giving instructions and information to one of the fire chiefs. When he finished, and the man in the red uniform and gold helmet ran off to follow his instructions, he turned to her.

She looked up into his tired, soot-covered face and said, "Where is your father?"

"I don't know," he said, turning to gaze at the fire. "He was here. A terrible night for him. His last ship gone up in smoke!"

"What happened?"

"No one knows yet. It started down below somewhere and spread before it was noticed," Donald said. "It'll be a total loss. And she didn't even get off the stays!"

"Are we insured?"

"Insurance will cover most of it," he said. "But it's my father who will be hurt most. This was his last personal effort."

"I know," she said. "I must find him!" And she began moving among the host of strangers, thinking she saw Bart somewhere and then finding it was someone else. Then she recognized one of the watchmen and went to them.

"Mrs. Gregg!" the man said, lifting his cap respectfully. "A terrible night."

"It is," she said. "Have you seen Mr. Bart Woods?"

The man looked upset. "I have, ma'am. I saw him just after I got here."

"Where?" she demanded, "Please tell me. I must find him!"

The old man looked sadly towards the blazing ship. "I don't think you will!"

"Why not?" her voice rose in panic.

"The last I saw of him he was walking alongside the yard; making straight for the ship, and her all flames from end to end! I shouted to him, but he paid no heed to me! Went straight on and I swear, you may not believe this, he went on board her! And that's the last I saw of him, or ever will if I know rightly!"

Had it not been for the crisp night air and the desire to get back to Donald, she would have fainted. She swayed a little, and the old man stared at her in alarm.

"You all right, ma'am?" he asked sharply.

"Yes," she said in a faint voice. "I will be. Just let me get away!" And she turned her back to the flames, heat, and smoke and began a desperate search for Donald. She found him again where the fire chiefs were conferring and clutched his arm. "Donald! Listen to me!"

"What?" he turned to her; she saw the fear in his face.

"He's on board that ship!" she said hysterically. "The watchman saw him go! He tried to stop him, and Bart wouldn't listen!"

Donald nodded. "I guessed he'd done it when we couldn't find him." His sooty face was highlighted by a sudden burst of flame as a large section of the burning vessel collapsed.

...

Winter came to London, and then another summer. The firm of Gregg, Kerr, and Brown had new yards—business was prospering. Donald and Julie married and bought a new house not far from her father's estate. He left his mother to live with a widowed cousin and the servants. She was so deep in spiritualism that she scarce had any time for the world of living in any case.

The body of Bart Woods was never found. In lieu of a burial, a special plaque was erected on the face of the office building in his honor. Anne and Count André were married in Paris and made their home there. She was already pregnant, and she confided to her mother that if it were a boy, she would surely call him Bart.

Becky and Davy Brown found themselves much as they had been at the start—they were both free and alone. But life had wrought many changes in them and in their views of life. Becky still loved Davy truly; the flame had ebbed over the decades, but there was still a spark there.

Davy invited her out to Tenby Hall for the weekend and promised that Donald and Julia would be joining them. But first he took her for a stroll in the gardens to show her some of his fine new flower beds. They paused by the big fountain in the middle of the gardens and smiled at their reflections in the rippling water.

Becky, looking at her slightly overweight figure, said with a rueful smile, "Hardly the girl who carried trays in the tavern!"

Davy chuckled. "I wouldn't want that girl now. She'd be far too young for me."

"What about me?"

"You're just exactly right," Davy said, embracing her. "And so you always will be for me!" She knew the circle had been completed—she was returning to her first love. The perilous loves that had brought her this far were already fading into memories—some bitter, some sweet!

A Sneak Peek from Crimson Romance
(From *Lord Monroe's Dark Tower* by Elf Ahearn)

Bournemouth, England—1818

If Claire Albright had one wish, it was that her heart would stop hammering against her ribs. One look from him with those troubled, brooding eyes and she would certainly faint. But if he was attentive or warm, perhaps she would cry. She took a deep breath. *Stop being ridiculous; you will neither faint nor cry.* Ignoring logic, her heart beat faster.

The vehicle drew to a bumpy stop at the exact point where a crenellated tower cast its toothy shadow. Feeling as if she were lowering herself into the jaws of a beast, Claire stepped from the coach, shivered in the chill shade, and approached the stairs to Bingham Hall. Two urns squatted like toads on either side. From each jutted the naked stems of flowers that had been ripped away. Droplets of moisture still oozed from the traumatized stalks.

Not a welcoming sight. Claire's fingers went cold, and feeling her knees grow weak, she clung to the stone balustrade like a sailor in a rough sea.

From inside the coach came the chipper voice of her chaperone, Mrs. Gower. "Smile dear, bright and happy."

Claire tried to force her trembling lips into a grin. "Be vibrant, not shy," her chaperone lectured during the ride. "Don't talk about herbs and cures—he'll take you for a midwife."

"But I am a midwife."

"Then you're not to mention it. No man wants a wife with a profession."

Swallowing, Claire paused to collect herself.

"Go on child!" urged Mrs. Gower's shrill voice, "*La*, he'll be married to someone else by the time you reach the knocker."

"Please hush," Claire whispered, her stomach churning as she lifted the knocker—a mermaid with its tail curled in an uncomfortable loop. But as her fingers brushed the mermaid's scales, a butler jolted the door open. Barely stifling a cry, Claire jumped back, and regaining her composure, pasted what she hoped was a 'bright' smile on rigid lips. "I'm here by invitation from the Viscountess Monroe and her son, Flavian Bourne, Viscount Monroe," she said, digging frantically into her reticule for a calling card.

"You must be Lady Claire Albright," the butler said, his eyes lighting with interest. "His lordship is awaiting your arrival. Please come in. I'll announce you at once."

But before she crossed the threshold, Lord Flavian Monroe hurried into the dim recesses of the hall. "Lady Albright," he said, his welcoming smile warming her icy nerves like a cordial on a cold day. He swept past the butler. "What a joy to see you. I've been waiting like a child for a sweetmeat." He took both her hands in his. Calloused and rough, his hold radiated heat through the chill in her bones. She couldn't help but laugh.

"My lord, I'll confess the horses seemed to trot a ponderous gait."

"A pretty pair of Cleveland bays, too. What a shame they didn't understand the urgency of your arrival."

She laughed again and bowed her head. How wonderful to see the haunted look she remembered gone from his eyes. If she gazed one second longer, she might stroke his chiseled cheek and shame herself. Oh, why did he have to be so spectacularly handsome? Chestnut hair swept back from a high forehead, serious brown eyes with a glint—like a bonfire burning miles away—and masculine, weathered cheeks that lacked the creamy blandness of most titled gentlemen.

La, my lord," cried Mrs. Gower, whose bulk stuffed the coach door, "what a splendid *pied-à-terre!*"

Flavian's gaze shifted to the chaperone. "Mrs. Gower, what a grand sight you are."

"Indeed," Mrs. Gower said, losing her balance on the coach stairs during a peel of flirty giggles. Two footmen dove to catch her. She bumbled onto the gravel, accidently tearing a gold frog on one man's livery, but managed to keep her footing. "My lord, it's impossible to figure, but I'll wager I've lost a full ten stone since we met last year at Lady Claire's sister's wedding."

"And that's why I mistook you for a sapling."

"Oh, you're a charmer," the chaperone gushed. "Out of my way, lassie, I'm taking him."

Flavian laughed with the same warm good humor Claire remembered teasing out of him during their walks at Cowick Hill two years ago. As the months plodded by and she hadn't heard from him, Claire had come to doubt the feeling of delight they'd shared in one another's company. What a relief to know she was mistaken.

As one footman assisted Mrs. Gower up the stairs, the other struggled with the oversized trunks strapped to the coach roof. Even loosening them from the roof seemed too much for the fellow.

Flavian rested a hand on Claire's back and winked down at her. "I'd like to impress your chaperone, if you'll indulge me a moment."

She dropped a small curtsey. "Impress to your heart's desire."

He swept down the stairs and standing beside the coach, said, "Hand it down, Hancock."

"Are you ready to swoon, Mrs. Gower?" he called over his shoulder. The woman batted away her escort and pivoted to watch the action.

The footman dragged the trunk to the edge of the roof, maneuvered it over the low rail, and straining not to let it drop, slid it at a dangerously fast rate toward his master. In one graceful motion, Flavian caught the wooden container and, single handedly, lowered it to the ground. "Now, the next." Red-faced and sweating, the footman repeated the procedure. When Flavian had both trunks on the ground, he positioned them on their ends and then stood between them. "Hold onto the railing Mrs. Gower, for I intend to amaze." Laughing, he bent his knees, and with fingers clutching each handle, he lifted the two trunks simultaneously.

"Oh *lawks*!" shrieked the chaperone, braying like a fishmonger's wife. "He's as bluff as bull beef."

Flavian managed a grin, though he gritted his teeth from the strain. When he took a step forward, and another, and another, till he started up the stairs, Claire could restrain her admiration no longer. "*La*, it must be fourteen stone you're carrying!"

"His lordship's the strongest man in all England!" cried the footman from atop the carriage.

Though the viscount's figure was long and lean, he clearly possessed strength beyond that of the typical man his size. A thrill ran through Claire as she pictured the ropes of muscle beneath his coat, unable to tear her eyes from the bulges beneath the fabric.

As Flavian approached the top of the stairs, he appeared to falter, almost tipping backward. Claire dashed to his side. "Careful, my lord!"

"Ha," he said, delighted that she'd fallen for his trick. At the last few stairs, he hoisted the trunks higher, broke into a trot, and then, turning for her benefit, lowered them slowly to the floor. Claire's hands went to her heart and she shook her head in amazement. "I am in awe. It took four men to load my baggage."

He grinned and stepped back into the sun. A bead of sweat raced toward his cheek, he huffed air, but otherwise acted as if he'd just lifted the down of a dandelion.

A slight rustle overhead distracted Claire, and at the same time, she felt a light tap on the back of her travel costume. She looked up to see the flicker of a face disappear inside a window on the third floor. The sash screeched in its casement, closing with a bang, and the face disappeared. Confused, she looked behind, and saw the desiccated body of a small, gray rat. Flavian's expression went dark; pain, worry, and anger flickered across his features before he composed himself with the shielded, haunted look she'd seen so often at Cowick Hill. He wrapped his arm around her waist and guided her into the house. "Clean that up, Marlow," he said to the butler.

What poor servant made that terrible mistake? Claire wondered, hoping no one would suffer dismissal for it. "It's quite all right," she said, trying to sound amused. "Our cats bring me similar presents all the time."

Instead of joining in her gaiety, Flavian's lips drew tight. "I'm so sorry. What an awful greeting."

Claire smiled, trying to cheer him. "Oh, forgive the perpetrator. Accidents happen, and nothing can dampen my pleasure in seeing you again."

"Isn't she sweet?" Mrs. Gower added. "Imagine what a lovely mistress of the house she'd make."

Claire cringed inwardly. It really was too bad her sister, Snap, was too young for a come out, and that her father refused to "abandon his research for a lot of London ne'er-do-wells." Why couldn't he make do without her mother just this once, when Claire was faced with the most important decision of a young lady's life; namely, to find a proper husband? She let a little sigh escape. Meanwhile, the tiniest speck of light had sneaked back into Flavian's eyes. Being burdened with Mrs. Gower wouldn't be quite so bad if the chaperone amused him.

"Now, what would you like to do?" he asked. "Settle into your rooms and freshen a bit?"

"Perfection," Mrs. Gower declared. "Your summons of Lady Claire has pricked my curiosity, my lord. Whatever could a handsome young man want so urgently with a beautiful, wealthy, unwed girl?"

Without a hint of amusement, Flavian turned his somber eyes on the chaperone. "Lady Claire and I will be discussing that privately."

• • •

Nincompoop, Flavian muttered to himself as he paced the marble floor of the reception hall. He gave his thigh a sharp slap and started back toward the bottom of the stairs. Why did he invite her here? Did he honestly believe those blue eyes wouldn't affect him; the tender rose of her cheek wouldn't stir emotions he'd let settle like sediment after he'd met her two years ago? *Nincompoop.*

His agitation was cut short by the vision of Claire floating down the stairs as gracefully as a ballerina. His stomach hopped when she fixed those portals to the sky on him and opened her lips in a smile as bright as stars on a summer night. Though the interior of Bingham Hall had been scrubbed and dusted in anticipation of her visit, no amount of suds and elbow grease could clear the stark gloom of its naked interior. Claire, in her pretty rose-colored linen, was like a Botticelli statue stranded in gray velvet. *Touch her,* his body cried out. Instead, he clasped his hands behind him and shifted weight, rocking a little as she approached. *Fool, fool, fool,* he thought, trying to fight the surge of emotion in his breast. He shifted his gaze to the diamond-shaped stoneware on the floor, but it did no good. Her face seemed etched in every tile. The scent of roses preceded her, but he didn't look up as the soft sound of her footfalls grew closer.

"My lord," she said, with music in her voice. For a moment he couldn't speak; his throat tight as a vise. *I'll keep her at arm's length. She won't be dragged into this den of misfortune.*

He moved forward to offer his hand as she stepped near. "May I take you on a tour of the house while your things are unpacked?"

Mrs. Gower heaved out of a wingchair in the parlor just off the reception hall, and put down her teacup with a clatter. "What a marvelous idea."

He proffered his arm, but the older woman waved it away. "You assist Lady Claire. She's able-bodied, but delicate."

Struggling to keep a straight face, he turned to his young guest. "Then, Lady Claire." She accepted his arm with such a graceful nod of her head he had to avert his eyes.

As they proceeded across the entrance hall, Mrs. Gower waddled behind at a pace that tried his naval discipline, halting at every feature and commenting on the architecture. "Lovely high ceilings," she said, "and I'm especially in favor of molding like this."

Claire appeared unfazed. At the fireplace halfway down the hall, she paused before a Sevres clock of biscuit porcelain with two loosely clothed lovers cavorting beneath a standing cupid. He knew she was giving Mrs. Gower time to catch up, but it pained him that the clock was the only decorative piece in the hall, or in fact, almost anywhere in the manor house. "Lovely. Is it French?" she asked.

Her question drew him from his musings. He nodded. "Mother used to adore collecting during her travels."

"Will she be joining us for dinner?"

Not trusting his features to remain neutral, he moved closer to the clock, so Claire got only a view of his back. "She stays in her apartments mostly. When I asked for her availability, she was taking an afternoon nap."

Mrs. Gower puffed up beside them. "Then I'm glad I'm here to see that you behave proper around the young lady."

With a courtly bow, he replied, "You are a welcome addition, Madam."

The chaperone tipped back her head and brayed. "You're a devil, you are."

A flicker of pain crossed Claire's features, but Flavian was grateful for Mrs. Gower's antics. She distracted him from the shabby furnishings and the vibrancy of Claire's slim elbow. "I'd like to take you to the long gallery upstairs," he said, dropping her arm.

Claire looked at him quizzically. "I should like to meet your ancestors." Her honest blue eyes sought his, no doubt questioning his distant behavior, and the realization pierced his heart. *You're a scoundrel, Monroe. She shouldn't be here at all.* He thrust his hands behind his back. "Then we're off."

"My late husband's family had a long gallery," Mrs. Gower said, trundling after them. "Floor to ceiling lords and ladies and the like. How they adored me. 'What happened to that wife of yours?' her ladyship would ask, and I'd say, 'Here I am!'"

"Mrs. Gower married my mother's cousin," Claire explained.

"Aye and I've spent a lifetime in London, so I know a thing or two. Her mother finds me invaluable as a guide to her young brood. Four girls and I'll see all of them wed and fat with babes."

He laughed and Claire's cheek went rosy—a most attractive hue. He tried to catch her eye, but she was lifting her skirt to ascend the stairs.

He led them through the arched entry to the long gallery. Sunlight poured through mullioned windows. Each rectangular beam stretched across the wooden floor and up the far wall, illuminating six massive tapestries. The hangings depicted religious scenes of varying horror and beauty. In one, Mary cradled her innocent babe; a few panels down, John the Baptist's vacant eyes looked heavenward as his severed head rested on a silver platter. Tacked over the tapestries were portraits of Flavian's ancestors: bloody tyrants, uniformed adventurers, gentle masters, fiery maidens, plain women, and pretty children. They were his history, and he was their future.

"Who is this intimidating gentleman?" Claire asked, stopping before a gilt sideboard above which hung a portrait of an officer in full dress. Behind him crashed a raging sea, the Union Jack whipping on the mast of the *HMS Indomitable*. Though canyons of flesh lined the man's face, beneath tufted white brows shone a pair of eyes as fierce as a badger's.

"That, Lady Claire, is my father, Admiral Gareth Geraint Monroe, Viscount of Bourne, God rest his soul." Flavian executed a sharp salute.

Claire's flute-like chuckle made him smile. "You salute as if you'd served."

"Starting at thirteen."

"My legs don't like the sea," Mrs. Gower interrupted, plunking into a heavily carved chair. "Myself, I find water bracing, but my legs won't go near it."

With a note of hurt, Claire said, "But you never mentioned you were in the Royal Navy."

Certain items of his past needed to be revealed; he'd known that before he invited her. It was only fair she knew something of his life. Shrugging, he replied, "The subject never arose."

"But we spent weeks together at Lord Hugh Davenport's house party, and through all our conversations—"

"My late husband never spoke of his time in the service," Mrs. Gower said. "He got a mighty wound in the buttocks—kept him mum."

"Then were you shot, my lord?"

"Not in the classic sense of the word." Unwilling to say more, he pointed at the next portrait. Before continuing his lecture, a small thud followed by a ping caught his attention. At the far end of the hall, a button rolled across the floor. Claire caught the movement and started down the gallery to investigate. "What was that?"

Flavian swept past her, picked up the button, and jammed it in his pocket. Louder and with more menace than he intended, he said, "It must have fallen off the tapestry."

Puzzled, Claire's brows lifted, and she gazed at him with questioning eyes. He took her arm and led her to a painting of a man with an arrogantly lifted chin. Restless eyes gazed beyond the canvas and a feathering of sandy hair curled back from a high, lined, forehead. "The rightful heir, my brother, Lancelot; may he also rest in peace."

"The artist brought such life to his face," Claire said.

"Yes." In fact, the only details the artist left out, Flavian thought sardonically, were the losing cards, which his brother should have clutched in his left hand while the wife of another man should occupy his right.

Claire touched Flavian's elbow. "How did he die?"

"Stupidly."

"Is that the Monroe got a hole put in him in a duel some years back?" Mrs. Gower chimed in. "Now, that was a scandal the gossip mongers…"

"It was he, a wound from which he failed…" Another light thud from the end of the gallery distracted him.

Claire walked quickly down the corridor. "Something hit that painting again." She peeked into the hall and heard running footsteps pounding down the staircase. "Is there a reason a servant would want me to see this portrait?"

Drawing breath, Flavian carefully regulated his expression. "That's Hernando de Vargas Duarte. He was a dear friend of mine who once saved my life. He's gone now."

"Oh dear, so many deaths," said Claire.

"He was drafted into Napoleon's Grand Army and died in Russia." Flavian studied Hernando's bearded face and thick eyebrows, marveling that the gentleness of his friend's almond-shaped eyes were so perfectly portrayed in paint. In those eyes, he still saw the command he'd obeyed seven years ago, and how bitterly he'd fought with his mother the night before his departure for Spain. "Look at the news," she'd said, beating the paper against her skirt. "Napoleon is everywhere in Spain. You cannot help *her*.' But that very night, he'd swung a cloak over his shoulders, and shouted, "I can't leave her in that misery. I owe Hernando that much and I owe her much more." Then he'd slammed the door deadening the sound of his mother's weeping.

A crash from somewhere downstairs broke the memory. Flavian raced toward the source two steps at a time, but when he reached the reception hall, it was empty. On the floor before the fireplace lay the shattered remains of the Sevres clock.

Curious to see what had fallen, Claire scurried after Flavian down the stairs. At the same time she arrived in the reception area, an elderly woman stepped through the door of an adjoining room. Thin and statuesque, the dowager held herself beautifully erect as she crossed the floor with small, pain-filled strides. Her eyes pierced Flavian with a look of extreme displeasure. "It's getting worse," she hissed before she saw Claire. Her son, squatting to pick up the ruined bits of porcelain, kept his head down in shame.

"Ah, my Lady Claire," the woman said, screwing her expression into a welcoming smile.

Flavian stood. "Allow me to introduce my mother, Lady Monroe."

Claire dropped into a curtsey, and then took Lady Monroe's outstretched hand. "It's a pleasure to make your acquaintance."

"And I yours, my dear. Was your journey uncomfortable?"

"Not at all."

"I'm so grateful to hear that. The roads can be so difficult these days; one has to be quite athletic to survive them."

"Your son told me you also traveled."

The woman shot a guarded glance at Flavian. "She did, but mother has been unable to get about as well as she used to."

Lady Monroe nodded her head in approval. "My health prevents me," she replied, laying particular emphasis on *health*.

"I'm so sorry about your Sevres clock. Lord Monroe said it was part of a collection you acquired during your trips abroad."

The elderly woman lowered her lids and the line of her mouth went taut. "It's a terrible pity," she said, almost in a whisper.

Just then, loud footsteps resounded from a hallway leading to the east wing of the house. A look of near panic lit Lady Monroe's pale eyes. "Take me to my rooms," she said, gripping Flavian's arm.

The footsteps grew closer.

Before Flavian could excuse himself, his mother was shuffling from the reception hall. "If you'll excuse us," he said, offering a quick nod before catching up to her. He turned back an instant later. "Would you meet me in the garden in about ten minutes? I'd like to talk to you."

Now it sounded as if someone was intentionally stomping his feet as he approached, making as much noise as humanly possible. Confused, Claire felt like a lost soul standing in the vast reception room. "Of course, but where am I to sleep?"

"God, this is inexcusable. Mother stop."

Instead, the elderly woman increased her laborious gait.

Marlow!" Flavian bellowed. "Marlow!" The pounding footfalls ceased immediately with only their echo reverberating through the marble interior. The noise was replaced by the distant vibration of doors opening and closing, and of someone approaching swiftly from the area of the kitchen. The butler burst into the reception hall, slightly out of breath. "My lord?"

Without turning, Lady Monroe waved an imperious hand in the air. "Take Lady Claire to her rooms and be sure she's settled and comfortable." As she was about to disappear into the east wing, she hesitated long enough to look back at Claire. "If you ever need anything, you may come to me, but I'm afraid my health will prevent me from being present often during your visit."

Claire returned her best smile. "Perhaps I can give you something to make you feel better?"

She pressed her frail body against her son with the possessiveness of a child to its nanny. "Flavian mentioned your interest in healing. How wonderful that would be, my dear. How wonderful…" Lady Monroe's eyes reddened, and as she turned away, Claire noticed the woman was trembling.

• • •

As Marlow swung the door open, the view of the garden made Claire pause. Though Bingham Hall held an impressive array of valuable furniture, its barren interior didn't seem to get any brighter even in the most persistent sunlight. But the garden eclipsed the grip of melancholy with flowers of every hue and color. Patches of blossom invited the eye to travel over the estate's impressive lawn. A massive copper beech grew near the house, and beneath its impossibly long limbs, were wooden benches for intimate conversation in the deep shade. In the distance, framed by the white trunks of sycamore, stood an antique stone bridge that crossed a canal on the left side of the lawn. Beyond it, a thick wood fringed the grass. In the center of the yard, the view ended as much as a quarter of a mile away, where a low hill supported a miniature Greek temple. Tucked beside the house to the right, a flower-festooned path ran into a formal garden.

Flavian stepped between two statues of women holding urns bursting with spring pansies and vine. "You look radiant," he said, beckoning her to join him.

Claire's heart jumped.

"You go ahead, dear," she heard Mrs. Gower squawk behind her. "But remove the shawl and pull your bodice down!"

Claire turned and tossed the shawl back to Mrs. Gower; it was too hot to wear anyway. She bit her lip and hurried down the stairs, praying Flavian didn't overhear her chaperone.

"My father had the estate landscaped by Capability Brown," Flavian explained as Claire gazed at the wild beauty of the grounds. "But he insisted on the preservation of my great-grandfather's formal garden."

There was such a lot of open space to cover on the grounds. Claire knew Mrs. Gower was hidden somewhere behind an invisible curtain, fretting about every flaw in her performance. Divided by thick hedges, the formal garden offered more immediate refuge. "What wonderful flowers," she said, leading Flavian down a graveled path between a riot of peonies, irises and lilacs. The sun-warmed blossoms suffused the air with gaudy perfume. The peonies especially were so ripe with scent and color Claire was almost embarrassed for them. They exposed their petals with open sensuality. "Immodest things aren't they?" she said, lifting the heavy head of a blossom and sniffing deeply.

"Forgive their forward nature," Flavian replied, chuckling. "They can't help themselves."

"You have my pardon," Claire told the flower. When she let it go, it drooped nearly to the walkway.

She strolled on, attracted down the path by a patch of yellow primrose. Flavian caught up to her. She couldn't keep a smile from her lips at the sight of him: the flecks of red in his curls, the ruddy flesh rounding his angular cheekbones and square chin.

He produced a peony from behind his back.

"Is this the one I forgave?"

"You were so kind; it couldn't bear the weight of sorrow when you left."

"Thank you." Her hand closed around the stem. It was cool with a woody flexibility that sprang under the weight of its showy flower. He'd given her a flower. Her heart filled until she had to swallow and look down. She hoped Flavian didn't notice the heat growing in her cheeks. "In China they use peony to cure all kinds of aliments. Stomachache, gall stones..." Then she remembered Mrs. Gower's warning about herbal remedies—that he'd reject her as a woman more interested in doctoring than in having babies of her own. "Why am I talking about all that on a lovely day like today?"

He moved closer, a keen look in his eyes. "Is healing a grim subject?"

"Only when it fails." She moved quickly to a patch of faded jonquils just ahead. "How spectacular they must have looked in full bloom."

She heard the crunch of gravel as he came up behind her. A tingle coursed through her spine. "But that doesn't happen often with you, I would imagine," he said.

Oh, why did she have to go and mention healing when he hadn't seen her in so long? Knowing she dabbled in such things probably accounted for his long silence in the first place. "It's just a hobby, you know, healing."

"When your sister, Ellie, was wounded two years ago, you seemed to know what to do."

Claire tried to think of something to distract him, but nothing came to mind. Sure that he'd react with cold brooding, she spread her arms hopelessly. "I do. I do know what to do."

Rather than retreating, he seemed pleased. "How did you come upon the art?"

"I have a mentor. One of our tenants at home is the local midwife, but everyone goes to her with all their ailments. When my older sister, Peggity, was born, father sent for the doctor. That man nearly killed my mother and the baby. All of the servants begged father to fetch the tenant woman, and she saved them. Both of them…Oh, but look at this beautiful garden. Why dwell on hardship in the midst of grandeur?"

The corners of his eyes narrowed. He plucked a spent stalk. "Narcissus. Does it have healing properties?"

She could not seem to dislodge him from the subject. Perhaps he wanted to assure himself she wasn't a medically minded bluestocking. "Are you interested in herbal remedies, my lord?"

A troubled look came into his eyes. He rolled the daffodil between thumb and pointer then shrugged. "Perhaps."

"Well, jonquils make your hands itch and turn scaly." Flavian looked surprised. "I'd toss that back if I were you."

He dropped the stalk into its bed. "Such a lovely flower possessing such sinister qualities…"

Steering her away from the patch of daffodils, he brought her to a square of herbs. "Now, come tell me everything you know about the rest of these innocent looking plants."

"That would be a very long conversation, indeed," Claire said.

He hesitated, seeming to consider something. "You're to make your come out this season, aren't you?"

"Oh dear, yes."

"Don't you want to?"

Claire's palms grew moist. "The truth is, crowds unnerve me. I'm not looking forward to London at all."

He laughed. "Then you don't mind stopping with me for a little while?"

"I feel as if I've won a reprieve, temporary though it may be," she said, sensing the heat spreading to her cheeks. "I'm disinclined to be on display."

"It's unnerving for both sexes."

"Ah, but the men hold all the cards."

He scratched his chin. "That's funny; I always feel the women have the power."

"But the men do the asking."

"And the women do the refusing."

They laughed together, and Claire sensed their emotions loop one around the other in a combination as sweet as butter and honey.

Feeling as fully blossomed as a peony, she eyed Flavian, tucked a hand beneath her chin, and swayed back and forth. If she didn't say something soon, she'd kiss him. For the sake of modesty, she looked down, but couldn't stop the gentle sway of her body. "At any rate, the idea of parading about trawling for a husband…"

"I quite understand," Flavian said, huskily. The hum of insects, busy in the hot sun, grew in intensity. He pivoted away, exhaled, and then bending down, snapped a single flower from a blue hyacinth.

"How about this flower and its healing properties…? Actually, that's not of interest right now. Come with me a moment." Taking her arm, he led her into a secluded alcove. A corset of lilac and forsythia shielded the area completely from the household windows. "Would you care to sit a moment?" he asked.

Claire noticed that his breath had quickened and his movements grown choppy. *Nerves?* She wondered. *Was he about to ask permission to court her?* Heart fluttering, she sat on the cool marble bench and laid the peony across her lap. He positioned himself next to her, his body so near she could feel his nervous energy.

"Let me look at you first," he said. Obliging, she turned towards him, but couldn't face him for the pounding in her heart. He took her hand—his fingers, dry and callused. Claire lowered her gaze and smoothed her skirt. "Claire, it's so wonderful to see you again. You've been in my thoughts constantly these two years..." He broke off, shaking his head and releasing her hand.

Fear clamped her chest. Healing was a concern to him. What a fool she'd been to admit to it. The *ton* never opened its doors to a woman with serious interests. "What a silly goose I am," she said.

"You?" Surprise registered on his face. "If anyone's the goose in this garden, it would be me. No, I've brought you here because... of course...I enjoy your company." He cleared his throat. "And... and I'm hoping you can help me."

A thin stream of disappointment darted through her bones. *You had no right to expect a request,* she scolded herself. *You're just dismayed you still have to go to London.* She lifted her chin and heartily replied, "If there's something I can do, it would be an honor."

"What a grand lady you are," he said. He took a deep breath and turned away. All at once, he seemed deeply shaken. Could that be water pooling in his eyes? Whatever would bring a man like Lord Monroe nearly to tears?

In her gentlest tone, she coaxed, "What is it, my lord?"

"I must seem ridiculous." He pressed his fingertips to his forehead.

"Please...let me help."

Rubbing his face vigorously, he recovered himself. "There is someone here who is troubled. Your knowledge of herbs and medicine..."

Claire laughed. "Oh, what a comfort! I thought you disliked me because I practice healing."

"Not at all," he said, "In fact, just the opposite."

"Oh, you're very different indeed. Mrs. Gower has been so worried you'd think ill of me."

He clutched her hand, rubbing the back fervently. "Nothing could induce me to do that. You are the finest young woman it's ever been my privilege…Well, the fact is, I'm at a loss where to turn…for this patient because it's a complicated…perhaps bad situation."

Claire took his hand and stilled its impassioned motion. "I've seen people die. I've seen the worst of sores and broken bones. Whatever your friend's disease, I won't shrink away."

He appeared so desperately worried. She prayed the patient wasn't suffering the way Mrs. Optkin did—the blood and the baby, so still and blue. Her hands started to sweat and she withdrew them from his. Swallowing, she looked directly into his face and smiled reassuringly. "Everything will be fine."

He studied her carefully. "This is a strange sort of sickness. You may be shocked.

My…"

"I can hear you," said a girlish voice behind them. A peal of giggles, and then a pretty young lady jumped from the path into the alcove. "I'm like a little cat—sniff, sniff, sniff, and then I pounce!" she declared.

"Abella, this is Lady Claire Albright. Lady Claire, my ward, Abella Carmencita Vargas-Duarte."

"I pleased to meet you," Abella cried, her voice tinged with a Spanish accent. "Vav, he talk about you. He say you…precocious?"

Claire didn't know how to respond. Flavian had never mentioned he had a ward. Why did he harbor such trivial matters as secrets? *How strange.* But the girl's lively good spirits swept all thought aside. About sixteen-years-old, her dark curls framed skin the color of freshly cut wood. Her smile lit the heart from the inside out. It was impossible not to smile back. "Precocious?" Claire said, chuckling, "my family finds me quite dull."

"Oh, they don't know you as I do," Abella said, with a cascade of giggles.

Claire laughed too, caught in the giddy tide of Abella's humor.

"*Precioso*," Flavian corrected. "'Lovely,' in your native tongue."

"Ah. Forgive me, Lady Claire. I make these mistakes, but I make up to you. Come hear me sing."

"I was speaking to Lady Claire privately," Flavian said gently. "I do hope you weren't eavesdropping."

Ignoring him, Abella widened her large brown eyes. "You on coach a long time, *si*? Oh, I make fresh like a child soon. You hear me sing." She stroked her throat like a shopkeeper displaying his finest wares. "*Muy bueno*. Forget all about that old coach." Taking Claire's hand she pulled her down the pebbled path.

"Actually," Flavian said, following them, "the birds stop chirping to hear Abella sing."

www.ingramcontent.com/pod-product-compliance
Lightning Source LLC
Chambersburg PA
CBHW010301100726
47904CB00011B/2693